The Singing Ship

THE SINGING SHIP

The Singing Ship

A NOVEL

REBECCA WINTERER

Del Sol Press

Winner of the 2016 Del Sol Press First Novel Prize

For Terri Molineux

THE SINGING SHIP

CONTENTS

THE SINGING SHIP

PROLOGUE

BEFORE THE PILGRIM FAMILY with their buttons, altars, and inventories; before royal families, prime-ministers and presidents, entertainment and sports stars, and reality TV personalities; before territories with sheep and cattle properties, mining and sugar cane industries and tourism along the coast; before policies about these people versus those people or even distinctions between foreign and native, us and them; before convicts and bushrangers, freemen and nouveau gentry; before the flu epidemic, the overland telegraph, and even before the ships from across the world arrived with Europeans, who were as generous with their beads as with their botany, buckshot, and bacteria—13,000 to 11,000 years before, to be precise—this ocean advanced a meter a day, the intertidal zone stretched, and those who were there on the Arafura Plain and the Great Australian Bight were forced to retreat.

How could they know of the massive ice floes, fragmented from the Antarctic ice sheet, melting as they drifted north and the lakes in the lobes of the ice shields of North America emptying and the seas' instantaneous rise? Their place, never a "plain" or "bight," was formed of the bodies of ancestors. The blood that coursed through their arteries and veins was as much theirs as ancestral. Bodies inseparable from place and past, they welcomed the water. They built great fires and sang and danced, and in this dialogue of corroboree—to the clacks of sticks, thuds of footfalls, and drone of digeridoos—elders led the celebration of the water and receding land. That's how they launched themselves on the voyage inland.

PART ONE

WEIGHING ANCHOR

THE SINGING SHIP

✦

THAT DAY WAS QUIETER than usual in the Casuals Department of Delton's Department Store. Mrs. Johnson, from Linens and Fabric, had already dropped off the box of buttons Robert Pilgrim had requested earlier in the week. He'd chosen for Audrey, his wife, three flower buttons with pink, purple, and yellow plastic petals respectively, a striped toucan button, a fish button with glazed green scales, and two bead buttons that resembled pearls.

The last time Delton's was this quiet there'd been an explosion at the mine outside Mt. Isaac in which four mechanics were killed. Robert knew the men by their widows. For a month after the accident, Casey Phelps and Julie McInerny had stopped shopping altogether. Mary O'Neil had replaced her white church veils with black ones, and Jan Tyndon had bought dozens of men's athletic socks as though stockpiling for all the years Jim wouldn't be buying them. Robert took pride in his insight about Mt. Isaac's private life and pleasure in the moments he could act upon this, like when he slipped matching gloves into Mrs. O'Neil's bag on the morning she bought the veils. Because she later returned to give Robert her husband's hardhat, he knew that his gesture was appreciated.

Robert called his supervisor to request an early tea break. "Go for it, Bob," Mr. Hamish Templeton said. It was the same tone he used when he said, "I'll pass your concerns on to the Delton family, but I wouldn't hold my breath," when Robert had mentioned his concerns about the lack of windows at Delton's and his worry about bush fires and his fear that he wouldn't have enough time to warn his customers if he couldn't see what was coming. Robert had made a scrapbook in which he'd pasted newspaper articles about fires and fire fatalities in Australian history: Black Friday, January 13, 1939, seventy-one lives, sixty-nine burnt mills, millions of acres of forest; 1943-44 fire flume in Blue Mountains, New South Wales, ten lives. He intended to present this as evidence to the Deltons, assured that they'd do the right thing once they realized what they were up against. He didn't feel it was necessary to divulge that he'd lost an uncle to fire. To play on people's sympathy didn't seem fair.

Robert, in the tearoom, was waiting for the tea to brew when Anthony, the new clerk from Glassware, shuffled in. Given his seniority, it wasn't fair to compare, but Robert felt the younger clerks, like Anthony, didn't take pride in the job. Robert wasn't going to boast, but besides appreciating individual nuances, he could juggle the customers at the register with those browsing along the aisles with the ones in various stages of undress in the dressing room so that each customer not only felt attended to, but pampered as well.

"Milk, Anthony?"

"Please, Mr. Pilgrim." Anthony was polite, at least.

"Anthony," Robert said, handing him a mug, "You've got to shower each female customer with the attention of a fiancé."

"Awh, yeah, definitely," Anthony replied, with a smirk.

"You've got to be sincere."

"I would be, too, Mr. Pilgrim."

Robert couldn't tell if Anthony was making fun of him or embarrassed. Of course, he was young for this talk. You needed a certain level of maturity to understand customer contact. Discrimination wasn't natural for some. Robert himself had taken some time to distinguish the needs of government workers coming from the council, school, and library; the blue-collar workers from the mine and petrol station; the shopkeepers and beauticians, retirees and dole collectors; and the property owners who drove up in utility trucks, but strutted in like cowboys. There were commonalities definitely, but the differences were where the sales were.

"Is Glass getting some good sales?" he asked, changing the subject.

"You know what you might find interesting, Mr. Pilgrim, is that there's a rumor that your customer, Belinda Black, was beaten up by her husband and is now in hospital."

Maybe it was the information or the tone, or the order it was said, or the slurping that followed it, but Robert felt uneasy. He stared at

Anthony's loose necktie that hung below the first button of his shirt, fighting a queasy sensation and reflexively reached for the button box on the inside pocket of his blazer. Belinda, hennaed hair alive with frizz and her brown freckles that melted into her rosy skin that melted into her thin lips, "beaten," Anthony had said. And your customer, he'd said that too, like he knew that Belinda frequently visited his department, sought out his opinions on products, awaited his recommendations while she slowly and deliberately licked the colored balm from her lips as though it were flavored.

Robert cleared his throat.

Anthony stirred more sugar into his tea then hit the spoon against his bottom teeth. *Tap, tap, tap.*

"This Black business is, right, awful," Robert finally rasped.

"Yeah, I thought you'd like to know, Mr. Pilgrim. I've noticed that you keep track of your customers." He'd noticed that, but had he noticed that she'd kept track of him? Robert wasn't going to say he was a victim here, but she had stalker qualities. Anthony must have noticed that she'd find any excuse to brush up against him, lean into him, gestures that even Audrey knew weren't respectful of the space Robert had built around himself. Still he had to be receptive to Belinda Black; she was a customer after all.

The whir of the air-conditioner's fan seemed louder. Robert's eyes watered, and Anthony had left his shirt untucked in back, slovenly, on purpose—was that possible? Robert felt overwhelmed with the messy implications of things. He mopped his eyes with the grubby tea towel from the counter, a normally foul act to him, and grimaced when Anthony said, "Anyhow, ta for the tea, Mr. Pilgrim."

"Right. Sure, Anthony, thanks. Thanks for the update."

Robert had seen signs of abuse a month earlier. There had been a bruise on Belinda's neck and a gash that ran like a shadow along the base of her lip. He'd pretended not to notice even while helping her choose a nylon scarf to cover the bruise. He'd said that the scarf's pastel flowers complemented her skin perfectly. And he'd said, "lovely colors," like that, even while noticing that her makeup was thick and that the rouge on her cheekbones hinted purple. She'd smiled at him sweetly, trustingly even. "Shall I show you the new non-balling jumpers from Brisbane?" he'd said. If he wished to be the man to comfort her here, offer his shoulder, he didn't know how to get beyond that restrained civility that defined, caged, and insulated him. Instead of a word of support, Robert politely sold her a batik scarf from Bali for $6.99, marked up three hundred percent. "Next week there'll be a sale if you'd like to wait," he'd said, gazing uncomfortably at the beige carpet between them.

When Belinda returned to Delton's two weeks later to buy a tie for her husband, she'd sought Robert's assistance. She'd asked him to model a few of them if he didn't mind, and he'd said, "Gladly," because he'd had some time to regret not reaching out to her in a way that settled right with him. He couldn't exactly say, "You'll be safe here, Mrs. Black," but certainly he could do more than he'd done. "I see you have a couple to be modeled then," he said, taking in the two ties she'd collected and following her to the empty women's dressing room. Her bruises had faded to yellow, barely noticeable now.

Robert first removed his tie. Belinda then slipped one of her ties over Robert's head and, with her hands between his vest and shirt, knotted and adjusted it for him. Then casually she'd said, "The longer ties are perfect for my husband, Freddie, but the colors are too vibrant for his taste. You're a color man, aren't you?"

"Men don't tend toward flashy colors," he'd said, professionally like that, struggling to ignore her fingertips and palms that lingered on his chest and to remember why and how he'd wished to be helpful here.

Of course, he should've said, "Is this the one, then? Let's take it back to the register and will that be cash or check, Mrs. Black?" He should've wondered if there were other customers in need of help and left to help them. Maybe here a shout for assistance, a call to Audrey or even Mr. Templeton as Belinda closed the dressing room door behind them. Of course, he should never have let Belinda kneel. He should've pulled her hands from his belt, zipper, and thighs as though they were stinging tentacles. He should've paid attention, no, remained on guard. Pulled himself from her generous mouth, but, you know—this pleasure—too pure, too pressing, impossible really to extricate yourself.

Robert leaned into the counter, resting his head in his hands. "Part of being a man is wandering," he could hear his father's voice. And like this was meant to be comforting: "You can't turn that off just because you're married. You're not a bloody faucet, Bob!"

✦

There was now no denying the air's texture. Bernadette Pilgrim felt contained and pressed by it. As she hiked further into the bush, her sweat collected and dripped from under her hardhat, the damp newspaper itched her brow, and her dress clung to her back. At a clump of eucalyptus trees, a kilometer beyond the ironbarks she'd seen earlier, Bernadette rested long enough to eat an orange, sweet and refreshing, which she documented in her notebook as "one orange consumed." Without her usual fastidiousness, she left the orange peels in the grass and, without consulting her log, decided to follow the Tropic of Capricorn, latitude 23° south, further west. That she'd looked this up earlier and had been proud that she shared Captain Sturt's keen attention to direction today meant little to her.

One hundred and twenty-seven years after Charles Sturt's expedition set out for the center of Australia, and two thousand three hundred kilometers east from his departure point, Moorundi, in the south west of Australia, Bernadette Pilgrim left Mount Isaac, Queensland, one week after her eleventh birthday.

Whereas Sturt and his colleagues wore trousers and long-sleeved shirts of linen sailcloth (waterproofed with linseed oil), black riding boots, and felt hats, Bernadette wore a cotton dress patterned with tiny blue medallions, newly polished school shoes, and a white hardhat held in place by balled up newspaper and a stained yellow ribbon.

Bernadette borrowed the hat from her father as protection from the magpies that would swoop and dive-bomb her. From her mother, Bernadette took a meter stick that had been chewed at both ends by the neighbor's terrier in case she happened upon an adder, taipan, or brown snake, which so far she hadn't. Naturally, the Sturt expedition was better equipped with Tranter revolvers, Terry's breech loaders, and knives crafted at Fitzroy Iron Works.

Bernadette, in the school notebook that she'd converted into an excursion log, listed the supplies she carried in a knapsack: two oranges for scurvy, a box of raisins and four slices of bread for hunger (explorers usually took flour but that wasn't practical), a flask of raspberry cordial for thirst, and two Arnotts Butter Biscuits for civility (a notion she'd picked up from the tea and sherry breaks of Captain Cook and his naturalist, Sir Joseph Banks, whose expeditions she'd also diligently studied).

On this day, unlike other of Bernadette's expedition days when she would stand on the top railing of the back fence casting her sights on the bush as if it were a vast coastline, she couldn't see a thing ahead of her. The flagrant crimson from the bottlebrush bristles and the golden wash of wattle blossoms were as lost to her as the amplitudes of wet and dry, the air's texture up against her skin, in her nostrils and throat. Even the dingy menthol smell of eucalyptus and the clicks, hums, sighs, rushes, and whistles of bush life couldn't draw her in. In the house behind her, the light from her parents' bedside lamp spilled into the hallway from under their door. The wood floors creaked from her father's weight as he paced. Or was he packing? She wasn't sure about this latter point, although she was confident that her mother had turned away, pretending sleep despite the dawn commotion. Her little sister, Jane, still slept in their room as though she weren't in a hammock on a boat that was dangerously keeled over. Typical, Bernadette thought.

When Bernadette finally climbed off the fence and entered the bush, she knew without looking back that the house was unmoored and lurching towards her. She walked onward, though, with the rectitude of Captain Sturt, noting the minutes to reach the clump of ironbark gum trees west of them. The twenty minutes that she'd typically log in her book, like Magellan or Cook or Vasco da Gamma recording their time of departure from Spain, England or Portugal, she didn't. Such rituals and affinities seemed juvenile now. "Silly, like silly little you."

✦

Motivations for expeditions change. Cook in 1769 in the Pacific was different than Cook in the Antarctic in 1773 and, of course, Cook in Bering Straits five years after that. Similarly, Sturt's motivations were different in 1828 and 1829 in New South Wales, and fifteen years later in 1844 in Central Australia.

Bernadette's would change also. She was six the first time she expressed her ambition as an explorer. She knew that on the back of the world map that hung in the hallway were continents with landscapes, peoples, and languages to discover and the prospect of adventure. "Funny that no one's searched the other side yet, Mum," she said, tapping the plastic frame. "Aren't they stupid!"

A day later, when Bernadette asked for supplies, her mother, Audrey, removed the map from the wall to reveal its bare wooden backing. She described the dimensions of the globe, which said without saying: "See Love, there are no places left to discover." Not convinced, Bernadette set her sights on the backyard, then the bush that backed up against the backyard, then the bush that surrounded their small town in central Queensland.

When Audrey caught Bernadette circumnavigating their fence, she sat her down and said, "Bernadette, a girl like you should fix her sights on things that can be done locally." She handed Bernadette wax paper, colored pens, and an atlas opened to the Hawaiian Islands and said, "Trace these, hey. Why travel when you can decorate your and Jane's room with tropical islands?"

Bernadette read explorer stories and studied their routes. In later years she included her sister, Ship Sailor Jane, and Jarri, her imaginary Aboriginal guide, for more expansive expeditions. She learned to be more discrete and protective about these forays, however, especially after her mother told her about Marcy.

"Bernadette, when I was your age I had a sheep called Marcy, knitted from oily wool with black shiny buttons for eyes. I loved her so much that I took her to the shops, beach, friends'—everywhere. One day, Henry, my brother—your uncle—wants me to play outside with him, but I'm playing with Marcy. He says, 'Come on, Audrey, I've got a frilly-neck lizard. Let's chase him and stick him.' So do you know what Henry does? He grabs Marcy and bites off her eye and spits it at me."

"What did you do, Mum?" Bernadette asked.

"I went with him to stick the frilly lizard. Dolls are dolls, Bernadette. You leave your childhood games. You must."

✦

Now beneath that eucalyptus littered with orange peels from her second orange, for Bernadette thinking back on this story, she might've thought of that one button spat, but also of all those other buttons that, just yesterday, she'd heard pop and spin across the kitchen floor; all her mother's collected buttons—not exactly spat, but spattered over the tiles. She might have heard her father's shout: "Get out, you silly! Get you and your sister away!" and felt again the hard concrete where he'd pushed her.

Bernadette stared up into the tree's canopy suspended hundreds of meters above her. How small I am, she thought. And then, I'm not hardly small because, a moment later, she walked deeper into the bush.

By the time Bernadette had passed into new territory, an insect drone—mostly of flies—had replaced the bright calls of early morning. Attracted by the orange's sticky residue, the flies persisted around her lips and nostrils. She tried to ignore them, reminding herself that this is what flies did in the outback and hadn't all Australian explorers encountered this and hadn't she herself encountered this on her previous expeditions? She conjured Ship Sailor Jane and Jarri. "We must set our mind against these critters. Onward!" she ordered, refocusing on the horizon and the large red rock that she'd targeted there for discovery and which, she'd decided, would vindicate her from her father's unfair dismissal.

Bernadette, like a ship, steered toward the rock through oaks now, not gums, and kangaroo and tussock grass as tall as her waist. She hummed "Botany Bay": "*Singing Tooral liooral liaddity, Singing Tooral liooral liay,*" with a joviality that, although false, meant to recall a mood that, for the life of her, she couldn't attain.

She swept her meter stick staff before her to flush out creatures, but stirred up dust and dry seeds instead. A paddock's length further her staff snagged in the grass, snapping her out of her song and the space within herself where she'd regained the confidence of an explorer. The meter stick became a bit of wood with faded markings for measuring fabric and the explorer became a child and Bernadette flung the stick high and far. What am I doing? This grass, these reptiles, my bush sense—where's it gone?

Can't I be Captain for once? Ship Sailor Jane intruded.

Please, Sailor! An expedition needs officers and crew, not two captains.

Please, can't I be?

You don't know enough.

I do so! Test me, come on, test me.

The number of hands hired for a 400-ton ship is not fifty men, Sailor, but one hundred.

To not starve, Sailor, you eat the weevils in the dry goods. You suck the orange to fight the scurvy.

If you pilfer food expect punishment. On expedition, it's all about food and water, Sailor. That's all it's about.

I know that, Bernadette—I've died of scurvy, I've died of starvation from shipwrecks, I've drowned in cyclones. How many mutinies do I have to be murdered in?

"Shut up," Bernadette whispered, striding ahead faster as though, with her own propulsion, she could regain that sense of herself that said, Yes, I will have to flog you for this, Jane. And, no, those buttons meant nothing. And, yes, I know exactly why I'm going where I'm going and I never needed a stick in the first place.

Bernadette, with destiny upon her, left her first hints of fear and regret in the grass as though she could leave them forever, saying to Jane:

"Most explorers who leave don't come back.

They meet bushrangers or ex-convicts out there.

They get diseases; their limbs rot off.

Poisonous snakes bite them.

They starve or die of thirst.

Aboriginals don't like explorers, Jane, they never have. Right, Jarri?

I'm only telling you this for your own good. No one else here will."

✦

It was Bernadette who informed Jane that their father had had the breakdown, telling her also that in families of explorers this was something you could expect. Bernadette was vague enough that Jane wasn't sure what she was referring to. Was it a condition that Bernadette had discovered in one of her explorer books and thought that the Pilgrims should have too? Jane didn't initially associate it with the day that their father pulled them from school, for that was the same day as their mum's button explosion. "Boom! Just like that— buttons everywhere," she'd told her best friend, Franca.

Naturally, Jane, as soon as she could, told Franca about this breakdown as well.

Franca then told Cynthia Clark, two years ahead of them in the fourth grade. Who told whose parents wasn't clear, but someone's parents were told because some parent explained to one child who cautioned another child who warned another child so that before Jane knew it, and without her understanding, at lunch she found herself in the center of a ring of girls singing, "Loony tunes! Loony tunes! Jane's dad is loony tunes!"

When Jane claimed there'd been a mistake, they sang louder. When she claimed that their dads were loony, too, they sang louder still, and when, finally, she tried to break out of the ring, they tightened it around her like a noose.

No one expected Jane to start dancing. But what came to her, as she made her first tentative moves, was the Aboriginal Dreamtime story that her mother had once read to her about Tiddalik, the giant frog, who'd drunk the earth's water and created a drought. *It's up to you, the dying creatures, to make Tiddalik laugh.* Old Wombat had advised them that if they could make him laugh he'd cough up the water and they'd be saved. Jane closed her eyes.

"Loony tunes!"

It was worth a try. The kookaburra told a wry anecdote in praise of amphibians, generally, and frogs, specifically. Jane swayed her head and mimicked the laughing call of the kookaburra: "koo-koo-koo-kaa-kaa-kaa" for the girls, who immediately parroted it back. The kangaroo, proud acrobat, jumped up and over Emu, the proud sprinter. Jane, now silenced, swung her arms above her, leaping up and down like a pogo stick.

"Dance! Dance!" the girls chanted.

No, not that either.

Blanket lizard paraded with his swollen belly. Jane quit the pogoing, thrust out her belly, and wriggled her hips almost immediately realizing that she didn't have enough of a belly to make this work ether. The eel Nabunum, though. She could be the eel dancing on the dry creek bed. Jane rolled her torso down and opening her arms spun clockwise and then counterclockwise staring into each of the girls' eyes as she turned.

The girls, finally speechless, backed away and, by the time the school bell rang marking the end of lunch, Jane was alone.

Just as Bernadette had always been an explorer, Jane was a dreamer. Early on Jane's arms and legs would flail and noises of distress or delight would push themselves from her sleeping torso as though inside her a tormentor or cajoler was expanding. That story her mum had told to distract and to entertain her had instead set off a new series of nightmares.

Jane dreamt she was the eel.

She dreamt of a man with a giant mouth laughing.

She dreamt she was a flood, a desert, and a pool with dead birds floating in it.

She was once the last person dancing, unable to stop.

Standing alone in the playground, Jane felt the essential distress of all these dreams without the clear recollection of any of them. As she queued with the other kids to file into the classroom, she wasn't particularly comforted that in the story Tiddalik had laughed at the eel and had replenished all the waterholes, rivers, and seas with the water he'd swallowed. Jane looked for Franca, who she noticed had slipped ahead of her in line behind Kerri Simpson. "Franca?" she called out, thankful that her friend hadn't joined the clique.

Franca turned slightly.

"Jane Pilgrim, you're the most loony Pilgrim of all; far loonier than your dad," she said in Jane's direction before turning back to Kerri.

✦

Nightmares offer their own distress that no piece of advice can easily assuage. When Jane became too scared to sleep, Audrey took her to the pediatrician, Dr. Bronson, who cut straight to the matter: "Your daughter suffers from a modicum of excess worry, which doesn't help sleep, and that deprivation of rest contributes to more worry so you've got yourself a circular event, where this begets that and that begets this until you've got yourself more than a modicum. Growing pains are seldom standard, Mrs. Pilgrim. Your Jane has nothing that time, a cup of warm milk with Milo, and some Children's Aspro won't cure."

Robert, skeptical about the benefits of chocolate milk, spoke with the parish priest, Father Malcolm. "Let's go talisman cure on this one," the priest said. "Kids like to know they've got a saint on their side. Not a guardian angel, mind you, that's too easy. If Jane constructs some altars to the saints, puts a bit of elbow grease in, see if she doesn't feel safer with our Godly Ladies and Gents looking out for her."

And sure enough, after Jane received *Stories of Saints* from her father and had begun to construct altars for the saints, she did forget the dreams that had undone her or even that she'd been undone. What she'd been gleaning of the awesome Dreamtime world where the backyard could lead out to a dinosaur feeding ground, the Milky Way as well as a pie shop and netball court, where she could be an eel, the desert as well as the sky above, mostly faded along with the voice that could weigh in on these things. Generally, but for the wise and holy men and women of our tribe, the sacred indivisibility of time, space, and matter isn't necessarily something kids or even grownups are expected to grasp for long.

✦

Mrs. Green clapped twice and greeted Jane's class with a, "Sit please!" Once they'd settled, she tapped her chalk on the desk and asked, "What would you do if there was a fire?" And immediately after: "I'm not going to wait all day, speak up!"

Jane tried again to catch Franca's eye. She wished Franca could understand why being a bird or animal was the only thing that occurred to her to make the girls leave her alone. She hadn't been trapped before so how would she know that a saintlier, non-loony way wouldn't occur to her? Next time she'd definitely channel a saint from one of her altars. After a while Jane gave up trying to connect with Franca, staring instead at the back of Gavin Mackay, who sat directly in front of her.

Mrs. Green drew three columns on the board. "What's the difference between a house fire, a bush fire, and a person on fire?" While she listed the household items of particular danger—stove-tops and kettles, candles and light sockets, hot metal and glass, chip oil— Jane ignored the notes that Franca and Kerri were now exchanging. As Mrs. Green warned them against matches, fireworks, and lightning bolts, Jane inhaled the sweet scent of the fire safety mimeographs that Mrs. Green had just distributed, ignoring that Franca and Kerri were doing the same. By the time that Mrs. Green explained that the best way to extinguish a fire is with water or smothering it with blankets or—"if it's you"—rolling on the ground, Jane grimly tracked a beetle that had landed on the back of Gavin's collar.

"The phone number to the Mt. Isaac Fire Department is 620-261," they recited. She watched it fall from Gavin and scuttle across the floor toward the windows.

"The Mackays could use Dalmatians," Jane had once overheard Mrs. Filo, their neighbor with the swing set, tell her mum. Later her mother had clarified that donations were gifts for poorer people. At the time, Jane had known that she was missing something, but now it seemed okay, a relief actually with all the Franca and Kerri activity to picture Gavin with a spotted dog with a cheerful red bow tied around its head. It was a relief then to imagine the altar she'd later construct for the Saint for Dogs.

Gavin twisted around and glared at Jane as though he knew that she was using him. His eye was inflamed and red, like the bow she'd imagined, except where it was stained yellow from Dettol disinfectant.

His damaged face embarrassed Jane—how it looked, how she hadn't noticed it before, and how it made her realize that she'd never tried to be his friend. She smiled self-consciously and he smiled back.

"And what, Mr. Mackay, are you doing?"

Gavin spun to the front, his left knee tensely jigging up and down.

"I just, I was…"

"Enough excuses, young man! I wasn't born yesterday when it comes to you Mackay brothers. Turn to your book exactly now. Please pretend that you care about fires!"

✦

At the last bell of the day, Jane quickly collected her port. She ran to the school's back fence, hoping that no one would see her slip out alone, and veered west toward the shady gum tree. There, Jane perched on the tree's exposed root and from her port removed the sketch of a dog with black spots that she'd secretly drawn in class. Gulping back a sob, she acknowledged that for any fire—Mrs. Greens', Father Malcolm's hell fires, and the wild fires her dad recorded—a massive supply of water would be required. *Don't muck about with self-pity, Ship Sailor Jane*, Bernadette admonished.

She searched for a stick that looked like a dog bone. More water than a fire hydrant contained, but less than that frog. She collected a couple of gum nuts to be used as dog treats. Maybe Moses, definitely Jesus, would step up with the water supply and definitely rely on her to manage the hoses. She slipped an elastic off the end of one plait. They would expect Jane to direct Bernadette, her parents, and really everybody in town to put out the flames. But Franca and Kerri—*control, Sailor*—and those other kids wouldn't be invited. She wrapped the dog sketch around the bone stick and secured it with her elastic. Hell would flood. But the doomed people would still survive with the flotation beds and inner tubes like those at the town pool. She scattered the dog treats at the base of the Dog Saint altar, propped now in the hook of a tree root. Sins like flames dissolve in water, which was exactly why God supplied inflatables. "Exactly why!" she repeated out loud.

"Exactly why what?" Gavin had stealthily crept up on her.

"What?" Jane jumped up trying to act natural.

Gavin crouched to examine Jane's project.

"It's an altar for the Dog Saint," she said.

"Who's that?" He poked the bundle.

"The saint who looks out for dogs."

"Is your dog sick or something?"

"We don't have a dog." Jane, blushing, stared down at her school shoes.

"Thanks a lot by the way, Jane." He'd flicked off the elastic and was now tracing the outline of the dog.

"For what?" She tried to sound tough.

He stuck the bone part of the altar emphatically back in the ground, ripping the paper. "I'm sure you know what!" Standing, he tossed her gum nuts in the grass.

Jane thought he couldn't know about the dog or the red bow. It's not all my fault that Mrs. Green got mad at him. Behind her ear, she hooked a strand of hair that had escaped from her plait and gripped her port so tightly that her knuckles blanched.

"You want to go to the river?" he asked.

Bernadette and the others would never agree to hold a hose for her and Franca wouldn't want to hold a hose for her and what did it mean that she and her Dad were loony anyway? The afternoon seemed strange suddenly, and the world where she would meet Franca after school and go on expedition with Bernadette and her mother would caution her not to stray from Franca's or Catechism or Brownies was already in another older time of her childhood. What did it matter what the "what" was? Gavin didn't seem to hold it against her. He wasn't even bothered by the altar. And then there was always the chance he might explain his face. As Gavin started down the path leaving barefoot imprints in the hot, red soil, she followed him.

"Yeah, sure," she said. "Let's go to the river."

✦

Audrey Pilgrim rested the maypole, a three-meter umbrella-style clothesline donated by Geraldine Moss, the town librarian, against her hip. She'd volunteered to assist Louisa Cawley, President of the Mt. Isaac May Day Committee, in choosing the maypole's position in Pickdill Paddock for Saturday's celebration.

While most residents of this small town in central Queensland anticipated May Day as a welcome break from the routines of weather, work, and school, Audrey invested herself in the celebration, believing that a spring ritual grounded children and adults in an essential way. Mrs. Markham, the primary school's headmistress, reinforced this on parade that week, describing to the student body how once May Day marked the day that Anglo Saxons sipped milk still warm from the cow and sucked gobs of honey from ancient pots. "Imagine, children, the decay on their poor teeth without a proper toothbrush!" Terence Becker, leader of the Boy Scout troop, focused on the "bright fire" of Beltane and sacrifices—"We're talking the sacrificial slaughter of magpies and wombats and the like"—made for abundance. He skipped the part about sacrifices concerning fertility as it might have brought up practices that parents and priests were more comfortable handling and which the mere thought of made Terrence's ears redden and his trousers tight. Not shy about matters, Joe Pearl, the publican at Mt. Isaac's Imperial Hotel, pronounced to his regulars: "Don't kid yourself, fellas, this is our holiday. Yeah, boughs of blossoms brought to decorate the maypole, right! The skyward symbol of life, right! Tell me that's not about the primacy of the rod."

"It's got to be perfect, Audrey. The placement," Louisa said. With one hand Audrey steadied the pole's sway, and with the other she pulled down her dress where it had begun to ride up.

"A maypole must be at the epicenter of the action. A maypole must draw all eyes to it. A perfectly placed maypole, Audrey, is magic!"

Audrey, with arms trembling, back muscles taut and still tightening—they had already traversed the dusty paddock five times—felt her enthusiasm wane at each pole re-position. Still she worked to retain a positive outlook as she imagined the maypole's colorful ribbons connecting her to Jane and Bernadette at Mount Isaac Primary School, to Robert at Delton's Department Store, and stretching as far as the coast and the Yeppoon cemetery to her parents and Nan, who had all died of old age, and her brother Henry, who'd been killed three years before by a drunk driver. With an optimism directed more at them than Louisa, Audrey responded:

"It's good to try out every spot. I see that. This pole is hardly heavy at all. Magic, I can see that. Yes, Louisa."

Audrey's incongruity wasn't isolated. May in the Southern Hemisphere is actually autumn, so the regenerative aspects of the May celebration, at least locally, insinuated themselves through the

21

suggestion of spring rather than the facts of it. For example, although there'd been no rain in Mt. Isaac for over thirteen months and the town's lawns and the scrub, on its outskirts, had faded and become brittle and brown, the red cone-shaped flowers of banksia trees still offered brightness here and there, as did the evergreen leaves of the eucalyptus trees that liberally covered the region. The early onset of morning frost and that damp chill, which seeped under blankets, through wool cardigans, pullovers, and trousers, were hopeful signs in this place. Only a hopeful community could look to the unchanging blue of the broad sky above them and see a new season with the possibility of rain.

When Robert voiced his concern about the amount of work she'd invest in the celebration, Audrey happily justified her activity. "On what other holiday can our girls join the Smith, MacNamara, Pakanovsky, and Phuong kids to dance around the maypole while their parents drink beer and eat barbeque together?" she asked him. "On what other day did the Mount Isaac State Primary and Secondary Schools, the mine, local businesses, and clubs build floats on the backs of truck beds and everybody who belonged to anything march in the parade down Main Street to the sounds of bagpipes, marching bands, or accordions? On what other day could you sit on a float in a beach or jungle scene, beside a giant fire hydrant or clover or amongst bauxite pieces scattered beside a massive cardboard bauxite boulder covered with red crepe paper?" Or, in her case, watch from the street beside Mary Ellen Keys who'd always scream, "Dominic, you're bigger than bold!" to her disabled son. "After a full morning typing contracts for Solicitor Simpson, I like to consider spring, Robert," she'd said. "I'm good at it."

"Definitely, Audrey, you are," Robert had replied, "but be mindful that overworked hands become rheumatic and stiff. Strained eyes don't automatically reverse themselves. Plus, spring is messy and entails a lot of washing up. Those May Day white peasant blouses, the grime notwithstanding, can be quite provocative. There's a reason that they say not to let the cat out of the bag. It'd be a shame if you needed the same remedy my mum did for her joint pain: ointment made from crushed eucalyptus leaves, chamomile blossoms, and lard."

Audrey's generous outlook helped her cope with all that bewildered her about Robert's responses. His solicitations were his way to acknowledge Audrey's stress in assisting Louisa with the May

Day activities, remembering, as he would, that Audrey had wished to direct them herself. This was his way to say, Audrey, I'm glad you've stuck origami flowers onto a two-meter globe for Jane's Brownie troop float; I'm impressed with your construction of the cardboard Egyptian pyramid for Bernadette's Grade Seven float; that wrap-around skirt and headdress lined with lace and fake pink flowers for Jane's maypole dance costume is exquisite. Creativity and industry like yours is unbeatable. Sexy even. I've got just the remedy if later your hands are sore.

Louisa directed Audrey four steps to the left and then three steps to the right. Yes, solicitations like Robert's signified a support as loving as his daily gifts of buttons, which he'd presented to her each day of their marriage. Who but him had that imagination, attention to detail, persistence, and reliability? She doubted if Louisa's husband or her boss, Solicitor Simpson, did that for their wives. Audrey felt more than the creep of fatigue. She looked over at the cluster of stripped-barked gum trees that rose over one hundred meters above the eastern section of the paddock, shrouded in morning mist.

She missed Robert: his touch, taste, the weight of his body. She couldn't pinpoint the day he'd stopped reaching for her, but Audrey was certain now that he'd consistently stopped, which disorientated her, as though, without warning, he'd pulled up anchor and set her adrift. She wondered for an instant if she might've been culpable, her longing too insistent or maybe not insistent enough. She felt a surge of doubt and a niggling fear that she, with all this craft, may've squandered her talents.

"That mist reminds me of fog on the north coast where I was raised," she quietly said.

"I was raised here." Louisa checked her wristwatch.

"Since you've never been, the beach in Yeppoon is worth seeing, especially the white ship sculpture above Keppel Bay. Robert and I went there for one of our first dates."

Louisa nudged her half a step left.

"Eerie music floats through the sculpture when it's windy, and I don't know how it happens"—and I don't know how I'm doing these petty projects when I had such plans for my own creative ones—"but that music lifts you to an ancient place and fills you with a feeling beyond hope."

Louisa dug a heel into the soil, glanced behind her out of the paddock to the bush where the town's development had stalled.

"Beyond hope, hey?"

"That's why it's called The Singing Ship. It's famous," Audrey added.

Louisa replied that she'd never heard of a singing sculpture and then recounted how one night when she was a girl she dreamt that she was Prime Minister of Australia.

"That very next day, Audrey, Milli Peterson sent a message from her property that she wanted to sell me her stallion. Father purchased it for me, too. Yours is a pretty dream, though." Louisa stared at Audrey with a fierceness that Audrey knew was largely absent from her own expression.

She hardened hers: "A) I didn't tell you a dream." Audrey's tone hardened too. "B) Let's put the pole right there under those trees. And C) I'm not getting any younger out here!" I did not give up my dreams, she thought. I still have chances!

Louisa looked with perplexity from Audrey to the trees.

"And if you carried Geraldine's clothesline for any amount of time, you'd understand the weight of it!" Audrey sharply added.

Both women blushed.

"I'd like you, Audrey, to keep the weight of the ritual in mind. And ribbons. And children. Twirling around the maypole with their ribbons in their outfits with their songs. Perhaps then you'll appreciate the importance of pole placement." Louisa's chin jutted forward with each emphatic phrase. "Spring is not a frivolous event!" she angrily declared.

"Autumn, Louisa! It's autumn!" Audrey shouted back at her. "This is real life here. Autumn!"

Louisa harrumphed and strutted away. As Audrey watched her go, she heard Jane clap and recite in unlikely accompaniment:

> *"Come, lasses and lads, get leave of your dads,*
> *And away to the Maypole hie!*
> *For every he has got him a she,*
> *And the fiddler's standing by!*
> *For Willie shall dance with Jane,*
> *And Johnny has got his Joan!*
> *To trip it, trip it, trip it, trip it, trip it up and down!"*

As Louisa disappeared between the nude trunks of eucalyptus trees and high grasses, Audrey said, "It's true I would've liked to have had a stallion." And then even though her mother replied: "What rubbish, dear. Isn't it enough to be Mummy's little helper and Daddy's little pet?" And then her father: "This is a fair country, Love. Some of us don't want stallions. Don't wish for what you shouldn't want!" And after that Robert: "The wildness of a stallion is far too dangerous," and Bernadette: "It'll be my stallion, not Jane's, Mum," and Jane's desperate how-can-that-be-fair look, Audrey declared to the empty field: "Yes! The Singing Ship made music! And I still want a stallion! And yes, Mum, Dad, Robert. Yes, Bernadette. Yes, Jane! Yes! I want!"

✦

Robert felt the walls closing in on him when he returned to Casuals after the tea break. He worried that Belinda's condition was a result of their tryst, if you could call it that. Freddie Black might. He worried that Freddie would be out for more vengeance and that unwittingly Robert had put his family at risk. He mopped the perspiration from his brow with the handkerchief that Audrey had embroidered with his initials, RJP—Robert John Pilgrim. He tried to discount these worries along with the smirk he now pictured on his father's face.

Sort the slacks into ascending sizes. Fold and stack the cardigan sweaters. Unpack the new shipment of blouses. He wished there were more customers, then he wished there were none. He attached prices on the new batch of blouses with a sticker gun. Did Freddie have a gun? That he hadn't used it on Belinda didn't mean he wouldn't use it on them. Take an inventory. There was definitely a shortage in size ten sleeveless dresses. Audrey's size, which was larger than Belinda's size six, which he wished he didn't know even though it was legitimately known for the purpose of customer insight.

He felt again for the buttons in his blazer. On the way, his hand passed over his chest, a man's chest like any other, and he pictured then all the men in his father's pub, where, for the first time, he saw himself and Freddie Black too, and in his mind's eye all their chests were as broad as oil drums and, please God no, each of their members was rock solid. He dumped the buttons in his palm and studied them like they might provide a remedy to his agitation and when they didn't he emptied them into his trouser pocket and called the personnel manager, Mrs. Dowley. "I have a fever," he said. "A flu." They agreed he'd better get home before he could infect anyone.

Robert arrived at Bernadette and Jane's school just after little lunch. Because Audrey handled the majority of school activities—the Parent-Teacher nights, fetes, athletic days, and the rest—he'd seldom been. He contributed to the girls' school readiness: their discipline in dress and homework—all key indicators for success. It's that insidious slackness that you most have to ward against. Slop. Not many fathers can claim to guard against that with their kids, he'd once boasted to Audrey.

The school secretary, Miss Sandle, greeted him from behind the registry desk in the front office.

"I'm here for my children," Robert said, noticing that she wore a stork pin from Delton's Accessories Department.

"Audrey's mother is here for an unexpected visit, and Audrey sent me for Jane and Bernadette. You know, for preparations and such."

Miss Sandle rifled through the roll book. "Back in a tic," she said.

Robert waited outside under the school's corrugated iron roof awning. He rubbed the fish button in his palm like a worry bead, his thumb deliberating on each ridge of its scales. "We had a good time fishing, didn't we?" He tried to capture that idyllic memory of fishing for bony breams at Mulga Creek with his father and brother, Stewart, in an effort to cap the onslaught of the more upsetting memories.

He looked up to see Miss Sandle approach with Bernadette and Jane. Bernadette strode with the confidence of Mr. Templeton. Poised, her thick black hair was pulled neatly into a single braid, her school uniform was pressed and clean, and her shoes were immaculately polished. Jane flicked her left pigtail behind her shoulder and waved at him. "Dad? Dad!" Robert didn't wave, but nodded in her direction, noting the stain on her uniform, one brown sock scrunched down at her ankle, which she paused to pull up, perhaps sensing that his gaze had fallen there.

The girls looked surprised to see him, but not alarmed. Miss Sandle clearly hadn't mentioned the visit of Nanna Rose, which was fortunate since she'd been dead for over five years.

"I shall take them from here. Thank you." Robert said more sternly than he intended and, as if to reverse the tone, once the three of them were alone on the sidewalk outside the school, he said, "Doesn't the cement feel warm?"

The sidewalk stretched before them, between the broad band of bitumen on one side and a line of golden wattles, planted by the

Garden Society, on the other. Behind the trees, pre-fab trailers painted the same off-white color peeked through, dull against the pale sky.

"What do you mean?" Jane said.

"What's going on, Dad?" Bernadette said.

He ushered them forward. "I mean, sometimes you can notice new things if you pay attention."

"What's going on? Where's Mum?"

"Home, Bernie." He didn't usually shorten Bernadette's name and he realized it probably sounded as foreign to her as it did to him.

"Why are we getting out of school early, Dad?" Jane asked.

"There's nothing new about hot cement." Bernadette scowled.

"Because Jane, like your Grand-Dad Jack used to say, there's no harm in a day of hooky."

"Why's that, Dad?" Jane asked, tugging up that same sock.

"Enough chit chat, girls," Robert said. "Let's head home so we can begin our Pilgrim family 'arvo,' as your Grand-Dad would say—our day of fun."

"It's eleven o'clock," Bernadette said.

"We'll sit: play games, read books, and what-not." He must've known he didn't sound like himself. "Your Mum will make cordial, and we'll eat biscuits and cake." He wasn't himself. He pictured his father roll a cigarette, grin at him and his mother, and his mother, with her arms rested on her belly as though it were a new counter, smiling at Jack then Robert and back at Jack. What do any of us know of each other? "We might even sing, girls." Audrey, this isn't like that; this isn't me.

"You only sing at Christmas and birthdays," Bernadette reminded him. "We're supposed to be in school."

"Could we have chocolate for our afternoon tea, Dad?" Jane said. "Could we have licorice and a milkshake, a strawberry one?"

"Where's Mum?" Bernadette glared at Jane.

The moment Marjorie Mead's Ford Falcon rounded the corner, for Robert it could only be Belinda's Freddie, aiming his vehicle at them like a weapon. Robert shoved his daughters across the path behind a wattle tree, blocking them from the driver's view. Later, Robert would insist to Audrey that he saw the car coming straight for them onto the sidewalk, so pushing them was simply a survival instinct. He'd insist that Mrs. Marjorie Mead from Elm Road, who'd splurged on silver bangles last Tuesday, was blind and a danger on the road, and her license should be revoked. Later still, at the Tremble Family Nursing Home, Robert would warn residents and staff alike to always be wary of their fun.

That day, as soon as Mrs. Mead was out of sight, he turned to his alarmed daughters, not registering their alarm, and said, "What a close call. Aren't we lucky!" He thought: I need to pull myself together. Bernadette and Jane silently wiped the gravel from their legs and gathered their ports from the sidewalk. Bernadette finally said, "Old women in cars can be very dangerous."

"Lucky she had the patron saint of cars with her," Jane added, not detecting Bernadette's sarcasm.

"Please already!" Robert snapped. Concerned that they wouldn't be safe until they were indoors, he gruffly redirected his daughters to the inside sidewalk and marched them home, guarding them as he'd done when they were toddlers. In air filled with the ratcheting of heavy machinery, punctuated by spurts of jack-hammering, carried on the wind from a construction site at the center of town, they walked the final blocks home, neither girl speaking, cautious of the shift they'd seen in their father.

✦

Robert immediately busied himself in the kitchen when he realized Audrey wasn't home. He opened and closed the cupboards, inspected the refrigerator, and turned the tap on and off twice. He'd promised the girls food and fun, but he couldn't focus on either with Audrey still in Freddie's sights. Bernadette left the kitchen by the second turn of the tap. Jane still waited for him and cordial and the possibility of cake.

"It's not too hot," he said. "I'm hardly sweating."

"Neither am I, Dad," Jane said, her face glistening.

Robert removed his blazer and loosened his tie. He set the buttons on the table like stakes in a bet.

"Do you remember Grand-Dad Jack, Jane?" He wanted her to leave.

"Nanna tied his leg onto the wheelchair with pieces of string." Jane arranged the buttons into a daisy shape with the fish and toucan in the center and the flower and bead buttons as petals. They'd be nice in an altar, she thought. "He must be glad to be in heaven."

"That's right." Robert had limited his family's visits with his parents until after his father's stroke.

"Remember how he fell on your lap, Dad?"

Reclined in a settler chair at one end of his parent's veranda, Robert had been ignoring his father seated in his wheelchair at the other end, ignoring him calling over to Robert with language that since his stroke slurred and didn't string together sensibly. He continued to ignore his father even as he propelled himself at Robert using his right arm and leg, his left side unusably contracted and weak. When their chairs collided, his father's body whipped forward and onto Robert's lap, his father's leg still entangled in the wheelchair. And his father chuckled.

"Nanna made roast beef and Yorkshire pudding," Jane added.

"Bugger you!" Robert blurted out to his father, who, he knew, had intentionally done that. "That's right, bugger you!"

To Jane, who stunned and solemn, and wondering—had to wonder—why her father had sworn at her, Robert ordered, "Get out! Go join your sister!" As soon as Robert heard the bedroom door close behind her, he said, "Bugger you," again and again, louder each time, until daughters and dread were gone from the room replaced by self-hatred of a magnitude that was impossible to quantify. What was odd and what Robert never confided to anyone later was that he had the strangest sensation of his father next to him, congratulating and consoling him at the same time.

✦

The sun, now white and high in the sky, bleached the color from the sky itself, as well as the trees, rocks, and brush that Bernadette passed. When she reached the red rock, Bernadette realized it wasn't a rock or red, but a huge termite mound, the orangey color of glaze on the cream buns at the school tuck shop.

Flushed and slightly lightheaded, she removed her knapsack and hardhat and rested against the dormant mound. She faced north where twenty-nine kilometers off was Moreen, the state-owned bauxite mine, and fifteen kilometers before that, Gilgin Downs, an abandoned cattle property at the base of the escarpment. Although not necessarily seeing it, what she looked out on, squinting into the distance, between bites of white bread and sips of red cordial, was an ancient unsettled bush that rolled indefinitely before her. Behind her, literally rough against her back, was that termite mound that she'd just discovered and that she'd sketch later because it was unusual, and a record would be needed. She decided this, but made no move to get her notebook.

Sir Joseph Banks, Bernadette's go-to naturalist, might've recorded that the termite mound was approximately seven meters tall with a circumference of one and a half meters, and then calculated its age and estimated the number of termites needed to build it. He might've surmised that the grass and spinifex nearby fueled their activity, and made some few notes on the effects of weather on the mound's surface, speculating about the working conditions inside the mound. He might've made a note to himself to find out if the termite mound had significance for the Natives. If there were a specimen to be found, Banks would've pinned it to the back of the tiny box he carried with him in the pocket of his long coat.

Bernadette stood and observed the termite mound from a distance. She meant to be as scientific as Sir Joseph Banks. The week before, she would've measured the mound's height with her meter stick. The week before, she'd still have a meter stick that she hadn't flung somewhere into the grass. Last week, she would've studied the mound's surface with a magnifying glass. Bernadette's magnifying glass lay in the drawer of her desk beside Jane's bed. It was an oversight that Banks, Sturt, any decent naturalist or explorer wouldn't tolerate, and that would definitely make it harder to accurately diagram the pattern of tiny holes that bored into the mound.

It wasn't as though she couldn't formulate hypotheses about the termite mound without tools. Bernadette still hadn't moved. Where the tunnels led, the nature of the rooms inside, and the possibility of a queen termite nesting in the cool center. *This is not a beehive, Pilgrim,* Sturt admonished her. Banks agreed. Okay, but this week is still like last week, she thought, although she felt less sure.

Bernadette scrounged for a sharp stick that she could use like a chisel to cut into the mound to get a cross-section so she could gather samples and test her hypotheses. Once she found the right stick, she stepped closer. The termite mound was rooted awkwardly before Bernadette, almost on top of her, like the earth's own boil. She poked it with the stick. Dry and as hard as rock, she was surprised that the first thing she pictured were millions of milk-colored termites, with the hard bodies of cockroaches, roiling beneath its surface. Her plan to investigate the termites seemed questionable then, and, with a pang of revulsion, unable to analyze or to ignore the mound, she struck it with her stick. "Bugger you! That's right bugger you," she berated it as she hit it.

As she hit it again, Bernadette now feared that the termites might somehow spread to her and burrow under her skin. Bernadette's head pounded under the drilling sun. She backed away from the termite mound as though it were all true and inevitable, her stick raised as though she was holding off a bushranger. Sweat poured from her. Bernadette didn't want to look at the termite mound, but feared taking her eyes off it. Is this it? Is this all? Is this what I've been looking for? Am I sun sick? A sweet watery pool in the back of her mouth. Dropping her stick, Bernadette squatted, then half kneeled, and threw up into the mineral rich red dirt of central Queensland. She knew right then that she was the loneliest explorer in the world and didn't want any part of it anymore.

The retreat of an explorer is seldom graceful. Magellan was killed on the island of Mindanao, defending his landing party's withdrawal. Cook was killed in the Sandwich Islands over the theft of a boat. There is a small list of Australian explorers who weren't killed, but never returned. It's likely that Bernadette, fallen back on her haunches and still queasy, didn't think of these men or the Native men and women who also died during these retreats.

She sat like she wouldn't soon rise. She didn't hum "Botany Bay" to recover herself. Tears streamed down her cheeks, fueling the ecstatic flies. She didn't care now if Cook or Sturt or whichever explorer Captain testified: "Your Majesty, she's too unprepared for serious exploration." She didn't care that she was off path and had been for a while. If needle-like grasses were to spear her calves, she would've let them. Bugger them. Thorns to tear and to stick to her dress, to scrape her skin, to pull her hair: good for them. She was eleven years old and alone in the bush with no one but Jane to miss her.

What now, Sir? Our horses are dead, and Jarri says the water's far from here. Ship Sailor Jane again, loaded with tin cups, kettles, and pans, and standing beside Jarri, their Aboriginal guide.

Even if Jane felt up for launching a rescue expedition after yesterday's trouble, it would take time. Bernadette knew that first there would be prayers and an altar to construct to the "Saint of Lost Explorers." The bullocks for the search party would have to be blessed and Jane would have to consult her best friend, Franca, to decide on the best route to Bernadette. "I'll be dead and eaten by dingoes by the time Jane arrives." The part of Bernadette impressed and consoled by Jane's industry and dedication, promised next time to use fake bindings on Jane's wrists when she mutinied, and to defend her when anyone yelled, "Bugger you!" at her.

"We'll manage, hey, Jarri," Bernadette said, again considering Jane with all her supplies at the same time pushing away images of her dad in all his buttons and glass and her mum grimly retreating. "Because that's what you do on such expeditions. Manage, hey." Jarri grinned. Bernadette spat the sandy grit from her mouth, temporarily upsetting the flies.

✦

Jane had hiked to the Meralamgee riverbed—the river had been dry for over eight years—twice with her Brownie troop. Gavin said that he'd gone plenty of times with his older brothers, Paul and Jimmy. As Jane trailed behind Gavin on the path, she told him how Mrs. Joy Laurel, their Brownie troop leader, had boiled a billy of hot cocoa for the troupe to drink with the damper pudding that they'd baked in tin foil in the hot coals, and how afterwards, they'd competed in three-legged races until Mimi Plumbe threw up.

Gavin told Jane that, like Mimi, sometimes his oldest brother, Paul, threw up in the riverbed. He told her that he was the official campfire builder for his brothers and that sometimes Paul paid him with sips of beer, which had the same bitter taste as cough medicine. Nearly every weekend, Gavin said, they exploded fireworks in the riverbed and laughed really, really hard because the explosions were so funny and "gargantuanic." Sure, afterwards it got colder, he said, and sure, he'd have to wait forever for his brothers to finish with the girls they'd brought, but it was worth it, he said, waiting.

"Did you ever nearly accidentally start a fire with the fireworks?" Jane asked.

"Oh, no! I'm very experienced," Gavin said.

Glancing at Gavin's tanned toes, Jane said, "I wish I could wear bare feet. My dad says it gives you flat feet not to wear shoes." She felt apprehensive mentioning her father.

Gavin studied her shoes for a time before he replied. "Oh, yeah, I convinced my Dad that shoes were a complete waste of time. I mean, I know everything, I mean, exactly everything that I'm walking on at every single minute of the day. You can't beat that!"

Jane thought of what she knew about Gavin and his family

besides the dog. Like the Pilgrims, they went to Saint Stephen's. Bernadette had noticed that Mr. Mackay dressed better than the rest of his family, even Mrs. Mackay, which had bothered her. Jane, today, thought that was a good sign, one that spoke of respectability. There was no way that other kids would circle Gavin and call his Dad loony.

Gavin was kicking up dirt with a devil-may-care attitude that spoke to Jane of freedom and of good fortune. She slowed, stopped, and setting her port in the dirt, stooped to undo her laces. She slipped off her shoes and peeled away her dusty socks. Delicately, she placed her pale feet on the hardened path. Heat shot into the pads of her feet, but she resisted the urge to pull up. She could see from Gavin that the pain would pass. Jane smiled at him conspiratorially.

"Your dad sounds nice," she said.

"I mean, I had to convince him," Gavin said, looking up at the tree beside him with affected casualness. He tapped his hands against his faded shorts, creating a rhythm that seemed to please him, grabbed her port, tossing her shoes and socks inside, and hoisting the bag onto his head, he glanced surreptitiously at Jane's feet and said, "I already knew that you didn't put butter on a burn."

Gavin carried Jane's school bag like a new sensation. He walked with the steady, deliberate gait of a person who people could follow and could share a good joke with. Jane's gait was the reverse. She limped and hopped in response to the sharp, hot ground: snippets of taunts, of Franca with Kerri, and of curses and buttons tripping along with her.

At the riverbed, Gavin helped Jane pack her cut and bruised feet in the cool damp sand.

"Hey, want to see what I have?" He dug into his pocket and, with the flourish of a magician, slowly opened his fingers. A neon-orange lighter with a yellow smiley face motto lay in his palm. Jane could see the fluid in the see-through container riding back and forth like a wave.

"It's my dad's," Gavin said.

"We're not allowed lighters or matches at our house," Jane said. "My dad's loony."

"Well, he gave it to me, 'cause you know, I'm the official fire maker in the family, like I said." Surprisingly, Jane didn't think of Mrs. Green's lecture or even of the effort and danger needed to douse that fire that she'd daydreamed about. She envisioned her altars—Dog Saint included—circled around her like the girls in that ring, and she pictured herself lighting each one.

"Let's build a fire!"

"Yeah? Sure?" he said.

"A big one," she said, freeing her feet from the sand, and jumping up. That all the saints she'd expected to stick up for her hadn't, that Franca hadn't either, was as clear to her as that Gavin had been sent to be her official fire-building friend.

After Jane and Gavin had gathered dead leaves and branches, uprooted handfuls of dry grass, and collected sticks and twigs; had stacked wood into a pyramid, under which they tucked the leaves and twigs—"tinder" as Mrs. Joy Laurel called it or "flash" as Gavin's brothers did—Gavin retrieved his lighter, nodded at Jane, and circled the pit at a processional pace, flicking the lighter on and off at even periods. Then with the precision of an official fire maker, he knelt and lit the leaves. Jane pressed her hands together and laughed as flames leapt, dived, crackled and spit, twisting and turning in all sizes of licks and shades of yellow, orange, blue, and red. "Here we go, here we go!" She laughed, her eyes shining.

After some time passed, Jane said, "Do you suppose Moses ever had a burning bush, Gav?"

He shrugged. "Dunno."

What if all the prayers that Jane had prayed at her altars—for Nan before and after she went to heaven, Grand-Dad with his bung leg and arm, for getting along better with Bernadette and a chance to lead on just one expedition, for world peace and hunger, unbaptized babies and animals in limbo; for how she didn't know what to do exactly about Nan and Grand-Dad's health, Bernadette's behavior, didn't understand exactly what the problem was with unbaptized babies and pets or how to solve the conflicted and starved world, didn't know how to control all the ungenerous feelings that overcame her that could be, as Father Malcolm said, "your guaranteed ticket to hell"—what if all these prayers had gone nowhere because there'd been no bush, no Jesus, no saints, no nothing?

Gavin spat like he'd seen his brothers do. "What's your dog saint say?"

Jane was embarrassed. Not only was she uncertain about the existence of God and her saints right then, but also she'd never imagined them speaking back to her as she'd prayed.

"Ruff! Ruff!!" Gavin grinned.

"The bush is an angel from God," Jane said matter-of-factly

masking her defensiveness. "In fact, the bush is God," she said, doubling down.

"Definitely. This fire is like that bush," Gavin earnestly responded. "It's a God sign." He looked at Jane and bayed like a hound.

Jane wanted to tell Gavin that Moses' fire was a one-time deal and that he really shouldn't make fun of the saints, but she held herself back because that was the type of thing Bernadette would've said and besides, he was her friend now.

A moment later, when Gavin began to spin in place beside the fire, it was as though for a second Jane was watching herself in the playground. He moved as slowly and gracefully as she'd imagined the eel, Nabunum. Wow, she thought. He didn't use his arms though. Instead he unbuttoned his shirt. Once it was undone, he dropped his shirt in the sand, and still turning, quickly pulled his stained singlet over his head and tossed it into the fire.

Gavin Mackay, across the smoky fire from Jane, wasn't himself without his shirt. His stomach and back covered with wounds weren't his. He had small and larger burns and fresh burns beside healing ones. Some were sharp edged and some circular. Some were solid red and others solid white while others were crusty and blackened and others wet with clear or gray-lime fluid. Jane couldn't recognize him for all his burns at first. She couldn't breathe.

Everything she knew to explain this—scalding water flying out of kettles, sparks spewing from toasters, flames erupting from barbecues, bushes, and homes; their Meralamgee campfire exploding and striking Gavin thousands of times on his back and belly; a plague of stigmata not seen on any one saint's body—fell away from Jane and, where she sat, all that remained was Gavin's face watching hers—wringing and still, screaming and silent, held and holding, for all he was worth.

It took some time for her to get to him. Jane eventually knelt before Gavin and, cradling her hands around his back, gently rested her cheek against his stomach. Know that for some who've been hurt so thoroughly, a kindness can draw attention to all the cruelty that's come before, and the kindness itself may seem cruel. Gavin slapped Jane away from him, shouting: "Shut up! Just shut up!" as though she was an endless stream of acid words.

✦

Audrey, abandoned in Pickdill Paddock with the maypole, welcomed the sight of the pick-up truck roaring into the paddock, sending clouds of dust flying. Three men emerged from the cab wearing shorts and singlets of red, yellow, and green, like a disarticulated traffic light while a fourth man, in khaki pants and a pale collared shirt, jumped off the truck bed, stacked with planks.

Audrey considered calling out a "Hello" to them, but was then struck by how peculiar she must appear, standing alone with a clothesline. As the men laid the plywood dance floor on the level ground under the gum trees less than sixty meters from her, the maypole grew taller and heavier.

When the hammers finally began, the noise offered Audrey the reprieve of anonymity. She looked to the area of bush where Louisa had disappeared. She'd be back soon. Audrey waited, cheering herself with the image of George Volasheski, standing in the corner of last year's dance floor squeezing out "Beer Barrel Polka" and "Bodje Moi" on his red accordion with mother-of-pearl panels, and the May dance with dear Jane and Bernadette weaving themselves and their bright ribbons between the other girls and boys around the maypole. After, she and Robert waltzed and toasted to their luck and love with champagne that cheerfully bubbled up under their noses.

When the hammering abruptly quit, Audrey felt like a schoolgirl who'd been caught daydreaming.

The khaki man looked towards her, squinting as though he were peering into the sun. Maybe he thought he was seeing a mirage: leaning against a mulga tree, an elegant, olive-skinned woman, whose disarming smile was that of the girl he'd left in Athens or Lisbon. He might recall the softness of her flesh and her earthen scent from the crook of her neck where at one time he'd buried his youthful face.

The khaki man turned back to his crew. "Don't be so foolish," Audrey gasped as an expanse of loneliness enveloped her. She and Robert didn't dance and rarely touched. The hammers resumed. I need to leave, she decided, still not moving.

The khaki man was now lumbering towards her, steady and unhurried as though he'd crossed the paddock already more times than he'd wished. He was broader and older than she'd assumed: his shoulders gathered in a hump and his arms hung like the bulky and uneven halves of a broken wreath; his belly filled his shirt and hung blandly over his belt. She noted the hair on his arms and knuckles was as dark and shaggy as the hair on his head. His face was thick and inscrutable, and when he was close enough, she could see that he looked at her as he might a fence post. There was no hint of the young boy's charm that she'd imagined. His jowls were thick and his double chin hung to his neck.

Audrey gripped the clothesline tighter as though it had become unstable. The khaki man, meanwhile, would see that she wasn't elegant either. In fact, he would see her widening, dulling, fraying, and frizzing before him. Her thin lips that had never contained her overbite, the wrinkles beside her eyes and mouth, the bulge of her waist in her snug wool cardigan were all openly displayed for him. If he looked hard enough he might even see the gout gelling in her ankles as it had done in her mother's and Nan's ankles.

"G'day," he said when he was no more than one and a half meters from her.

"Good afternoon," Audrey said, intently examining the maypole as though she were gathering its dimensions to report to him.

"Fickle weather; one minute it's hot; a second later, cold," he said, looking toward his crew.

Audrey glanced at her nails, drained of color and felt a shiver travel over her torso as though his observation recommended it. Though she didn't respond directly to him, she felt an affinity with him for his plain talk of weather.

"I just can't decide how much of the maypole to bury," she said. "You know, what if it's not tall enough or too tall..."

"Yeah, that'd be a problem." He circled her, taking the situation into account.

"You've made the dance floor, I see."

"That's right." He was an arm's length from her now.

"A good position, too," she said, cautiously praising him.

"I thought so." The hammering paused and resumed.

He moved closer and patted the pole as though gauging its ability to resist him, and stepped beside her. Although she was chilled, her face burned, and she felt her own hot breath shallow in her throat. He could be a threat, this man. She searched again for Louisa and saw the workman in red light a cigarette. She saw the high branches of the eucalyptus trees bend towards her in a breeze she couldn't feel. The khaki man kicked a rock away with his work-boot caked in clay. This mundane action reassured Audrey and set off a strange yearning in her. When he quietly stepped behind her, she concentrated on his belly that grazed her back and the heat that poured from him, arriving seconds before his breath of cigarettes. She remembered her Nan's legs and how swollen they'd been from what she'd been told were years of lollies, chocolates, and cakes and she remembered the dreams of her own legs bulging with square chocolate bars and gob stoppers that rolled under her skin like ball bearings. Nan's legs and her legs didn't matter to this man. She was olive-skinned and elegant. And, not like Robert, he was wonderfully earthy and rich.

The khaki man clamped his arms around her like a vise, and she was squeezed between his elbows as he held the pole with one hand and with the other hand turned the clothesline's knob until the clothesline opened above them like a giant umbrella with spokes and sky patterned fabric. In this awkward backwards embrace, they stood for a time with Audrey barely breathing, her stomach free falling, and her mind filling again with images of ribbons now fluttering in accompaniment with the music of The Singing Ship.

Audrey, suspended in the moment, said nothing when the khaki man finally let the clothesline tilt and fall away from them.

"I just wanted to do that," he said and chuckled. "You just leave it there, Mrs. Pilgrim. Mrs. Cawley told me to go ahead and plant it where you stood."

There are caverns so deep where darkness penetrates every pore and shame drips from the walls and pools on the floor. Audrey stood mutely in this cavern, observing the ground as though she could see it. Somewhere deep inside here, spring and stallions defunct, she wondered if there were bats.

✦

When Audrey pulled the station wagon into the gravel drive and saw Robert, she was still discombobulated enough not to immediately recognize that he was too. This changed quickly for as he opened her door, instead of greeting her, he glared at her dress' mollusk shell print as though each shell pronounced some mistake of his, and said, "Get inside." As Robert grabbed a bag of groceries from the back seat, Audrey reflexively brushed the invisibly fine paddock dust from her dress and hurried after him, thinking something is terribly wrong; someone is dead.

Robert set the groceries by the sink and again washed his hands and forearms with dish soap. He commanded himself to slow down even as his anxiety sped him into a cul-de-sac within himself, where the kitchen's stuffiness only added to the closeness of that dressing room with the fire raging towards them and that boyhood bedroom from which there was no escape.

Robert ran cold water over his head and drank directly from the tap. Audrey stood warily by the screen door watching his bizarre behavior.

"Robert?" Audrey delicately inquired, afraid of what he had to say.

She waited a beat then in an attempt to regain normalcy said, "Do you know that Louisa Cawley has never been to the coast?"

No courtship is ever identical as no couple is completely alike. Two months after Robert Pilgrim had met Audrey McBride at Sunday mass, she'd invited him on a day trip to the coastal town of Yeppoon, 45 kilometers northeast of Rockhampton. She'd packed a picnic basket with egg, bacon, and beet sandwiches and cupcakes—two kinds: apple spice and chocolate fudge.

"Remember our picnic, Robert?"

They'd laid out a blanket on the headland, overlooking Keppel Bay, beside The Singing Ship sculpture, which white as bleached cuttlebone represented Captain Cook's ship, the *Endeavor*. She'd confided in Robert that one day she'd like to be an artist and she told him that Captain Cook first sailed through Keppel Bay almost 200 years before. The grandness and hopefulness of this event resonated with each of them: Robert, who, like Cook, had embarked on a fresh path and she, who was looking to make hers.

"The ship?"

That day there was an on-shore breeze, which hummed in the pipe organs concealed in the ship's mast and rigging. Music and light emanated from the structure: dazzling and soothing and connecting them. He'd taken and squeezed her hand. She'd said, I can tell you're a good man, Robert Pilgrim. I could love you if you just asked me to.

"Robert?"

"We have many insects that I've never noticed here before," he answered.

Robert spoke louder then as though Audrey couldn't hear and like it was the most natural transition added, "So Belinda Black was practically murdered by her husband."

Audrey had told Bernadette all about Captain Cook and their family's connection to that voyage when she realized her daughter's interest in exploration. Later Bernadette had come back to her with a library book and a quote from Cook about their Keppel Bay:

In this Bay is good anchorage where there is a sufficient depth of water.

"So first, Audrey, there was my concern for our family's safety and second, secondly…" Robert wanted to tell her that Freddie Black threatened every family in Mt. Isaac. He wanted to tell her that the fire had missed them, and that because only four men died at the mine that day, hundreds had survived. He wanted to tell her he'd done the right thing and reported the abuse and given Mrs. Black a free scarf. He wanted to say he had seven new buttons for her. Seven. And that hadn't he protected the girls and weren't they safe in their rooms now and hadn't he done the best he could? He wanted a different start, a fresh name, her ship with her—it could only be with her—out of there, out of this that he'd made.

"What's this all about, Robert?"

"I'm a moral man, Audrey."

"What are you talking about?"

"There's been a lapse," he said.

She opened a window, dismissing his concern about bugs. This autumn now felt unnaturally hot. One minute it's hot; a second later, cold. She shuddered.

"With Belinda. Mrs. Black."

Audrey turned back to him, gripping her dress as though there was some danger that her arms might fly loose.

"Belinda and myself," he said.

"What is this, Robert?" She couldn't believe this was happening. And now.

"A lapse," he repeated.

"What are you telling me?" Her own voice cracking, Audrey said, "Can't you speak normally to me, Robert? Can't you say, Audrey, how was your morning? How did you get along with the maypole arrangements? Can't you say, here, Audrey, I bought you flowers I've missed you that much? Maybe I can take you out of this stuffy house to lunch perhaps? Can't you say, Look how lovely you look, Audrey! Let me lift you into my arms…." She gripped the edge of the counter as though she might now fly off.

"Just once," he whispered. "An accident. You know, relations."

"Relations?"

"Not relations, an encounter," he said.

She scrutinized Robert's face.

He turned from her to the groceries. He refrigerated the milk and eggs. He stacked the fruit on the counter beside the sink. Setting the scaly pineapple on its base, he thought of all the sacrifices he'd made for Audrey and the girls. He was better than his own father. She had to see that.

"Listen," he said, "I'm just concerned that our family isn't safe." He lifted the pineapple again, transferring it from hand to hand.

Audrey hadn't moved.

"Once Black is under detention we can breathe a lot easier. Move on. Right, Audrey?"

He knew he wasn't making sense, but to start explaining, well, how could he reverse this? An apology? Just inadequate. He detected some departure, a shadow in Audrey's face, which, though he didn't understand it, somehow angered him. What did she want? For him to admit that he'd gone out of his way to seduce Belinda, and Belinda deserved to get beaten, and the Pilgrim family deserved vengeance? Ridiculous! A slippery slope is what it was, like his father had said. A blow job, for goodness' sake. Hardly anything.

"Those insects are sure loud," Robert announced.

Audrey shuddered again.

"Are you cold? I could get you a thicker jumper, Audrey."

Ignoring him, Audrey walked across the kitchen to the pantry where she kept food items as well as some of her jars of buttons. She chose a clear mason jar through which Robert recognized some of the buttons he'd given her over the last year. There were round and square, opaque and clear, metal and shell, and fancy and plain buttons of a wide array of colors, shapes, sizes, and textures. She'd told him once that they were jewels to her, and it was true that, many days, he'd felt like a king giving them to her. At Bernadette and Jane's births, Robert had bought Audrey heart-shaped buttons made with real gold plating, which hadn't been easy to find.

Now Robert watched Audrey lift the jar as though it were a chalice. As he watched her hold the weight of hundreds of days in her hands, she felt the weight of those hundreds of days bearing down on her. Disbelieving what was playing out before him, in that momentary delay, Robert rushed forward too late to stop the jar from dropping from her hands and exploding on the tiles at their feet, glass and buttons busting across the room in every direction. Before the sound of spinning had stopped, Audrey had grabbed a second and third jar and hurled them at his feet.

Audrey stepped back and numbly watched him. With handfuls of buttons and glass shards, on the floor on his knees Robert pleaded, "Audrey, please, please, look how many buttons we've got." It was only when he looked up at her—she had already turned—that Robert glimpsed Jane and Bernadette watching from the hallway, and he shouted at Bernadette: "Get out, you silly! Get you and your sister away!" as that same raw cry of his childhood caught in his throat.

✦

Bernadette, in the dense and shadeless scrub that day, was no longer aware of Ship Sailor Jane and Jarri. As her head baked, her skin burned, her thoughts loosely drifted, neither was she aware of Captain Sturt, who was snacking on a ration of salt meat and Banks, who was examining his termite specimen. As shadows formed and shifted around them, Bernadette's breathing eased, and, eventually, all that remained of her tears were the dirt streaks down her cheeks. Even the flies seemed to have let up. It was only when Bernadette heard rustling behind her—not Sturt shaking open his map, though maybe—that Bernadette came out of her stupor and turned, before she could think I shouldn't turn or I should turn slowly in case there's a brown snake.

Standing before Bernadette was a bird, unlike any bird she'd seen, staring at her through eyes the same transparent blue as the crystal ocean over the northern reefs. Its porcelain white beak was pointed and sharp as a dagger. Its black and purple feathers gleamed as though someone had meticulously polished each one. When a gust of wind swept through the scrub, stirring dust and leaves, this bird, as tall as Bernadette's school ruler, jumped towards her on its flesh-colored legs.

Bernadette didn't flinch. She held the bird in her sights, even as she noticed that behind it, undetected by her before, lay a nest of twigs and sticks arranged like a room: high walls and a floor with a circular mat. Bernadette couldn't make out the back of its nest, but a glint of blue drew her in. A male bowerbird, she whispered under her breath to her companions, who had handily resurfaced for her now that she had something to share. The bird hopped back to the entry of his nest and sprang back and forth over the threshold. Bernadette wasn't sure if this was his bowerbird dance for her, but she wished it was. He continued to spring back and forth towards her and away and, just as she wished he would be still and stare at her again with those eyes, there was a gust of wind and he flew off.

Bernadette waited for a time for the bowerbird to fly back. She remained perfectly still so as not to discourage him. She didn't look up, but pictured him circling above watching her and his nest. She listened for the flap of his wings and rush of air on his descent. She waited and waited until too curious to wait any longer—Sturt didn't need to nudge her—Bernadette crept up to the bower and, on her belly, scooted as close as she could to the entrance so she could examine it. She tentatively reached in and gently felt the sides and floor of the bower, careful not to disturb anything.

Inside, hidden in the back, she found a collection of blue objects. A snakeskin—possibly from a taipan—with a faded blue-brown diamond pattern was tucked into the edge of a wall. Beside it, were a cicada case and a short vibrant blue feather from a fairy wren. There was a scrap of ribbon that Bernadette recognized as a first prize ribbon from someone's athletic day even though the gold lettering had crumbled away. A bottle top and shard of glass lay together. Perhaps from the same soft drink bottle, she thought, although she couldn't picture how the bowerbird had collected them both. Probing further, beneath a layer of leaves, she discovered a cracked marble of searing blue, and observing it in her palm then replacing it, Bernadette imagined treasure brought back from exotic islands, piled high in the holds of wooden ships: azure, cobalt, indigo, and sapphire.

Under a sun that bent away from her and cast longer shadows now, not fifteen meters from that termite mound, seven and half kilometers from Mt. Isaac, and two thousand three hundred kilometers less seven and a half from Moorundi, Bernadette lay before the bower and, in her notebook, sketched it and the bowerbird. She filled five pages and their margins with her drawings and observations, written in tiny script. When she finished—Ship Sailor, Jarri, and Sturt waiting, Banks had bailed to his ship—she repacked her knapsack, collected her hardhat, and considered heading to India around Cape Horn, setting out across the globe to find Australia, New Zealand, and a passage across the Antarctic Circle. Before she headed home and inland to discover the country's center—Captain Sturt had already studied their map—on the floor of the bower, Bernadette left a strip of hem that she'd torn from her blue dress.

✦

For Jane and Gavin at the riverbed, stars arrived without the moon. Too early for an owl, a mopoke "mopoked." Gavin lay curled in the sand, guarding his burned torso and sobbing unevenly. Jane, a distance from him, sat with her own stinging feet tucked under her.

The fire popped. Like buttons bounced off the floor. Moses had definitely left this fire. Jane didn't know where she'd come up with the idea that he might be good with fire management anyhow. She sifted a handful of sand through her fingers like her dad had with the buttons and glass. Funny that her mum hadn't tried to bandage his cuts. Gavin sighed. Was it the same funny as her dad pushing her and Bernadette over, and cursing at her? Jane looked over at Gavin again. Who did this to you? Hurry-up, Bernadette, here I am. We've gone a bit too far this time, Captain.

To Gavin, Jane said, "Don't worry, Gavin, we'll be fine." Jane, like Bernadette, trusted her sister would come for her as long as she knew that Jane was out there. She also trusted that Bernadette had already deciphered one "funny" factor from another and might even later explain it to her.

In the trees closest to them, there was a screel and, in the branches, a frantic fluttering of wings. Jane reflexively cast out a quick prayer to Jesus and Moses: "Get me and Gavin home please," and after, promised, "We'll be good and come home straight after school from now on. I can vouch for him." She immediately regretted adding that last part, aware that Gavin wouldn't care to be vouched for.

Jane waited, twisting her right plait and wriggling her toes in the sand under her. She tried to conjure up some of her saints but, since they hadn't been helpful earlier, chances weren't great that they could help them now. She continued to wait, for what felt like hours and when nothing happened in, say, forty seconds, Jane tried again. "Dear Jesus and Dear Moses, I know we shouldn't have come out here alone and on a school night. We're sorry so please help us." She sounded petulant this time.

After this, though, there was no waiting. Jane collected Gavin's shirt and gingerly draped it over him. Her saints wouldn't be afraid or reluctant, she decided. Her saints would just take the hand of Moses or Jesus, even if it didn't seem like it was there, even if it was bloody from right off the cross. She couldn't expect Jesus or Moses to come down to the Meralamgee riverbed and say, "Hey Jane, hey Gavin, this way please!" It was actually a relief that her saints had had it worse than her. If she'd realized earlier that they could talk, they might've told her that and saved her some time.

Jane made her way to the riverbank, where she'd earlier seen a branch that could work as a torch. She set the end of it into the fire, which she fed with more sticks. While she waited for the branch to light, she dusted off her feet and pulled on her socks and shoes. Although her feet hurt, the hurt wasn't remotely comparable to Gavin's hurts, so she braced and continued dressing them. She wished again that she'd had the foresight to tell Bernadette where she was going that day, like that had been a possibility. Finally, with the lit branch, she went to Gavin and said, "Let's go home."

He stared into the ball of midges that swarmed on the sand before him.

She tugged on his arm and pulled him sort of seated. "Here!" Before he had a chance to argue or repel her, she'd thrust the branch into his right hand.

"You have to take us home now, Gavin," she said as though he was deaf. "Lead us back!"

Beside the fire in the Meralamgee riverbed, Jane waited for Gavin. She knew that fire had burned into his body. She knew that their fire could build into a huge conflagration and burn them and all of Mt. Isaac to the ground just like Mrs. Green had warned. But standing there right then, Jane trusted that this fire, while not Moses' bush, would not harm anyone. The other darker things Jane knew, or glimpsed knowing, she would learn later at this same riverbed. But for now, when Jane turned back to Gavin, holding the torch high in the sky before him, she said, "Rightie-oh, Gav," and together they'd climbed up the riverbank and trudged towards home. Gavin held their light as Jane told him the story of the frog, Tiddalik, and chattered to him about streams and water holes and the really excellent flotation toys at the town pool that he'd have to try with her next time they swam.

✦

After Audrey saw Robert off at the bus station for his journey to Billum Downs, his brother's property near Longreach, and after Bernadette appeared later that day at the backdoor just as Audrey was about to organize a search party, and after Audrey did organize a search party for Jane, who was found with a schoolmate safe and healthy albeit a bit dusted up, the next day, a beleaguered Audrey decided to visit Belinda Black at the hospital.

In the back seat of her station wagon, she'd loaded Bernadette's bedside lamp, which had exploded with a loud pop the night before. She planned to see Dan, the Fix-It-Man, before or after or maybe, no, not instead, and was dressed quite formally for this in her Sunday dress. She'd pulled her brown hair into a soft bun fixed with two red enamel clips. Her eye shadow was a shade darker than usual as was her blush, which was a shade lighter than the deep rose of her lips. As she loaded herself into the car, a warm breeze swept up and over her, and as she drove past Jane and Bernadette's school, she saw the eucalyptus and wattles, lining the sidewalk, sway and bend. The early wind forecast more. By late afternoon, a continuous ream of red dirt would engulf Mt. Isaac, obscuring each neighbor's house. For weeks after, the town's residents would clean the film from themselves and their possessions, and there would be no other topic. Robert, at his brother's, would miss this.

Audrey and Robert had decided to say that Robert was "ill" so he could qualify for a leave from work, and grant Audrey the separation from him that she needed. Audrey had extrapolated this scenario picturing Robert in a hospital awaiting electro-shock therapy: electrodes placed at his temples and a rubber mouthpiece, stuffed into his mouth like the end of a snorkel. She'd even insinuated to Bernadette that her father had had a "little" breakdown and was off "mending himself." This was okay, she told herself, since Jane and Bernadette had already seen him in that insensible kitchen scene of buttons and broken glass. And what else was she to do with her anger.

Audrey, unsettled as the air around her, drove past the Tindle Road turn-off for Dan's Repair Shop.

The problem was that Audrey never knew Robert was away from himself until it was too late. There were signs she could say now, but you could always say that looking back.

Belinda, she'd seen only once before at Delton's. Audrey better remembered that Robert had worn his favorite gray vest and that she'd brought him a pickle and pork sausage sandwich along with a slice of apple-nut cake, covered with vanilla icing flavored with orange rind. She believed she'd looked nice that day, but she wasn't definite about this. Belinda had been standing with him—to the left or the right—she couldn't remember that or Belinda's dress or height or even hair color, although now, after going over it countless times, she'd settled on a mini-skirt, average height, and dirty blond—a color that she'd never liked.

Audrey circled the Mount Isaac Hospital twice before she parked. There she re-emphasized to herself that Belinda wasn't pretty. She was plain and had fat fleshy arms, and wore short shorts with the seam up her bum, and slapped around in rubber thongs that left her feet gray-brown and sweaty smelling. "No man likes that," she announced.

Though the air by now was filled with flying particles, the hospital and even the hedge surrounding it maintained the solidity of a granite monument. That has to be assuring to patients and visitors, Audrey thought, feeling little assured. For an instant, any worth of solidity seemed dubious.

Audrey pulled from her purse a packet of family photographs of their holiday to Brisbane: Jane and Bernadette jointly holding a koala at the Lone Pine Sanctuary; Jane perched on Robert's shoulders at the Brisbane Exhibition, the state fair; the family before a sheep exhibit the same day. "Don't drop her," she'd said to Robert, recalling now the smell of manure and wet wool that day and that Jane had asked if they couldn't take a lamb home and that Bernadette had replied that they'd first have to shave its wool, slaughter and skin it so that they'd get proper lamb chops. After, predictably, Jane had been inconsolable and, although Robert had ordered her to stop, she cried all afternoon—at the other livestock displays, the baked goods and preservatives section, and even in the sample bag pavilion, where bags filled with lollies, chocolates, and toys were given away for free.

These are persuasive photos, though, Audrey thought, watching a scrap of paper scrape along the gravel and bank against the hospital curb.

If the photos weren't enough, she still had the buttons. She handled the jar as though it were a grenade. See this yellow sunflower one, she'd say, this is the day when Robert and I planted a wattle tree and discussed the girls' future. This clear button he gave me on Bernadette's Holy Communion day. The glass bead button is the day we gave Bernadette a bicycle. This is Jane's Grade One recital, and the pink button, the pink one with the ornate red rim, is last year's wedding anniversary.

Audrey stopped. There had to be a button in the jar from the day of Robert and Belinda's tryst. She turned the jar over and away, watching the buttons fall together and apart. How would she be able to identify that day or the days preceding it, when he must've been tempted, or the days after, when he must've thought about Belinda? There could be ten or more uncertain buttons in that jar. Audrey placed it back in her purse and prepared to drive to Dan's but didn't. That there were definitely more than ten buttons when Audrey had been away from herself, jars of buttons in fact… She got out and slammed the car door behind her.

When Audrey stepped off the elevator onto the Women's Floor, an orderly cut in front of her with a gurney, an overhead page for Dr. Velli was being repeated, and behind the nurses' station, the staff chatted amiably. Audrey waited in front of the station beside a couple, too young for the hospital and too underdressed for a dust storm, she decided, noting the girl's sleeveless sundress and the boy's worn tee-shirt and stubbie shorts. A matronly woman in a floral dress spoke evenly to them across the counter. The way the boy leaned protectively toward the girl was much like how Robert had shielded her from that drunken grazier at the Brisbane exhibition. "We're not here for trouble, Mister," he'd said, and stepped between Audrey and the man. The grazier had promptly stood aside and watched, unfocused, as they'd passed.

"Excuse me. Hello?"

Audrey tried to get the attention of the blond nurse, who, in her white uniform, resembled a cream bun. When the nurse, ignoring her, stepped behind a brunette one and struck up a conversation with a doctor, Audrey momentarily felt that all these people conspired against her. Beside her, Audrey overheard the words "home" and "they'll take good care of her" and "you don't want to be changing grownup nappies, do you," and she thought of her own mother, who had been immaculate about her appearance until the day she died. Audrey's mouth was dry. This floral woman appeared to be the only hospital person capable of crossing the counter; she even leaned over it to pat the girl's hand. Social Worker, her badge said.

Outside Belinda's room Audrey paused. Even though she knew a femme fatale in that room was unlikely, Audrey couldn't be comforted that Belinda was ugly or even that that mattered. What if Belinda wanted to be with Robert and he wanted to be with her, too? Belinda had been hurt. There was that. This hospital. Was there a better dress that Audrey might've worn; did it matter? She chewed the lipstick from her bottom lip.

The room smelled of bedpans mixed with disinfectant. A blue-green curtain was drawn around the only occupied bed in the room. Audrey cleared her throat and said, "Excuse me, hello, are you awake?" as she swept the curtain open.

Belinda was splayed in an awkward arrangement of casts, covers, pillows, and pain. The pillows had slipped from under her right leg with its full leg cast as well as her left arm with its right-angle cast. Both listed heavily away from her, bruises spilling from the ends of each. The worst one seemed to flow up against gravity into her neck and jaw, pooling in her eye socket. When Belinda turned to Audrey, her movement was as deliberate and slow as one whose joints are thickened by pain.

Audrey observed her dumbly, gripping her handbag.

"Having a good gawk, are we?" Belinda said in a surprisingly loud voice. "How many bloody times do you people have to hear it? I mean, can't you check with the last person who saw me, or the one before that, or the other "other" ones? Bloody hell."

Audrey cleared her throat. "I'm sorry, I…"

"This is the last time. Do you get that?" Belinda turned back to the window as Audrey shifted onto the balls of her feet. She knew that this was a confusion that she could easily dispel. Tell Belinda, no, no, I'm not the social worker you probably think I am. Tell her, no, you don't have to tell me your tale; you've been through so much. How can anyone expect you to tell it again? So easy to jump in really; so right.

"Aren't you going to take notes? I mean it. This is the last time!"

Audrey pushed aside the jar and photos, looking for the steno pad she knew was at the bottom of her bag. She flipped past the grocery list—minced meat, tomato sauce, Milo, onions, tissues, milk—to a blank page, and stood officially posed and ready to transcribe.

Belinda reported to Audrey the accidental fall off the kitchen counter—she'd been up there cleaning the high cupboards—and onto the slick linoleum, and the support of her husband, Freddie, and how he'd said, "Belinda, I'll stick by you and look after you all the while you're healing. That's the least a bloke can do." She reported how Freddie had to leave after he found her because the sight of her was "too awful" for him—"He's very sensitive you know"—but that was only temporary, "his being gone." "That's the least a bloke can do," she repeated twice with respect to his care for her, and, "That's how much he cares," three times, with respect to his sensitivity about her.

Belinda rocked and cradled her casted arm as she spoke, then looked calmly at Audrey and demanded a cigarette.

A social worker would've ignored Belinda's request, but acknowledged the contradictions in her story, recommended moving out then counseling, and given her a "safe" number to call once Belinda had refused both. A social worker would've wished her well then left.

The sky was dark with red dirt funneling through the air. The aluminum windows rattled.

"Where's your hospital badge?" Belinda asked.

"We, my family. Well, have you ever been to the Brisbane Exhibition? Because we have, and our family shared a lot of very significant moments, which you just can't appreciate," Audrey answered.

"Yeah?" Belinda drew the word out, as though she were a woman of infinite patience.

"And that might be really difficult for you to get, but you weren't there for the rides or exhibits or when we all had ice cream surprises and Jane cried. You didn't see Robert protect us from that lout. You can't possibly know how he protects us."

It sounded so much like, "That's how much he cares," that Audrey stopped.

Belinda flicked the black specks of dried blood from the bedcovers onto the floor with the back of her hand.

"You seduced my husband, Robert. From Delton's."

"You're an uppity bitch to come here."

Audrey couldn't picture what this woman had been like before the beating.

"What's it like to gawk at an ugly ratbag dog like me? Good?"

"Robert from Delton's."

Belinda sighed and rested her head on the backboard of the bed. Her pillows lay on the floor.

"Yeah, yeah, I remember. Robbie, who sold me the lovely scarf." It began as another sigh, then developed into a low rumble at the back of her throat. Pretty soon Belinda's shoulders were quivering in a mirthless chuckle.

"I blew him 'cause he was nice to me." Her now exasperated laugh wrenched her body so much that her leg was pushed precariously close to the edge of the bed. "He noticed my bruises so he picked out a scarf to cover them, and he sold it to me! He said next week would be better because the scarf would be on sale then."

The two women looked at each other.

Belinda stopped laughing.

"I don't know why I did it," she quietly said and looked out the window. "I do things."

Audrey moved to Belinda's bedside and picked up the pillows that lay beside it.

"Piss the fuck off now," Belinda whispered to her as Audrey helped Belinda reposition in bed. "You have no right to pity me."

"I don't," Audrey replied. And because it seemed like something both women needed, Audrey added, "I easily hate you."

Hate was hard to have for Belinda or Robert just then. Audrey could too easily see Robert's struggle between the decorum of his clerk role and that of a decent man who might intervene in the face of uncertain outcomes. Whether duty or sympathy—Audrey couldn't allow the possibility of lust just yet—led him into the dressing room with the girl that day, it was his own weakness—yes, lust here—that prevented his decency. There, in the quiet of the hospital room, rattled by wind and highflying sand, Belinda had begun to silently cry, and as Audrey left her, Audrey couldn't help but think of her daughter Jane's inconsolable tears at the Brisbane Exhibition. She couldn't help but understand that all of their dramas weren't essentially hers and that she hadn't been awake in her own story for a great while.

✦

The Central County Gazette article about May Day reported that the sky on Saturday was bluer than anyone could remember and that the temperature was "unseasonably warm." It said that the entire town of Mt. Isaac was at Pickdill Paddock celebrating May Day and that Eleanor Ramsay won first prize for her trifle recipe, and the best float went to the Girl Guides for their floral globe. Joe's Pub at the Imperial Hotel, of course, got an honorable mention for its giant Styrofoam stubbie holder. Yahoo! Bill's Brumbies played some excellent reels and "By Jove, can those Mt. Isaac people dance!" Roddy McPhearson, the bagpipe player, at the western corner of the paddock was also said to be remarkable. There was an abundance of tucker and grog, it said, and the egg-in-spoon and three-legged races were the most competitive this reporter had seen. Last, but not least, the maypole placement was perfect, and the kids who performed were to be commended. A special thanks was given to the May Day Committee, in particular, Louisa Cawley, for all her hard work. "What a marvelous day!"

PART TWO

THE VOYAGE OUT

✦

THE CAR RIDE to the bus station in Claremont was mostly silent. Audrey and Robert had left before dawn while the girls still slept with the plan that Audrey would be back by the time they awoke. It was as dark in the car as it was outside. "Won't Stewart be surprised to see me show up?" Robert's brother owned a cattle station called Billum Downs, approximately eight hundred kilometers west of Mt. Isaac, which was a full day's journey with a bus transfer and the lift that Robert would have to arrange from Morella, the nearest post office to Stewart's. He wanted some assurance from Audrey that the connections would be fine, which would somehow be an assurance that they would be fine. "The weather forecasters say that this unseasonable heat is about to break. Wouldn't rain be good, Audrey?"

✦

Robert and Stewart were the sons of Marjorie and Jack Thatle. Robert never was a "wild colonial boy" like his brother, but he wasn't a shy boy either, just average like most everyone else in the middle of the in-between distance from Longreach to Rockhampton. He kept to himself like some, self-reliant and contained. Home was their parent's hotel, which was also the shop, the pub, the post office, and the brothel, although the latter was not actually said outright in particular company, and there was some question as to whether their mother actually knew.

"Men need servicing. S'truth, no point denying it," Jack would say when Marjorie and the other "ladies" of the neighboring properties weren't present. Timing was key. On the second week of August, Marjorie would take the boys to the coast to visit her aging parents, who, she felt, depended on their visits for all those intangible reasons that children believe their aging parents must depend on them and often do. On this second week, like clockwork, men from properties, mines, and other sundry occupations across this middle distance would arrive at Jack's along with a truckful of "girls." They'd converge on the Thatle Hotel, newly converted whorehouse, for a week of sex for cash. Robert's father on more poetic days would describe the week as "a festival of fun," "a bugger-you-all fuck fest," "a find-and-fuck-your-filly-fest."

The year that Robert had stayed behind with his father, he was ten, almost eleven. "These things are indelicate, like a belch or burst boil," Jack had told Robert, who he called Bob even though Marjorie had named him Robert after Robert Menzies, Australia's Winston Churchill, who, Jack claimed, wasn't Australian enough to be Prime Minister. Robert, when he had first heard about the festivities, was filled with curiosity as any boy would be to discover the nature of "these things." These things were secret and powerful and could change his known world into something quite extraordinary.

Just after Marjorie and Stewart had left on the bus for the coast, young Robert Thatle got his first glance. He watched a neighbor, John Aggsbit, and his mate, Charlie, drive up with a utility truck stuffed with tents and cots. Robert helped them construct the canvas tents and arrange them in a row, like a barracks, and place a cot in each one. He helped his father to carry beer and booze from the back shed, to stabilize the hog as it was skewered on the spit for roasting, and to corral a lamb to be slaughtered for later. He didn't question why his father had packed all his mum's valuables into a suitcase and hid it under the kitchen floor. When they had stacked the finer furniture against a wall in each of their rooms, Robert had thought they were opening up a dance floor or, even better, a wrestling ring.

Before "the bird," "the sheila," "the slag" truck came, it's fair to say that Robert Thatle was filled with excitement and anticipation for all that was unspoken, but promised in the hotel grounds that had fast become a temporary campground, a spontaneous carnival with campfires dotting the area.

"Jack, this must be your boy."

"Yeah, that's Bob."

"Good on you, Bob."

"Boyo, are you going to see something worthwhile."

"You stay out by the water tower, make room for the real visitors, Bob. You'll be right." Something worthwhile was worth the displacement from his room and home. Something worthwhile was arriving with the men, who, as soon as they threw down their swags, took up drinking and gambling and shooting off their mouths until their fists got involved. They were festive and tense. Although young Robert couldn't discern the full scope of that tension, he too was excited.

That year there was a bet on in the pub. Nell, the escort of the transportation that was due, had promised Jack there'd be at least two virgins. Betting for virgins was a big money stake, a specialty bet, and only the fellas with cash to spare were in. Most blokes, it was true, were happy to go a lot for cheap.

The truck, when it arrived, was an open flatbed livestock truck, filled with women and girls.

"What, you could get, fit, say, twenty, twenty-three merinos in there," said one bloke.

"Forget it, think in terms of cows, mate. We're talking ten that way, and then at the back end, wait, yeah, another ten and what, that's what, thirty-four or so?"

"Shut your drunken mugs, boys," said someone else. "Sheilas are here! Look alert."

This shout had triggered a bigger shout among the men and they had welcomed the truck with a chorus of hoots and whistles, letting the dust from the truck settle over them. The women—they knew what was expected—gave a flash show of chests and hips, lips and tongues, a wayward displacement of skirts and stockings that had stuck to their hot, grimy skin. On numbers and composition, there had been about fifteen or so: a few white ones, a few black, fewer young ones, two girls, one, who, when the truck drove up, crouched behind the other women, smashed against the cab to be as small as she could.

Darren O'Doyle and Nell Nesmith stepped out of the truck cab and, like royalty, were applauded and hoorayed. Darren had smiled proudly at his flatbed merchandise, and his smile expanded when he began to calculate the returns for the week for, without a doubt, he was faced with "a mob of horny buggers." Nell—head whore, impromptu nurse, mother, sister, confidant for the women—searched over the heads of the crowd for Jack Thatle, and when she found him, broke through the crowd and was in his arms in seconds. What Robert saw was a robust woman mashed against his father and his father holding her there by her two buttocks and tasting her face as though he were hungry.

The shock and betrayal for his mother and family that Robert had felt, mixed with a strange titillating awakening in him. When Jack and Nell finally disengaged from each other and Jack had called Bob over, Robert had moved slowly, carefully, as though the air was viscous and poison both. And when Jack had said, "Nell, this is my son Bob," and Nell had smiled grandly at him, reaching for his hand, Robert froze. Jack said, "Come on boy, mind your manners. Say g'day to Nell! Say g'day, Bob!"

"Good day."

He said this and had allowed Nell to pump his hand enthusiastically but, he'd been distracted—horrified and intrigued—by the shiny wet dirt streaks all over Nell's face where his father's tongue had been.

Darren O'Doyle, as usual, had divvied up the women to men, had created schedules and lines where indicated, had collected payments for the variety of his services, and had organized the house scene for the more prized girls and the tents for the cheaper ones. Jack manned the bar, and Nell helped with the food. It wasn't clear if Jack received a special rate, but it was clear that Nell, while at the Thatle's, was exclusively his. Robert was the "go-for boy" and what he saw when he got things—booze, buckets of water, condiments, and condoms—he kept to himself since he had always been self-contained.

Harry Pickery won the bet and paid three hundred quid for one virgin for an entire night. It was decided that the other one would be pro-rated. Two hundred for the first go, one eighty for the second, and after that, down by twenty quid each session until she stabilized at sixty, which was still expensive but worth it given her age. "Nine," Darren had boasted although he'd never admit that before an authority. "Not that they'd bloody care," he claimed. "Black girls are worthless even to their own. I should know; I've recruited them." He snorted, taking another shot of whiskey.

But what Darren O'Doyle called a recruitment trip was always kidnapping, sometimes blatant, sometimes not. He bragged that he could as easily steal a girl off the streets as find and corrupt a "fringe dweller" group, getting them as drunk on methylated spirits as possible, and then bargain and bet the kids away from their parents, an event not likely to be remembered until morning when he and the girls were gone. It would have been just, had Darren in due course been thrown in jail or, for those with more vengeful tastes, been fatally stabbed by some girl, woman or parent who had been abused by him; but Darren eventually settled in Bundaberg and, with his saved money, bought a hardware shop. He had a happy marriage, three healthy children, and by the time he died of natural causes—congestive heart failure—he'd been a member of the city council and had been presented with a special pin for his civic mindedness.

Later that day, the bar-talk circulated back to Robert.

"Jack, have you given your boy a go?"

"What's that?"

"You know, has your boy had a go with one of the girls?"

Jack looked back at Bob who was bent over a barrel of soap water in which he was rinsing beer glasses.

"Plenty of time for that, I reckon."

"Do you have a bird in mind?"

Jack hadn't given it much thought, but the men at the bar were quite happy to think about it and describe graphically who was good for what and where. Some of the men were becoming quite sentimental about when they lost their virginity and to whom and some even welled up with emotion and actual tears. Okay, one actually. And he was well and truly mocked afterwards, when he'd come back from that lonely soulful place that was familiar to most of these men although rarely acknowledged.

"Bob, who do you fancy?" John Aggsbit called over to him.

"Give the man an answer," Jack said gruffly to Robert when it was clear he didn't intend to.

"Yeah, who's little Jack going to go for?" said someone else further down the bar.

"No one."

"Hey? What did he say?"

"Who's Naomi? Is that who he said?"

Jack had topped off the pint he was filling and had turned to Bob, "What did you say, son?"

"I said no one." Robert rinsed the glass as though the bar hadn't gone silent and his father wasn't watching him queerly.

"You're a bloody joker, aren't you," Jack said with boisterous humor he didn't feel.

"What, does he think these slags are too below him, does he?" one bloke said.

"Maybe he thinks they're good enough for us, but not for him," said another.

"Yeah, how'd he get so high and mighty all of a sudden?"

Jack could see this was going nowhere good. He leaned towards the men, and lowering his voice said, "Fellas, I don't like to admit this particularly, but Bob here, well, Bob's a bit nervous about this virginity situation." The men had nodded and soberly sipped their beer or dragged off their cigarettes giving some time to that thought.

"I could see that," said one.

"My own brother was skittish that way," said another.

"Do you have a plan then, Jack?" John asked. The men were now rallied around Bob's situation.

"Oh yeah," Jack said.

"A virgin with a virgin isn't such a bad idea," said one bloke close to the door. And, as if this was the funniest joke ever, the men guffawed, ordered another round, and started sharing virgin jokes and limericks until someone started up a bawdy rendition of the song, "Wild Rover No More." Robert's face burned but had remained hidden from the men, his back to the bar, his hands submerged in gray water.

At four the next morning, Robert's father had found him asleep in a blanket under the water tower. He brought tea that Nell had brewed especially for the boy.

"Come on, son, wake yourself," he'd said, passing the tea to Robert, who was sleepy and disorientated at first. "We've got ourselves a bit of business."

They headed to the house where Nell met them and took the teacup from Robert. They escorted him to Stewart's bedroom where the door was closed and the light off.

"Go on then, Bob. Get in there. She'll be right. Don't take too long. She's a bit prime if you get me?"

Robert, still drowsy, didn't speak or move to the door. Jack finally shoved him forward and Robert obediently entered his brother's dark room.

It was silent except for his and the girl's breathing. Maybe Robert thought desire would arrive with the touch of the girl, different than his own private touches. Robert made his way to the bed and pulled down his trousers, but this is as far as he got. When he reached for her what he found, what he touched was a liquid smear that he couldn't identify at first. He stood with a hand upon her, upon this, and what Jack and Nell heard outside was a whimper that they had cheerfully interpreted as sex. A rank smell rose from her, then them, as Robert began vomiting onto himself and the floor by her bedside.

When Robert stumbled to the light at the door and his whimper had grown into a full keen, Jack and Nell burst in. Under that bright light were two children: one girl awash in blood, scum, and piss and one boy dry heaving against the wall.

Nell immediately set to the care of the nine-year-old child, Mary Tucker, as Jack lifted his son out of the room. When Darren, awakened by the cries, had walked in and objected because someone was scheduled, Nell put him off. "She needs to be cleaned." She didn't say cared for or protected, but cleaned.

Did Robert hear the same thing? In no time, three days, Robert assisted Jack in hosing out the pub and mopping each room in the house before they rearranged the furniture back to how it was. He gathered the sheets caked with muck of little variety and put them in a pot to boil. He hosed the cots and helped break down tents and load them onto John's truck. They were cleaning the Thatle Hotel before the next occupants, Marjorie and Stewart, arrived, just like Mary Tucker, cleaned before her next "customers."

✦

"Come on, Jane. Let's go."

Even before they'd stepped out of the yard, Jane felt the morning heat press on her as well as the sedating effects of the scent of baking eucalyptus leaves. She shrugged, rolled her eyes, and yawned. She would've liked to have slept longer. An extra cup of tea with another Iced Vovo, her favorite shortbread biscuit with the coconut raspberry icing, would've set her perfectly for the day. Bernadette had given her a plate of them wrapped in cellophane and embellished with a ribbon for her fifteenth birthday the day before.

"Bernadette, why don't you sleep more?"

"I sleep plenty, little Miss Sloth."

"Seriously, Bernadette, what's not to be got from waiting an hour?"

Bernadette looked to the sky as though she were confirming the time. "It's mid-morning, Jane. And hot."

Theoretically, Jane knew that she'd miss Bernadette once she left for university the next day, but she also anticipated an ease in the household that just wasn't possible with Bernadette around. Already that morning Bernadette had pointed out how hard their mum still worked at Solicitor Simpson's, which Jane could tell wounded both parents although she wasn't sure why or even that Bernadette had set out to do that. Already Bernadette had lectured her about the difference between certain Australian trees and certain American ones, even as she'd insisted they had no time for dilly-dallying, no time for an Iced Vovo.

"You'll miss me when I'm gone, Jane."

"Yeah, but we still could've left later."

As they ventured out of the yard into the still hot day, Bernadette's main objective was to memorize all aspects of their journey to the riverbed. An exercise of recall, a tool to sharpen your mind, practice precision not sentimentality, Bernadette told herself. Although she envisioned herself immersed in Brisbane's bold urban life, she still planned to be prepared for that one evening when she might miss this place, when she'd want to recreate each turn of the trail, each section of brush with the insect, bird, and animal life along the way. She wasn't sure how she'd capture the floral and acrid smells, the bush rhythms, the mix of hush and music that was all around them only that she intended to. She couldn't stand that she might be stuck in her dormitory where the bleeps and barks of traffic seeped in and not be able to remember this world of her comfort.

"Would you like me to share with you the words of Saint Paul," Jane said, bending to pick a stalk of grass to chew.

"No, not really, Jane."

"Paul a.k.a. Saul."

"No thanks." Creatures were hibernating from the heat.

"It's just that it might be a good thing for you to consider, Bernadette, you know, the idea of charity as it relates to dragging your only sister from her birthday biscuits:

> *Charity suffereth long, and is kind; charity envieth*
> *not; charity vaunteth not itself, is not puffed up,*
> *Doth not behave itself unseemly; seeketh not her own, is not easily*
> *provoked, thinketh no evil...*"

Jane continued reciting sections of 1 Corinthians, occasionally stopping to consider Bernadette's discoveries: the echidna prints: four five-fingered claws that you could see from the channels in the dirt could rip into a hard termite mound as though it were as malleable as cookie dough. "Its tube-like snout and tongue, we've got to consider that," said Bernadette, looking provocatively at Jane. "You know that its tongue operates with the same hydraulic principle as a penis?"

"Piss off, Bernadette" was the response.

The previous week Bernadette and her friend, Felicity, lost their virginity to Gerry Wilden, the lifeguard at the pool. They'd planned it. They chose him for his nice body, which is to say, tanned with pimples, but not enough to be off-putting, tall enough to be exactly one head height over Felicity and almost as tall as Bernadette, and nice, which is to say, slightly shy, which you'd want so there'd be no boasting afterwards. "Reputation is key, Bernadette," Felicity had said. They and Gerry had spent the last month of the school holidays brokering the details as though they were at a market. Felicity saying, "Yes, of course, you want sex to correspond to love, Bernadette, but how realistic is that? It's not reasonable to put such pressure on the first time." Bernadette, of course, curious, and a great believer of reason (also not having a love prospect on her horizon), agreed, and although right after, when the whole thing seemed terribly disappointing—even for the sake of love—she could see now that it gave her a whole new perspective, maturity even, that separated her from the likes of Jane.

"Bernadette, I mean, have you ever heard so many words ending in eth? Listen: suffereth, envieth, vaunteth, seeketh, thinketh. You have to wonder how great it would be if we still spoke like that. What's a bet that the post-Paul peoples dropped the "eth" because it slowed them down? I doth thinketh to haveth a chat would soundeth silly-eth."

"Stop!" Bernadette's arm shot out like a boom on a boat. Before them was a spider web, two and a half to three meters across, anchored on one side to the branches of a wattle tree and, on the other, to the dead limb of a burnt hollow eucalyptus trunk. "Koalas like spots like that," Bernadette said.

"Not to mention snakes," Jane added. While they examined the web's contents: black beetles, butterflies, and bush flies—eleven of them—and two spindly legged spiders, the bush around them vibrated as did the web and they too, really. Perfectly comfortable with themselves and together, the sisters blended into this outback tableau with the web, trees, and grasses: the colors of their clothes and flesh blending into the oranges and reds, yellows and browns, and black and greens of the living bush around them.

Bernadette jotted a few observations into her book while Jane carefully sidestepped around the web so as not to disturb it.

"Do you know why I like Corinthians, Bernadette?" Bernadette had overtaken Jane on the path, re-establishing her lead and pace towards the riverbed.

"You can't beat the drama of a proud man knocked off his high horse, blinded and saved."

Bernadette thought it'd be nice to see a platypus for once at the riverbed, or to have the riverbed filled with water so there could be a platypus, or nice to have a river that she and Jane could swim in. That would be the type of memory she'd like to have for Brisbane. You are all sentiment, fool girl, she thought, squatting then to examine a shock of tussock grass, which she sketched because its lean and sensual form appealed to her as did the tiny bugs that clung to the stalks and sheaths that barely moved in the humid air, but moved enough that to those creatures it must have felt like a swing.

"*Rejoiceth not in iniquity, but rejoiceth in the truth; Beareth all things, believeth all things, hopeth all things, endureth all things.* So great all those *eths*."

Bernadette scowled. They were almost to the riverbed; the slight drop in temperature, a familiar sign that each girl registered, but didn't acknowledge.

"Rejoiceth, beareth, hopeth, endureth: aren't you even curious to know what *eth* means?"

"It's a suffix, meaning custom or habit," Bernadette said.

Bernadette had a knack to, with a word, momentarily shift Jane's awareness. Her chatter to Bernadette was chatter and meant as little to Jane as it did to Bernadette. Jane pulled another stalk of grass from the bank, deciding that she'd admit to Bernadette that there was an element of silliness to what she said, that parts of her concept of religion were still childish, no, under-developed, and that maybe her appreciation of this verse wasn't about its meaning per se, but the pleasure of the rhyme. Jane pictured the Iced Vovo she'd eat when they got home and said, "Isn't rhyme fun, Bernadette?"

Bernadette didn't respond. At the bank of the riverbed, she'd paused; her head cocked slightly, a hand raised in warning.

✦

The first time that Bernadette lied about her father's death she was standing in the registration line at Queens University. She'd arrived in Brisbane only a couple of days before, and had already been assigned a room in the first-year dorm. It surprised her how easily it slipped out. She'd been speaking with the girl in front of her whose bone structure made Bernadette feel as though she had none, whose clear complexion highlighted Bernadette's cover-up make-up, and whose tapered tailored dress made Bernadette conscious of her own frock, sewn two years before in Home Economics. The girl had said, "It must be hard for your parents that you're so far away." Bernadette had simply corrected her. "Hard for my mum. My dad's been dead for a while." When the girl had blushed, Bernadette had looked away and said, "No worries." She'd felt better, though, calmer.

The distance from Mount Isaac to Brisbane was roughly 965 kilometers as the crow flies, but much further on the dirt and bitumen roads that mapped the old explorer routes. Bernadette's journey began with the hour drive to Claremont, where her parents and Jane saw her off at the bus terminal, which was actually a wood platform beside Dawn and Sally's Ballet Studio. The bus to Mackay took three hours. She'd changed to another bus that arrived in Rockhampton four and a half hours later. There she'd stayed the night with her mother's cousin, Hillary, and the next morning took the Brisbane bus. This leg had lasted eight and a quarter hours with stops at the coastal towns of Bundaberg, Maryborough, and Gympie.

It was this distance that gave Bernadette some flexibility with facts. A week after registration at a mixer for first years held in the basement of the student union, she found herself telling James, a Brisbane boy, how her father had died. As supervisor for dragline operations at the open-cut coalmine east of Mt. Isaac, her father had been responsible for the dragline: that five-story monster, the ninety-meter boom, the bucket bigger than a trailer, and its half a meter-thick rods of iron the height of a person and the length of two train cabooses. When one of his mechanics caught his leg in coal near the foot of the dragline, it was up to her father to pull him loose. He did that but slipped under the foot as he did. "He saved a man but died himself. Imagine," she said. "How unlucky, but lucky that a man was saved."

While James' furrowed eyebrows suggested concern, his eyes traveled behind Bernadette to the fledgling cliques forming as new students searched for their own. It was difficult for her family,

Bernadette added. The company had compensated them. Neighbors and friends had brought casseroles and cakes for weeks after. "Sympathy has its own rewards, James," she'd said.

Although Bernadette realized she'd overdone it with the casseroles, she could tell James was impressed. He'd stopped scanning the crowd over her shoulder and instead focused on her with an approving look. When she finished, James gently squeezed her arm and said, "Hey listen, I'd like you to meet some of my friends from Brisbane. They'll love you." The beer tasted perfect then, and, in the crush of festive students, Bernadette felt perfectly comfortable. The reality of her father alive at home or at Delton's Department Store, the reality of her father at all, had no place here.

The next time Bernadette mentioned her father's death was at a party two months later. By then she'd used her student grant check to equip herself with the necessities of urban social life. She'd bought one linen and two cotton sundresses, two skirts, four tops, one pair of plastic sandals, one pair of leather sandals, a ball gown, and what can only be described as a dressage outfit: jodhpur pants, leather riding boots, and a fashionable turtleneck and jumper. She'd splurged on a wide-brimmed straw hat, imported from London, with two separate, but equally beautiful scarves that wrapped around its brim, and, after her face healed, dispensed with the make-up her Mum had given her.

Along with her outfits her accent changed. Her vowels contracted and elongated in her throat until she sounded as British as any private school girl from Brisbane might. It's true that Bernadette had abandoned her Mt. Isaac self, but who can judge if these movements away from herself weren't just the steps towards becoming herself?

The night of the St. Lucia party was humid, and Bernadette, in her new skirt and sleeveless top, was striking amidst the throng of students. She leaned against the wood bar on a rickety stool and as she wove tales of her childhood—of bush birds that drew blood and of daily escapes from poisonous spiders and snakes—her gray eyes perused the crowd with a combination of query and challenge.

She was on her third rum and coke when Andrew Pocklington, a second-year law student, pulled a stool beside hers, effectively cutting her away from her band of listeners. He'd been waiting for just the right moment to resume the banter they had begun over the prior two parties.

"Well?" he said.

"Pins," she said. "Once my history teacher was angry at me for a map display I'd made with pins."

"Yes?"

"Mr. Thompson said, 'That tide of red topped pins flooding the map, those were sewing pins!'"

"For what now?" Andrew considered that she might need another drink, that black hair like hers was sophisticated, even sexy, and that, with her, it didn't bother him that he hadn't thought to make a pin display himself.

"It was the flu epidemic of 1918. I wanted to see the one with the many, and if there was a place on the globe you could escape the epidemic."

"With pins?"

"I overheard Miss Perry, my English teacher, defend me: 'That's how it was, Mr. Thompson. It's not her fault that that's the way it was.'"

Andrew said, "Funny, Bernadette, you don't strike me as someone who needs defending."

"I'm not!" she retorted. "Where's my drink, mate?" she demanded with a softer tone, needing a moment to regain her composure.

As Andrew rose to refill their drinks from the bar behind them, Bernadette forced herself back to the pin scene, debarring more disturbing ones. Mr. Thompson's anger had been justified, she knew, because as hard as she'd tried to express the truth of that history, her map couldn't do it. Without enough red pins, she'd had to cover the other colored pins with tiny red hoods that she'd stayed up past midnight sewing.

"Agree with me here, Bernadette," he said, handing her a refill. "They're flying Dalmatians, those magpies in King George Square."

"Those birds are flying Dalmatians, Andrew."

"And lizards?" he said.

"Hard, scaly, and green as dinosaurs, Andrew."

"Yes," he said, "but by the time you hear the rush of wind and wings, it's too late. The magpie is on you."

"Yes." She tilted her head to the side as though conjuring the image. "But, when you catch the eye of a goanna, it's also too late. He'll not release you from his gaze."

Andrew stared at her with a wide white smile. Bernadette laughed, her head flung back—his lips shiny and red, she'd noticed that, along with his blond hair, blonder against his tan—then smoothed her peasant skirt. His gaze didn't falter from her even as he sipped his gin and tonic and the student beside him bumped him. I want to tell him something important, Bernadette nervously realized, aware she was attracted to him.

"Andrew, have I told you about my father," she said. "He was an opal prospector, who led an expedition to the north of Coober Pedy." Bernadette described to Andrew how the land around Coober Pedy was like a dried-up sea that crunched like hardened salt when you walked on it, and that the heat was so extreme that people lived underground to escape it. "Under there, they have kitchenettes and bedrooms," she said. "They have showers." She told him that her father, in search of new deposits, left with a guide. Instead of driving a utility truck, or ute, as usual, they rode camels because the terrain was that rugged. They were equipped for the expedition, and certainly, they couldn't be more prepared. No one knew what went wrong, only something did. Her father and the guide disappeared in the Great Victoria Desert.

"Wasn't there a search, Bernadette?"

"For over a month."

Bernadette and Andrew quietly sipped their drinks as disco music thumped around them. They no longer looked at each other; their eyes followed the array of students dancing on the wood floor before them. Bernadette felt ill.

"The first opal that Dad brought back for me was as black as tar, except for a flash of red. That's rare."

Even though Bernadette knew her father wasn't dead, she felt a cry loose in her chest, flying up into the hollows of her throat, and she swallowed it back. This grief couldn't last. She wouldn't let it. She willed it back into the thick and steady stream of her heart's blood. Andrew, by then, had leaned over and kissed her.

Bernadette couldn't know that Andrew, with this kiss, was, for the first time, swept up in a feeling that he couldn't control. As a Pocklington, he had pressures that couldn't easily be teased from his lineage: Anglican, with a hardy roster of barristers, judges, and politicians. Born to weigh things—degrees of equality, suitability, and aesthetics—important things; where you were positioned after a social interaction, Andrew's mother, Gillian, especially emphasized, was critical.

Listening to Bernadette, Andrew had forgotten the swirl of social maneuvers: those considerations of where he should be and with whom, even how he appeared leaning towards her in the din of that party at Ngarra Hall. The story of her father's death had transported him to a still, secret world where he felt calm and present. When he leaned to kiss her, it wasn't for Bernadette that he was reaching, but for that place she'd created.

As part of their courtship, Bernadette and Andrew would meet for beers at the Norwich and would walk along the banks of the Brisbane River. Here once, Andrew pointed out the stretch of river where his crew team rowed and Bernadette once pointed out the flock of galahs in the jacaranda trees ahead. They'd stood beneath the lavender boughs that day and observed the birds in their flutter of gray wings, inflated pink chests, and head crests like crowns, twirl and somersault in the air above them. They'd exchanged a look of lightness and possibility as though here was some joy that they could share, too. When Bernadette mentioned that galahs form permanent pair bonds in nature, Andrew had grabbed her hands and spun her around, as though they were swing dancing. Even after they'd stopped it was as though they'd continued to twirl and somersault towards each other.

In love, more surprising than their physical pleasure—pleasure Bernadette had hardly expected based on her previous findings—were the strange tales Andrew told Bernadette in those early months. He told her, for example, that on the morning of her father's funeral he and his mother, Gillian, had brought seafood canapés over to the Pilgrim's house. Gillian had also brought French champagne, "Delamotte Blanc de Blancs," specially chilled, for on a hot day in November, even at a funeral, that touch would be perfect, necessary even. Andrew told Bernadette that her mother, Audrey, had said, "You're too kind," to him and his mother, and he'd felt happy because they had been kind.

Andrew told Bernadette that he'd joined one of the search expeditions for her father. In a Range Rover, packed with supplies, they'd driven out to the Great Victoria Desert, stopping only in Coober Pedy. Some of the underground homes had caved in and there was a possibility that her father and his guide could have been in one of those. There were the cave-ins that occurred when people were inside and those when people fell through from the top. Bernadette's father and guide could have died in either circumstance though it would be impossible to verify which one.

Once he told her that he'd found camel bones and a compass out in the desert. The face of the compass was cracked, embedded with tiny grains of sand that sparkled like jewels in the light. There was no monogram, however, no identifying feature to tie it to her father. Bad luck.

Another night, as Bernadette assembled the buttons to send to her mother for the quilt that Audrey had been sewing since Bernadette's childhood, Andrew told her that Audrey had agreed to let the Pocklingtons use this quilt at his family reunion. "Of course, you're all invited," he'd said. "We'll spread the blanket across the lawn at the City Botanic Gardens, and lie there, drinking champagne and eating hors-d'oeuvres. It'll be so good," he said, snapping the button from his shirt cuff and handing it to her.

Two days after this, Bernadette and Andrew were studying across from each other at a long table in the St. Lucia Library reading room when Andrew grabbed her arm from across the table and whispered, "Bernadette, I don't mind telling you that I know something about justice."

"Settle down, mate," she urged good-humoredly. "You are studying to become a barrister."

"My father's a judge." His tone of urgency was new. "You know that, don't you?"

"Sure," she said, although she didn't actually, since Andrew only guardedly spoke about his father, who lived in Melbourne.

"A judge can get things done, Bernadette. What a judge can do is startling if you think about it. And my father is good." Andrew said, "If he finds out who murdered your father, he'll send him away for life." He assured Bernadette three times that week that she could count on this.

What Bernadette and Andrew each thought about Andrew's fabrications and assurances based on her father's death that wasn't a death, commingled in some other reality where facts could be unmade and remade, and passion could possibly buoy them or, at least, persuade them that that wasn't that, but *this*, this is what it is, and it's all right, comforting actually—kind mothers and dead heroic fathers defended by the just living ones.

When Andrew arrived at Bernadette's room, he was more agitated than usual. He settled in the chair beside her bed, complained about the smell of camels from his last trip to the Great Victoria and boasted about his remedy of dipping a handkerchief in Vicks Mentholatum to counter the smell. Bernadette informed him that every schoolgirl knew that remedy, which annoyed him a little although he didn't say so. "That camel spat at me," he complained, "and tried to buck me off by sitting." And as though reliving this scene, he jumped up from the chair and exclaimed, "Impossible to stay astride them, Bernadette. Camels!"

Before Andrew could say another word, Bernadette caught his hand and kissed it, and then standing, she leaned into him and kissed his full red lips. She looked at him then, her eyes resting in his in such a way that he felt suddenly uncomfortable and looked away.

"What is it?" he asked evenly.

When she tried to answer him, she couldn't. Maybe she wanted to tell him that he was the best camel driver she knew or that, yes, the Pilgrims would be delighted to come to the Pocklington picnic or maybe that she was just grateful that he'd made up those things and that she finally understood that between him and his judge father she could be assured some comfort and safety. She could finally just tell Andrew the truth of her trauma. Unfortunate how voices can fail at these critical times: Bernadette stood tongue-tied and slightly horrified that the pressure of her emotions was borne out solely by her unbidden tears.

Andrew pulled her into his arms. With her wet cheek against his chin, the weight of her head at the base of his throat, and her admission, "I'm so angry, Andrew. How can you stand it? There's so much anger," he braced, thinking, I shouldn't be bracing. But with her look, tears, and words, his world shifted and although he couldn't say what had changed, something had, which made him anxious because he couldn't know how they were changing and to what, which made him brace against her more and say, "Stop this, now, Bernadette. Stop, hey."

When she continued, "I couldn't see. Not me or you. I couldn't. That's how angry—fucking blind with it," he recoiled still more from her and told her that she could see anything she liked.

"Andrew. Can we stop pretending, now?" How ready she was to unburden herself with him.

Bernadette cried unabashedly into his chest, surrendering completely to the comfort of his presence. So profound was her sense of solace that she didn't notice Andrew's retreat. It threw her then, when not long after this, Andrew unpeeled himself from her arms and avoiding her eyes said, "I have to go: I have an essay to complete and there's a meeting with my study group, and I must ring my parents. They're expecting a call."

"Of course, you must," she answered, slowly recognizing it. As Andrew let himself out, Bernadette numbly sat at the edge of her bed. After an indeterminate time, she let herself fall back.

When friends later asked Bernadette what had happened with Andrew, Bernadette either replied that it was private and would change the subject or, if it was a better day for her, she might ask the friend: "Do you know the words to 'On the Road to Gundagai?'" And if they didn't, which they usually didn't to this version, she'd recite the first two lines for them:

> *"In a week the spree was over and the cheque was all*
> *knocked down,*
> *So we shouldered our Matildas, and we turned our back*
> *on town."*

This was guaranteed to make her friends laugh. God, stop, Bernadette. You can't be serious. Too funny!

And when Andrew's friends asked him, he would say, "I acted properly. How can you date a girl who, the entire time you date them, never sees you? What sort of relationship is that? I could have been anybody. It's certainly not like she appreciated she was with a Pocklington."

To one well-intentioned boyfriend who came after, Bernadette would bristle when he'd inquire about her past: "What part of love or love's losses isn't private?" she'd say.

✦

When Audrey Pilgrim reached across the counter to hand Dan, the Fix-It-Man, her broken lamp, he noticed the slip of hair at the side of her face, loosened from her bun. He said, "Didn't expect to see anyone on a day like this," and he looked beyond Mrs. Pilgrim to the sand storm outside his shop and felt sorry for them both then—him in a repair shop, in the back O'Bourke, and this woman, who clearly could believe that repairs would be important on a day like this. Shame life, sometimes, he thought. And when he carefully guided that scrap of gritty hair—he could feel the sand in it between his fingers—

behind her ear (an action borne from no more than an inclination for order, or so he told himself), Audrey caught his hand and rested her face in his palm. And as he thought, Steady on, she sighed, registering the warmth of his hand, then pulled away and silently walked out just as she'd done from the hospital less than half an hour before.

Strange providence that after she left Dan's, Audrey found herself driving behind the man in the white ute. He'd cut her off as she pulled out of the parking lot. At first when he'd turned, she'd planned to turn too. Left, then right at the Esso Station, then straight on Howard, but where she should've turned right at the florist she didn't, choosing to continue behind him, feeling more provoked than invited. As they drove past the sign that welcomed visitors to Mt. Isaac, it was clear that a dialogue had begun between the drivers on that empty stretch of the western highway, eucalyptus and brush fanning out on either side of them, below a sun that baked the tarmac until it bubbled amidst dirt flying at them from all sides. Clear also was that there would be no turning back from where Audrey's dialogue with this man would take her.

The following day, Audrey drove an hour to the Woolworths in Claremont to purchase that first blanket that would become part of a quilt that would one day cover a wall at the National Gallery in Canberra and be described as a "fine example of contemporary Australian folk art." She chose the cheapest blanket: an acrylic-polyester mix with the silky shiny borders. She chose rose because she knew instinctively that her buttons would set well on that color, and she bought a large pail of multi-colored thread that was on sale. The first blanket cost thirteen dollars and eighty-five cents and, with inflation over the years, the last blanket cost forty dollars even. Audrey never varied the blanket color although, ten years into the project, the Chinese manufacturers, Bedding & Beyond, changed the dye so that the rose was less dusky and more pink. Each blanket, once button covered, Audrey would stitch with twine to the last, creating blanket-sized quilt patches of three meters by three meters.

The night after Audrey had bought her supplies, at the end of dinner after clearing and washing the plates, she collected a jar of buttons from the pantry and emptied it onto the kitchen table. She divided the buttons by color then roughly matched them to the equivalent spools of thread. That these buttons documented each day of her marriage wasn't what struck her as strange, but that she'd stored them loose for so many years in bottles and jars. It would be right now to fix them down. She didn't consider how she'd arrange them. That didn't seem to matter yet.

✦

Audrey's boss, Solicitor Simpson, many weeks later, would be hard pressed to say what day his secretary, hired for her skills in dictation, typing, and organization and valued for her unobtrusiveness and invisibility, became so pronounced to him that he could no longer concentrate on his work. He suspected that on a day that she typically looked away from him, she didn't. Or was it the other way around? One day their eyes met, and Mrs. Pilgrim, really quite shockingly, didn't look away. Solicitor Simpson became less certain of what he understood, for how was it that one day she wasn't there and the next she was a solid, scented presence with a whirl of mysterious thoughts and emotions bound discretely across the room from him? How was it that his attention could so singularly be swept up in this presence at her desk outside his door, when the tray with tea was set before him, when she asked, "Mr. Simpson, should I call Sally Fredericks for the deposition this week or would next week suit you better?"

One late afternoon as Solicitor Simpson and Audrey were finishing up the day's business, Solicitor Simpson asked her into his office. Lately, he'd felt her eyes—neither hurried nor reluctant— luxuriate on his face and then share a look with him that until she'd shared with him, he hadn't realized he hadn't been sharing with anyone, and, that on his own, he'd been very lonely. He stood before Audrey, who calmly regarded him. "I'm a clumsy… Mrs. Pilgrim, a blind man. Please, see what you've done."

She moved past him to the windows where she closed the blinds as she did each day. The blinds didn't feel different, but everything else did: the shuttered view that necessarily shut out Robert and the girls, the intimacy of the darkened office, the expectant man behind her, and she herself insensibly awake. That a transformation had occurred in Audrey Pilgrim since her visit with Belinda and that exchange with the ute driver was becoming clear.

"What I've done?" Solicitor Simpson didn't reply, perhaps struggling with his own moral compass. Though change she had, even as Audrey appreciated the heat and pressure of her boss's arms around her, she couldn't fathom why her heightened senses would deprive someone else of theirs. She had no answer as to why her heightened senses precluded even the existence of Robert and therefore any guilt or regret that most would argue that she should've had. Most likely she hadn't even formulated that question.

In fact, with the certainty that Audrey dedicated herself to sewing the button quilt in those early years so did she concede to this desire, which, now awake in a manner almost painful, now unfettered by the constraints of oath and as acute as her awareness of life's finiteness, freed her to sleep with other men. Even as Audrey sewed the history of her marriage and family into round and swirling waves of buttons on the blanket's rose-colored background, outside the house, she sought the textures of bodies—to feel them, to feel herself against them. She told herself it wasn't reactionary and certainly it wasn't spiteful or lasting, for that matter. Her essential longing to hold and to be held she could no longer deny or contain. Occupation and disposition didn't seem to matter. Whether it was the repairman or solicitor, miner or grazier, musician or teacher, Audrey sought the tastes and heat of their mouths mixing with hers—salt, sweet, bitter, and sour—as palatable as the behavior of their bodies with hers.

✦

Audrey's journey to buy quilt supplies at Woolworths, although technically further, was nowhere as far as the distance Audrey had traveled the day before, when she'd visited Belinda and met the driver of the ute. That night of her return from Claremont, as Audrey sorted her buttons and thread, Bernadette watched from the doorway unaware of any changes in her mother. She hummed under her breath a tune that Audrey couldn't identify and she eyed Audrey critically, Audrey knew, because she'd reached that stage when she could see that adults could be unfair and unkind, confused and mistaken, yet still pretend to be none of these.

"I'm going to make a quilt," Audrey said, although that seemed obvious. She felt curious about Bernadette suddenly, as though she hadn't mothered her for almost twelve years. "What's the song, Love?" She wondered if she'd missed the time of genuine connection with her daughter and would ever know if Bernadette had already come up against her contradictions and ambivalent passions.

"What about the four missing buttons? When's Dad coming home?"

Audrey caught her breath, out of depth suddenly in the murky swirl of things she might have to explain. She reached for the blanket at her feet and removed it from its clear plastic wrapping as though the wrapping might tear or the blanket break.

"How long will he be broken down?"

Overcome with a mix of shame, shyness, and guilt—that reluctance in herself to speak freely with Bernadette—Audrey carefully refolded the blanket's stiff packaging. She set it aside, stared hard at her daughter while silently making a path through her own contradictions and ambivalent passions to tell Bernadette about the telegram that she'd sent to the Morella Post Office that morning, requesting Robert's return and to assure Bernadette that though it might take a while for the message to reach Robert, she was confident that, despite the distance, it would. "Your father will be waiting," she said. "He's healthy. Not actually broken down, Bernadette. He'll be home soon."

Audrey pushed back the chair and stood to unfold the blanket. Robert, at the General Supply in Longreach, buying buttons for each day he was away (fifteen by the time of his return), immodest about the time and attention he'd spend choosing each button under that shopkeeper's suspicious stare, was an image entirely too personal to share with her daughter.

"He'll be home soon, love," Audrey repeated, careful to rein in that sympathy, that habit she had for Robert.

Bernadette walked over to her and picked up the opposite corners of the blanket. Each of them stepped back letting the cloth stretch between them. Bernadette had resumed humming, "*Singing Tooral liooral liaddity, Singing Tooral liooral liay.*"

"'Botany Bay,' Love?" They shook the creases from the blanket that had been folded long enough that the creases were discolored.

"Do you remember that book about Cook at Keppel Bay?" Audrey asked.

"*In this Bay is good anchorage where there is a sufficient depth of water,*" they recited in unison, Bernadette smiling triumphantly. Audrey returned her smile, grateful for this unexpected fellowship.

✦

On learning of Audrey's quilt, some men would slip her buttons stolen from their wives' sewing boxes or pull them off their shirts and coats with bravado or shyness or the first emotion covering the second because some of these men felt more strongly for Audrey than she knew or cared. Occasionally, the men's wives, not understanding the extent of their connection with Audrey and some who did, would send along their own buttons. Audrey accepted all that was offered, for with each of these encounters Audrey sewed herself into the world as though she'd spent her life floating and loose, adapting and malleable above it.

There were no dreams here any longer. The connections Audrey pursued and discovered just as much revealed her loneliness along with the loneliness of some of the men with whom she slept. Audrey translated these into that quilt, using her men and their buttons, transforming each of them into something less lonely, sewing them together in a permanent community, undoubtedly more for her comfort than theirs.

As a natural course, Audrey spent less time involved with school and community associations. Eventually, Audrey resigned from her position with Solicitor Simpson in order to quilt full-time. Although the changes in Audrey weren't directly addressed in the Pilgrim home, her daughters and husband well noted that by the time Bernadette left for university, Audrey's quilt was as big as three single bed blankets. When Jane moved away from Mt. Isaac three years later, the quilt had grown to eight blankets. The rumors of Audrey's secret life Robert actively ignored while the girls completely dismissed them in disbelief.

Her neighbor, Doreen, was more vocal. She told Audrey that "she'd changed" and that "wouldn't she be better joining up with a quilting bee" and "why wasn't she participating in Mt. Isaac society anymore?" And that, finally, "there were incriminating rumors if she'd care to listen." Audrey, guileless perhaps, suspected that Doreen felt excluded so she invited her to tea one afternoon. Retrieving the quilt from the front room, Audrey unfolded a section of it for her to see. "I'm quite happy doing this, Doreen. See, once you get started, there are so many possibilities of beauty."

Doreen stared at it, her jaw slack. "I'm shocked, Audrey," she said. "This, this is native or abstract. It's a cheap bit of blanket with shiny buttons on it. Hardly a quilt! And hardly an excuse!"

Audrey also stared at her quilt. Finally, she repeated Doreen's admonishment. "Yes, hardly," as though she too could see the impracticality of such a non-quilty quilt, as though she too might criticize herself—but for what, though?—what luck or lack of it to desire contact and to be driven now to quilt and what luck or lack of luck that she felt no choice in these matters, and, surprising this—even with dismayed Doreen before her—Audrey Pilgrim no longer cared what people thought even as she did care, for with each button she sewed to the blankets Audrey closed a distance between them and herself and, unbeknownst to them and only half-perceived by Audrey, them with each other.

As Audrey showed Doreen out that day, where once she would've dwelled in the criticisms she knew that Doreen carried to the other women in town—"Not a bit of remorse and I'm telling you—about that quilt thing—there's no backing or blocking or appliqué. I didn't see any baskets or lilies or Mexican Star block or, even, angels or Chinese lanterns. How can you have a quilt without lovebirds or rainbows or ribbon pathways? What about birds and butterflies or the morning star cushion?"—Audrey instead turned to the interplay of red buttons with purple, flat buttons with moundy ones, and the difficulties of using these to express motion and depth on a still flat blanket.

✦

Nothing was smooth that first night that Audrey started sewing the button quilt. It was quiet without Robert. She still felt physically uncomfortable. Under the overhead light the buttons seemed to lose definition and color. Bernadette must've noticed too for after she'd helped Audrey unfold the blanket, she moved the standing lamp from the lounge room, and set it beside the table next to Audrey's chair. By then Jane had wordlessly wandered in, and had claimed the spot across from Audrey. From a paper bag in her lap, Jane pulled out tools and supplies to construct an altar: scissors, crayons, a cereal box, a paper doll, glue pot, and a shard of glass. Audrey swept a pile of buttons further down the table to make more room for her.

"For Saint Rita, Mum," Jane answered as though Audrey had asked. "I read that she's the patron saint of desperate cases, but she's good to pray to if you need skin wounds healed."

Bernadette gave Jane the what-planet-are-you-from look.

"Jesus sent a thorn from his Crown of Thorns into Rita's forehead, which festered and stank and made her an outcast with the nuns. But when she died, and this is true, her smell turned forever to the sweet scent of roses. To this day you can see and smell her in Italy." Jane lined up the crayons: Carnation Pink, Jazzberry Jam, and

Wild Strawberry beside the paper doll and placed the shard above the doll's head as though she were prepping for surgery. "The glass is for the thorn and I'm going to color roses all over her body."

She then peered at Audrey and Bernadette through the glass piece that could only have come from a broken jar. It was only a sliver. There was no way to honestly see through it. Audrey pulled the longest needle from the packet. Jane would have to contend with the glare from the lamp. Yet Jane was looking. See her, Audrey admonished herself, allowing then the image of Jane further ensconcing herself in devotion and prayer, glue and glass to sink in. The blanket's dense fabric would require the sharpest of needles. A wider eye would be easier to thread.

"Good, Jane. Saint Rita it'll be then," Audrey finally replied, and I can, I will, under her breath as she slowly edged to the cave's opening, and "Did you get enough to eat tonight, Love?" hand trembling as that first button was sewn down.

✦

Over time peoples' attitudes to Audrey and her quilt changed. It wasn't just Robert who brought her buttons or later, Bernadette sending them from Brisbane and Jane from Toowoomba. Or Audrey's lovers during that stage. Friends and committee members, hearing of Audrey's quilt, would bring by envelopes of odd buttons, hoping that she'd invite them in to see it, which, after Doreen, Audrey never did. Buttons arrived from most neighbors, other "friends" and acquaintances, and even from people who never liked Audrey and would be reluctant to admit a connection to her, no less a button contribution. Somehow the word spread about Audrey's project (rumor had it that Louisa Cawley had a hand in this) because, after a while, Brownie, Girl Guide, and even Scout troops throughout the state were sending her envelopes filled with buttons. Auxiliary groups, police and firemen's wives, the local chapters of both the Teacher's and Mine Mechanic's Unions, the Prison Reform Society, the Drought Research Group, and the bottlers at the Castlemaine Brewery donated buttons to Audrey as well. Robert documented that Audrey once exchanged a packet of family buttons for some collected and made by Claremont's Aboriginal Spirit and Ancestor Group, and that buttons arrived from as far away as Japan, Kenya, and the States.

When the Bishop heard about Audrey Pilgrim—and he did

through Sister Jacinta at Saint Ursula's Convent and Andrew Pocklington, a solicitor from Brisbane, with whom he'd occasionally share a drink—he thought it might be a nice trope for a future sermon. That very Easter the Bishop requested that each parish in Queensland donate a packet of buttons to Audrey Pilgrim, the artist from Mount Isaac.

✦

The table and its contents blurred. This is our love here, Audrey knew. And was it too late to embrace her daughters, assuring them of her love; too unkind now to question Bernadette's certitude, opening her to all the emotional turmoil that would come eventually unsolicited, too cynical to question Jane's faith? Eyes level—a mother should not cry before her children—Audrey gestured at the buttons and blanket. "See these…" She gestured again. "These are ours." Jane didn't see what her mother had meant as her sights were still filled with the wounds of Gavin and the redemptive possibilities of her altar. Bernadette didn't see how these buttons had anything to do with her. "Ours," Audrey repeated to her daughters.

✦

Jane and Robert first visited Bernadette four months after she'd moved to Brisbane. It was supposed to be a family visit, but on the way Audrey had decided to stop in Rockhampton to help her cousin, Hillary, who was in the process of moving. Bernadette met them on the steps outside her dormitory and, as she brusquely led them up to her room, she told them about her favorite course, "Australians at War." "The demand for our boys' bravery and their subsequent suffering was a result of poor planning by those in charge," she'd just asserted in a British accent that Jane found confusing, when two of her hall mates dropped by to greet them. Bernadette then announced that after their father's death they were lucky their uncle lived nearby in Tangorin. She gestured gratefully toward their father and, as her friends looked on sympathetically, said: "This is my Uncle Bob, and my sister, Jane."

Neither Jane nor Robert were prepared for this. Jane found herself nodding as if to say "Yes, aren't we lucky," and "Yes, I am Jane," while thinking Tangorin is not even close to Mt. Isaac. Robert ignored Bernadette or appeared not to hear because he'd turned his back to the group of younger people and was arranging the pens and pencils on Bernadette's desk: blues together, blacks together, reds together, and lead pencils according to height.

Like most siblings, Jane and Bernadette had a history of battles. Besides fighting about the details and dynamics of their expeditions into the bush, they argued about Jane's altars, which, placed liberally about the house, Bernadette disparaged as "the signs of an untidy mind that was ill-equipped to survive the outback," and which Jane defended as "the gateways to heavenly communications, lost to minds as unholy as Bernadette's." Later they argued about Jane's intercessions with their parents, which Bernadette likened to a puppy with a ball wanting someone to play with her and which Jane justified as a righteous impulse to unify and connect what shouldn't be broken.

"That's not an insight that a sister who's as oblivious as a giant pre-historic toad could have. Right, Tiddalik, I mean, Bernadette?" she'd rejoin, a barb that was guaranteed to annoy Bernadette. These battles laid the foundation for the biggest one, where all their pain and differences were most at stake and, as is often the case, the one that tied them most.

That day Bernadette wore the beige fisherman's jumper, jodhpur trousers, and riding boots as though she had a horse out back or had just stepped in from her cattle property. It wasn't just Bernadette's incongruence to her urban setting that troubled Jane, but the unusual brightness and authority of her eyes as she made her pronouncement. For Jane, this was just one more bloody Bernadette memory, and she was angry—angry at Bernadette for doing this and being this, angry at her father for letting Bernadette get away with it, and angry at God that this should be some plan of His. Much later, when Jane shared the experience with Sister Jacinta, the Head Nun at the Presentation convent in Toowoomba, Sister Jacinta had said, "Experiences, like visions, aren't chosen. Be grateful for what you receive. Though, yes, your sister does sound delusional."

That day when their father had left the girls alone, Jane confronted Bernadette.

Bernadette had stood poised and aloof, gracing Jane with an elliptical smile that denied nothing. Jane became apoplectic. "Are you out of your bloody mind? Don't you get that this, that this has real, serious implications? We just can't go around pretending we're not who we are or have other people be what they're not. Bloody bugger Bernadette!"

✦

Just after Jane's twentieth birthday she traveled again to Brisbane to let Bernadette know that she'd been accepted to join the Congregation of the Sisters of the Presentation of the Blessed Virgin Mary in Toowoomba. She carried with her a bundle of her own letters that Bernadette had returned to her unopened in the offhand chance that Bernadette would finally be able to receive them. Jane suspected her own motives weren't completely virtuous and that she might be setting herself up. Still, that Bernadette might feel remorse, be curious about the content of her letters, and even wish to reestablish their relationship, even if she was still unwilling to acknowledge their father, was worth the risk. Over the phone, Bernadette had been amenable to meeting, which definitely was a positive sign.

Bernadette politely welcomed Jane into her office at the university, which Bernadette had been assigned to complete her dissertation. They exchanged niceties about the weather and Jane's trip after which Jane told Bernadette her good news in the course of telling Bernadette that she would be staying overnight at the local Presentation convent. In the silent room, the sound of laughter from the courtyard outside the window floated up to them. As Jane looked around the office at the over-packed bookcases and the posters which lined the walls: the Aboriginal Land Movement, the African National Congress, and the Palestinian Liberation Organization, she felt encouraged by the ease of their companionship.

"It's because of the assault, isn't it?" Bernadette leaned back in her chair and patiently waited for Jane to explain her decision. She was just as oblivious to the struggles on the wall as she was to the fact that Jane had just flinched.

Disbelieving that Bernadette's understanding of her was fixed in time four years earlier, because of "their" assault—not just hers, Jane ignored the question. Instead she calmly reminded Bernadette of the length of her faith, which she counted now—fourteen years—from age six to twenty, reminded her that faith was personal and so individual that it shouldn't need to be justified.

Jane paused, fighting an urge to fling her letters at her sister, which, if she'd bothered to read, explained it all. What would Captain Bernadette like to hear? That yes, Jane once constructed altars to fend off the demons of her nightmares and yes, Jane made altars as an entreaty for each and every Gavin concealed by clean shirts or frocks.

Would it be helpful for the Captain to know that Jane needed that Jane to get to the next one, to this one? Did she really care that Jane had learned that those altars often blinded people to the need and suffering around them, and that in the end it was actions that mattered.

Bernadette chewed the end of her biro then examined the wet etched cap. There was no chance that for Bernadette's sake Jane would revisit that unaccountably uncomfortable table where her mother would name the donors of buttons so that Jane could pass them to her father to document for his quilt button inventory. There was no chance she would mention the difficulties of remaining open and kind in that schoolyard marked by intolerance and cruelty. If there was a point in telling Bernadette that she'd sewn the Southern Cross in buttons into their Mum's quilt for them and their abusers, right then Jane couldn't see it.

Instead, with as much strained cheerfulness as she could muster, Jane informed Bernadette of her lengthy communication with the Sisters and the extensive bout of introspection and justification for them to even consider her. Not that she did it solely for their consideration, no, that wasn't how it was. Just after Jane mentioned that she'd had to earn her teacher's credential to qualify to serve in this community of teaching nuns and was about to divulge how she'd had to be quite convincing, which hadn't been easy, Bernadette interrupted: "You're joining out of weakness. We both know that. And that's just a no-go."

Memories are stored vertically, fluid and accessible from the strangest depths. Jane heard a younger Bernadette in her captain persona pronounce that there'd been a mutiny on this expedition and that Jane had been brainwashed to the other side. As Bernadette added, "Think carefully, Jane. Be logical," Jane saw the Captain grimly pacing back and forth in front of her in their back yard, Jane's wrists chaffing from the shoelace bindings.

Meanwhile, across the desk from her, Bernadette, restacking the graduate student essays, told Jane that she was throwing away liberty, comfort, and intimacy—"Kids, Jane—a perfectly good life." Bernadette didn't notice the color rise in Jane's cheeks and earlobes. "The world is your oyster now that you've earned a teaching credential." Or that her eyes watered or that she swallowed continuously as though something the size of a gum-nut were lodged at the back of her throat. "I can't say enough about career planning," is what Bernadette actually said when Jane burst forth with, "Don't worry, Bernadette, a husband in Jesus is better than none at all," adding fiercely, "No sane person would ever venture out with you! You can bet on that!" And then: "You really are a bloody insensitive toad!" which she punctuated by slamming her bundle of letters to the ground.

Jane remembered Bernadette's stunned expression that, in the same instant, said, what are you talking about and aren't you a traitor and who'll be my back-up and I did my best. She remembered the immediacy with which this expression became cold and distant and how Bernadette rose and walked stiffly the two steps to the bookshelf saying, "If you're not going to be concerned about your life, why should I?" These words would sneak up on Jane at odd times: when she was scraping food off the cutlery in the nun's dining room, at the Sign of Peace in Mass, when she was sponge bathing Sister Theodore. Once when her student, Katrina, was reciting "The Exile's Lament," Bernadette's words smacked her in the face so hard that her eyes smarted.

> *But your names shall still live, though like writing in water,*
> *When confined to the notes of the tame cockatoo,*
> *Each wattle-scrub echo repeats to the other*
> *Your names, and each breeze hears me sighing anew.*

When Jane arrived at the Sisters of the Presentation of the Blessed Virgin Mary in Toowoomba, the regional city on the edge of the fertile Darling Downs, Saint Ursula's Convent, a wide and ruddy building of aged red brick, housed a mix of women mostly from Australia, but also from Ireland. Foreign and various in age and habit, the older nuns wore the pre-Vatican II floor-length black habit with the belt of beads, while the younger ones wore theirs shortened and of a lighter cotton more amenable to the tropics. The older nuns, from farther shores, had names that sounded dusty and strange to the younger women, who'd arrived at the convent from across town or, at most, from a property one or two hundred kilometers away. Jane had traveled from Mt. Isaac by two buses—four hours and fifteen minutes total.

Jane longed for the depth of history that the Presentation Sisters' roll of names offered: names that not only recorded for her the Sisters' history in Toowoomba, but also wound through the green and rocky hills of Ireland to Rome and the Romans, with their velvet robes, Latin Masses, and incense that wafted above congregations toward the dome ceiling of the Basilica. The younger nuns, the Annes, Clares, Elizabeths, and Marys came in time after Theresa, Raymond, Jacinta, Michael, Mary, and Agnes, who came after Geneviere, Brigid, Magnus, Gertrude, Bartholemew, Mary, Margaret-Mary, Theodore, and Scholastica.

Jane and her friends came next on the convent's rolls. At the end of her novitiate, Jane took her vows of chastity, poverty, and obedience and became Sister Ava, with Lily, who remained Sister Lily, and Brenda, who became Sister Anne. For the Holy Sacrament of Orders ceremony, overseen by Bishop Gray, accompanied by Mrs. McDonald on the pipe organ, and in a church filled with the sweet aroma of jasmine from the altar centerpiece mixed with Jerusalem incense, Jane's parents, fresh from Mt. Isaac, sat in the third row of St. Ursula's, behind Lily's two sisters and four brothers, who beamed at them with teeth that showed a familial gap.

That Bernadette hadn't come, wasn't beside her parents on the pew, was a fact that Jane pushed away with a prayer that begged her to arrive, even as it said, Forget you, Bernadette Pilgrim; forgive me, God, but forget her. What sorrow she felt, she hid in a fixed smile that lasted the day as though an orthodontist had wired it there.

At the end of the ceremony, after Bishop Gray had left the reception, Mother Superior gathered the girls again and congratulated each one, blessing their rings as though the bishop had forgotten. Jane, now Sister Ava, stood quietly with her parents, watching Sister Scholastica and Sister Brigid snort and wheeze with laughter while Sister Jacinta glared at them. "We have to go, Love," her mother finally said, and taking Jane's hand, pressed a round object into her palm that Jane knew without looking was a button.

"Sew it in, Mum," she said, pushing it back to her. "It'll be nice in your quilt."

Jane felt a quickening in her chest. By the simple act of pushing that button away, she pushed them away and pushed herself away from them and a series of choices that she'd never again see. Maybe though, by pushing that button away, she would move beyond her role in the family. She would no longer have to be that Jane—as pivotal to Jane's faith as she had been—a conduit of sorts, sitting between them: accommodating and unseen.

But was this true or just a story that she'd told herself about herself? A self-fulfilling prophesy?

"Hold still, Love," her mum had said as she made alterations to that May Day dress so long ago. "You don't want me to stick you accidentally." Her mother had kissed her on the peak of her forehead after they'd decided that Jane looked unbeatable, better than Bernadette even.

And the day after Bernadette left for university, she'd said: "You must miss Bernadette. You girls certainly wore yourselves out with that hike yesterday. You must've crawled through the brambles that the two of you got so scratched up."

And after that: "If you like, Jane, you can sew something on the quilt. It's yours too, you know." Hadn't Jane had two opportunities to tell her mother about what had happened and hadn't Jane each time chosen not to? Unseen, if she'd been that, had been her choice.

Then there was her father providing her with his fire data for her lecture: "Fires: Destruction and Regeneration in the Australian Bush" at Teacher's College. The garden book that he'd borrowed for her had been thoughtful too.

"You look a little pale, Love."

"Mum, it was good to sew that Southern Cross with you."

"Sure, Jane, it was for me too, that you wanted to do that."

"Mum?" Jane felt overwhelmed. Uncertain of what she truly understood.

"Beautiful what you made," Audrey continued, overcome with tenderness for Jane, her dear altar maker, who'd finally arrived where, it seemed so long ago now, she'd set out to go.

"I'm fine, anyhow. You know, the excitement."

"Good for you, Love." Audrey paused, then added, "She'll come around, Jane. Bernadette is stubborn, but she will."

Robert, as though awaiting a cue, stepped forward, placing a manila folder into Jane's hands. "Yes, Jane—Sister—what a fine day for you this is, for us." The familiar scent of his aftershave stayed between them as did his emphasis on "Sister," which, yes, she was now, of course.

"Go on, Sister, open it up." Inside the folder was a sheet of paper titled "Inventory of Altars" with a list of the names, locations, and construction materials of some of her childhood altars. Jane, eyes filling with tears, glimpsed there her younger self earnestly fabricating solace and safe havens with her flimsy coarse tools.

"Ta, Dad," she said with that smile. Here I am, Bernadette, she thought.

✦

After Bernadette's break up with Andrew, she left Brisbane as she had Mt. Isaac. She packed her briefcase with her books and maps and buried herself in the basement of the St. Lucia library at Queens University. She staked out a carrel against the windowless wall and below the low ceiling with pipes the width of medicine balls and banks of fluorescent lights.

On August 10, 1844, Bernadette left behind the facts of her past, and loaded herself onto the back of a bullock dray along with the supplies and surveying equipment of explorer Charles Sturt as he left Adelaide to find the Inland Sea. She chose Sturt because, lead on her first expeditions into the bush, he was one of the few explorers who she trusted. He was also the only explorer to bank his life and family's fortune on his knowledge of birds. Whatever brazenness that was, she wanted.

"I've seen them," Sturt said, beaming at Bernadette. "Flocks of them flying northwest: crested parraquets, with yellow heads and gray bodies, ears of orange and wing patches of white."

He told Bernadette that while exploring in the Macquarie-Darling area, fifteen years earlier in 1829, he'd observed flock after flock of parraquets—"cockatiels to you, Pilgrim"— fly north past drought stricken lands to Australia's center. In Adelaide, eleven years after that, he'd observed the migration habits of the black-tailed water hen, which, like the cockatiels, came and went from the north. Three years later, he'd told Sir George Gipps, a former Governor of the Colony, that Lake Torrens had always seemed to him an estuary connected with the inland sea. *"This sea, I wrote in my journal, has made a fertile land, a Mecca for birds."*

Almost a decade and a half after his initial request, Sturt told Bernadette, Lord Stanley authorized the Central Australian Expedition. "What a man with vision!" he declared.

"Good he wasn't a more cautious man." Bernadette congratulated him, glad that, at least, she wouldn't be held up.

"The point, Pilgrim, is the thoroughness of your observations and the scope of your patience and persistence," Sturt replied, to her surprise.

Besides Sturt, Bernadette left with his assistant Poole, the medical officer Browne, two native guides, a draftsman, a storekeeper, a collector and armorer, an overseer of stock, two servants, two sailors—one in charge of horses—and five bullock drivers. Also included were eleven horses, thirty-two bullocks, five drays, one horse dray, one light cart, and a boat.

"Andrew Pocklington and his cases of "Delamotte Blanc de Blancs," should be barred. Champagne plus a boat is too heavy," she said, aware that even without the booze, the weight of the stores was approximately seven tons, unaware that she'd unwittingly opened the door to him.

"Certainly the boat may seem cumbersome now," Sturt said, taking no notice of her. "And certainly it will be when you carry it over gullies and sand dunes, for example. But what a tremendous time saver for our survey of the land around the sea," he cheerfully added. Bernadette watched the sullen sailors load the boat onto the dray. She hushed two students, who made no effort to lower their voices as they sauntered by her carrel. She wrote the initials A.P. in a margin and crossed them out.

Once their party was finally on the way, travelling east and north along the Murray River past Lake Victoria to the Darling River, delays were routine. Cattle and horses strayed and had to be retrieved from the brush or extracted from the wild cattle herds. Despite herself, Andrew Pocklington stowed away. Much like the drays bogged down in the sandy cliffs above the river flats, he had to be extracted from sludge nearby.

Bernadette, chagrined, tried to distance herself from his appearance, joining the men to clear the dense mallee. With her scythe, rocking in her chair, she slashed the vegetation until the air was thick with debris. Although their eyes stung, their faces itched and their limbs ached, Sturt allowed few breaks. She was relieved that Andrew, in his sunglasses and with his face lotion with SPF protection, might be spared some of their discomfort before she was angry that he might be spared.

Next, the party had to contend with a series of hills between the Murray and Darling Rivers. Once the uphill routes were cleared, the drays had to be hauled up. Over and over the bullock drivers would have to hitch, unhitch, lead, and re-hitch two teams of bullocks to either the dray at the top of the hill or the one at the bottom.

Sturt volunteered Bernadette.

"Wouldn't let my sister do that," said one, still glad to hand her the lead rope.

"For a lass, she's not bad but," another said after he'd watched her descend with the lumbering beasts.

"Yeah, bulls don't mind her," said another.

"What sort of stupid bull would you be if you didn't?" said another, eyeing Bernadette from under the brim of his felt hat with something other than admiration.

Bernadette, wary now, anxiety ramping, tugged the rope, uncertain why she'd listened to Sturt. Of course, now there was no sign of Andrew. Tap it; ignore them, forge on, she insisted, this essay is yours, she thought, fighting her impulse to leave the library and call Andrew.

For each leg of Sturt's inland expedition, Bernadette and the party were forced to adapt. After the hill relays, when heavy rains arrived, the Murray River swelled into a muddy torrent and creeks and streams sprung up like a lattice around them, they adapted to the slues of ankle and knee high water, the boggy embankments, and the sweet pungency of their unwashed bodies. They adapted to the racket that flocks of galahs, parrots, and glossy black cockatoos made above the Murray's green banks; a clamor to be shouted over until the party adapted again, resorting to gestures and looks, unnerving to Bernadette for all the dangers she knew that could be masked by nature and in the silence of men.

Bernadette skipped lectures. She spent her time in the library in an incessant discourse with Sturt and his men about the direction and logistics of the expedition, careful to avoid the topic of the stowaway. For the other students studying in the basement nearby, there was nothing discourse-like about her mumbling. For Ted Ackers, an anatomy student, who had the reserved carrel closest, this mumbling had developed into a persistent hum, as though he'd unwittingly set up beside a beehive.

"Gentlemen!" Sturt called the group to attention the first evening of their three-month stay at the township of Menindee on the Darling River. "Should any member of this party have carnal interaction with native man or woman they will forfeit their salary from that day forthwith. Understood?"

"Excuse me. Excuse me."

The officers solemnly assented as though they'd come up with the mandate themselves, while the other men responded by not responding, their expressions reminding Bernadette of the bullocks' nearsighted ones, of Andrew as he pulled away from her that last night, of—she stopped herself.

"Hey! Hello? Are you aware you're talking to yourself? Mumbling!" Ted repeated, too emphatically for the library. The girl, pale and bedraggled, for the first time looked up at him, the dark circles around her eyes accentuating their pitch center.

"Matters of intimacy complicate our relationship out here," Sturt confided to Bernadette, who was distracted by the sailor's growl, the cough to disguise it, and this intense redheaded fellow who was stooped over her. "Compromises our position," Sturt reiterated, directing her attention to the stowaway, who was flirting now with a woman on the steps of the depot. Bernadette didn't know how to interpret the sailor's response, couldn't decipher what the redhead had said, and wasn't sure still how not to feel compromised by Andrew. Intimacy, no question, was painful and unworkable. "Yes, I agree," she said out loud to Sturt.

"You mumble!" Ted responded, not anticipating her response. "But of course you knew that about your mumbling." Ted was embarrassed. He also hadn't expected to be attracted to her, even as part of him warned: Watch out, mate, this girl needs a lot of light and sleep.

"Alright, whatever." Bernadette dismissed him, still unclear what the issue was, turning back to Sturt's Journal and her notes. "What a funny misnomer to name a red-tailed cockatoo, glossy black," Sturt said to Bernadette as Ted Ackers walked away, already searching for a reason to return.

After Menindee and Sturt's survey and establishment of the existence of the Barrier Range and the Grey Range that formed the Murray-Darling river basin, they continued north to Flood's Creek and further north to Depôt Glen. As they followed the Darling River it gradually shrunk to a muddy ditch. The trees thinned, giving out to an expanse of barren, shadeless land. The less there was of water, the more it was on everyone's mind.

The Scottish armorer, who'd cursed the haar, now longed for the sodden fog, while the servants made absurd bargains for water:

"I'd cut off a hand for a bucket of water."

"Yeah, take my arm—the whole thing for that same bucket."

"Get out. I'll give me arm and me leg."

"What about you?" The sailor in charge of horses looked to Bernadette. He could see Stowaway Andrew behind her guzzling champagne, oblivious to their thirst. It didn't matter to the sailor that she had declined Andrew's drink offer, and was aware of his and everybody's thirst.

"I'm sure water is close," she said, repeating Sturt's earlier announcement, with a twinge of guilt.

Bernadette's library mate, Ted Ackers, paradoxically took frequent fountain breaks. He tried to time his comings and goings with hers. Although he could tell that this girl was intent on a world apart from the library, he liked the proximity of their arms when they passed and hoped that eventually she might too.

Their expedition became stranded at Depôt Glen. With no rain for seven months, conditions deteriorating, Bernadette spotted Jane on the other side of camp.

"She has no business being here," Bernadette complained to Sturt following him in search of water 107 kilometers one way, 144 kilometers another way, and 160 kilometers again. She had to be hallucinating to see Jane in that landscape from Sturt's journal on land *"denuded of trees excepting a few box trees that grew at the edges of the dry flooded flats or on the banks of dry creeks,"* or to see Jane stumble across salsolaceous plains, or Jane wade across sand hills. At the same time that Sturt ordered the rationing of the depot's brackish and diseased water, Bernadette ordered Jane to go back.

The Captain, Mr. Poole, and Mr. Browne developed scurvy. Their gums swelled, the metallic taste, the blinding headaches, and, especially for Poole, his profuse nosebleeds had worsened. Bernadette watched the storekeeper cut the flour and tea rations for the rest of them to compensate for the reduction of salt meat in the officers' diet, ignoring the salmon and cucumber, and wasabi shrimp and avocado canapés that Andrew nibbled on. She ate the apples and sausage rolls that she found on her desk. Meanwhile, Sturt ordered three more ration cuts.

"Stowaway doesn't belong with us at Depôt Glen," Sturt finally reprimanded Bernadette. She didn't know what to say. She was more ashamed that she'd needed to bring Andrew, than by Andrew himself. She was also ashamed that she was still reluctant for him to go despite himself and that her weakness was now plain for everybody to see.

"The point, Pilgrim," Sturt, dabbed fresh blood from a nosebleed, then impatient and annoyed by her reticence, snapped: "Are you with us or with him, Pilgrim?" Bernadette, avoiding his stare, looked away to see Jane assisting the storekeeper by the water hole.

"You, Captain!" she said, essentially aware of herself suddenly with him and them in Depôt Glen. Standing, she directed Sturt's attention to the flock of water hens that was alighting beside Jane at their waterhole.

"Beautiful!" Sturt appreciatively noted that some birds flew north, the direction they were also headed. "We are within 160 to 240 kilometers of the Inland Sea, Pilgrim," he said, before shooting two of them.

Andrew was gone.

Jane, impervious to danger, had disappeared again.

Sturt handed the dead water hens to Bernadette to spread on a neutral colored blanket so he could paint them. She knew that, because Sturt's sight was filled with the promise of birds, he couldn't see the desperate looks of his men as she filtered their water through a rag for his art project. She realized that, because his sight was filled with the promise of birds, he couldn't see these birds. Bernadette saw, but she didn't care. They'd come too far.

The birds' sticky blood was familiar. She arranged the bodies— she knew how to do this—to hide their wounds. Where is she? We smell fetid. We rearrange ourselves. Where'd you go, Jane? Then, as she unhinged that last bird's wing to spread flat for the portrait: I won't care; I'm not caring.

✦

While Robert waited for Jane on the bench outside Bernadette's residential hall, he played with a pencil from Bernadette's jar that in his rush to leave he'd held on to. He'd said: "Right, I'll just give you two some time to visit. I'll wait downstairs. Good digs, Bernadette. Your mum would approve. Keep up the studies." By the time he'd made his exit, Bernadette's hall mates had left and Jane stood before her sister, her mouth agape with incredulity.

The harder Robert Pilgrim worked to stay ahead of events, the more he seemed doomed to be forever behind them. Still, he was optimistic that the future could always be better and that somehow he could control that. Even as he was resting on the bench watching the students walk by that day, although he felt disturbed by Bernadette's disavowal, he also felt comforted by the familiarity of her actions like it was something he might've expected. She was smart, his Bernadette. He trusted that.

The pencil tip was dull, the graphite worn down. He looked around to see if there was a newsagent nearby that might sell a sharpener. He could sort out the pencil situation. A new box of pencils would be a nice hand off to Bernadette to show her that he understood, to convey without saying that he regretted letting her and Jane down the way he had, and that if anyone understood the need to swap out your personal details, it was he.

"Hello there! Bernadette's Uncle Bob, right?" The pencil snapped. Robert, stupefied, looked up from the broken pieces to the young lady smiling at him.

"Gabrielle. I'm Gabrielle Sullivan. We just met upstairs." She shook his hand and plopped herself on the bench beside him.

"Yes, of course. Hello again, Gabrielle."

"Bernadette's told us so much about her childhood in the outback. So exciting!"

"Yes, for sure." He slipped the pencil pieces into his blazer pocket.

"Excitement and danger go hand in hand out there." He wondered what Bernadette had shared with her.

"Being raised here in the suburbs, the biggest thrill has been hugging the koalas at the Lone Pine Sanctuary. Seriously dull!" She smiled expectantly at him.

Robert felt curiously natural transforming into Uncle Bob right then, and peculiarly comfortable as Uncle Bob sharing with this girl intimate family stories that had never been shared. He proceeded to tell Gabrielle Sullivan about the bushfire that swept through his Uncle Ian's property claiming his life. He told her that although he hadn't been close with his uncle, it had been tremendously hard for his father, who, on hearing the news had rushed out back like he might be sick. Robert didn't tell Gabrielle how his father had howled and shouted like he'd lost his mind, sharing only that after he came back in, he was as quiet as a grave. He told her how their mum assured them that it'd be at least a bottle of whiskey before he got back to himself. "The medicinal applications of whiskey shouldn't be discounted. I've learned that."

"Sure," Gabrielle said as though she knew that too.

"That's when I began to record and map the fires in the region from the news reports I heard over the wireless and from the talk of my father's customers at the post office and pub," Bob recalled.

"Your Uncle Ian would be glad something good has come of this, Bob; you looking out for us the way you do," his father had privately said to him. Robert had been so full of things he wanted to tell his father that he hadn't known how to start. Robert looked over at Gabrielle. Strange the ease Robert felt as Bob, like somehow this uncle, his namesake, had just been waiting to lead him back to his family.

"I have a brother, Stewart," he added.

Gabrielle said she didn't have a brother but could imagine that if she lost one of her sisters—she had five—she'd definitely be devastated. She didn't seem to notice that Bob said "have" a brother versus "had" a brother. "Fire is so unpredictable and lethal. So sad," she quietly said.

After they'd sat in silence for a beat, Uncle Bob then went on to tell her about his father's pub and how it had transformed once during the August holidays. He whitewashed the story a bit, okay a lot, but he told the true bare bones of the event, which was still disturbing. "Horrific!" Gabrielle exclaimed. "Bernadette never mentioned a brothel: does she know? Do you think it was related to him losing his brother? I've read that grief can have a powerful effect and not necessarily in a positive way."

Robert considered that. Not likely, he thought, not replying. He didn't know why he'd shared these stories that were neither "exciting" nor "thrilling" in any happy sense with this girl. Was he testing one version of his father against another like one would clearly win out? It was impossible though to separate one from the other, the good from the bad.

"Do you mind if we just keep this between us, Gabrielle." He paused, adding, "Bernadette has been through so much already losing a father. I don't want her to have to contend with this and think any less of her grand-dad." Sooner or later Bernadette and Jane would have to weigh his own attributes and actions, he knew, face their own Jack Thatle predicament.

"Sure. Sure." Gabrielle said.

"Sorry, this is all a bit too exciting in the end, yeah?"

"I guess," she agreed. After a minute or so of silence, Gabrielle excused herself. She felt inexplicably burdened by the stories Bernadette's uncle had told her. I'm too young for those, she realized as she walked towards class. She got about twenty meters before she turned back. "Maturity," her mum liked to say, "isn't a noun. You have to be willing to look each situation in the face to gain any amount of traction on the process."

"Mr. Pilgrim," she said re-approaching him. "I just want to say how terribly sorry I am about your brother and your dad's brother and the way things turned out at your father's pub."

"Thanks, I appreciate you saying that, Gabrielle. I really do."

After Gabrielle left, although there was a surge of activity because of the change of classes, Robert's world on the bench was as still and quiet as the confessional after Father Malcolm absolved you of your sins. Because Robert had never told anyone about his uncle's death or his father's pub—not Audrey, not even Father Malcolm—he could neither have predicted his sense of relief nor the depth of longing he felt then for his mum and dad. He could never have predicted his chagrin at severing himself and his family from the goodness that was also Thatle. Robert pictured his daughters upstairs—fighting, he knew. A box of pencils could in no way convey his worry for all that they would have to sort out.

✦

There was a hush over the Pilgrim place. It was late afternoon and the heat was palpable. With the humidity this high, Audrey felt like she was being steamed. She'd just returned from assisting Solicitor Simpson with a case as a favor to him. They hadn't been intimate for years, and for years he still hadn't had the air-conditioner in his office repaired. No wonder his pregnant secretary, Angie, couldn't help out. Even if she didn't have morning sickness, she would've developed heat stroke in no time in that environment. Audrey's blouse was soaked with sweat. She looked forward to a cold shower and a change of clothes, and maybe half an hour before dinner to sew.

Thankfully it was slightly cooler inside the house. As always, Audrey had kept the blinds down to retain any chill from the night and early morning air. She wasn't surprised at the quiet. The girls she knew had hiked earlier in the day and would be recovering. Audrey smiled. More likely Robert would be napping, recovering from the workweek. The girls didn't need much if any so-called recovery. Probably they'd be lounging in their rooms: Jane with her Bible and books and Bernadette, who could say. Only that she better have finished packing for tomorrow's trip to Brisbane. University, imagine.

Audrey stopped in the kitchen for a glass of ice water. They'd have salad and cold cuts for dinner on a day as hot as this. She pulled out the fruit salad to give it a stir. From the kitchen window, she saw movement in the yard. Robert was leaning against the far fence. He looked deep in thought. Audrey hadn't considered how he'd be taking Bernadette's departure. She hadn't given much thought to Robert's relationship with Bernadette at all, but of course, he would be feeling sad that she'd be going. Just seeing him out there—Audrey didn't want to dwell on the emptiness that was coming—she finished her water and headed to the shower. One of the girls must've just showered; the bathroom tiles were wet and the air still muggy.

Both Bernadette and Jane's doors were closed. Audrey had come to expect that from Bernadette. She was a typical teenager and private and, quite frankly, had been closing her bedroom door to her and Robert from as early as she could reach the doorknob. Audrey didn't take it personally. She liked the independence of Bernadette. She wished she could have been as confident and self-assured as her at that age.

Audrey heard the washer. The laundry door was shut as well, which wasn't typical. Already, freshly showered, she had begun to sweat. In fact, it wasn't clear if the water had ever dried. The curse and beauty of the tropics, right Audrey? Bernadette, always organized, was probably finishing some last-minute laundry. Audrey opened the door. Bernadette spun around to face her. She was overdressed in baggy athletic gear; her hair was still wet from the shower, although the gash on her lip and scratch on her cheek were the first things Audrey saw.

"Can't you see I'm doing laundry?" Bernadette's voice was defensive and high.

"Love? Are you all right?" Audrey stepped towards her. "What happened?"

"I'm washing!" Bernadette shouted at her.

"I see that," Audrey said carefully.

"And I'm leaving!"

"Yes, but…" Audrey slowly raised her hand to calm her.

"Seriously?" Bernadette, sarcastic now, then defiant: "No buts! I'm gone!"

Audrey was speechless. She didn't know how to reconcile the carefree Bernadette of the morning with this embattled and wounded one.

"What happened, Bernadette? Is Jane okay?"

"Fine! We're fine!" Bernadette said working hard now for control. "We fell." She searched for the words to both explain and to escape this, opting for what she knew would be believable. "We had a fight, and tumbled, but we're fine now. There were brambles. It's steep, the riverbank."

"Okay, Love," Audrey said carefully again. "If you're okay for now, let me check on Jane."

Bernadette pushed past her to Jane's door. "We're fine! Leave us alone! Can't you respect our privacy?" She was shouting again. And before she backed into Jane's bedroom and slammed the door against Audrey, she added, "Respect us, okay, Mum? Just do that! That's all we're asking!"

The girls didn't come out for dinner or for the rest of the evening. When Audrey asked Robert what he knew of the girl's fight, he said he couldn't say. "It was bad, though," he said, he saw that. Neither of them said or ate much. Audrey returned to work on her quilt as a necessary antidote to the unhappiness she felt all around her. Before Audrey retired for the night, she checked on the girls. She cautiously opened Jane's door. She sighed, releasing a breath that she hadn't realized she'd been holding. How peaceful her daughters were in sleep curled up together: Bernadette's arm draped over Jane and Jane clasping Bernadette's hand with both of hers.

✦

In Toowoomba, Jane, now Sister Ava, was no longer alone. She, Sister Lily, and Sister Anne moved into the Presentation community as a unit. Although separately they prayed, taught, and assisted the other nuns and the priest, together they planned lessons, corrected exams and essays, and compared notes about each of their separate activities. They were light-hearted about the business of religious life. And sometimes they were disciplined for their lack of discipline for which the penance was prayer and chores, but no harm done, really. These were easy days. Sister Jacinta, not too happily, labeled them the "giggling gerties." The older nuns in the community of St. Ursula's were at times drawn to them and at other times repelled. Ava, Lily, and Anne, so chuffed with themselves, didn't notice either way.

Only two years after they'd taken their vows, Sister Lily reverted to being Lily, marrying John, a lay volunteer in the parish. The day after she moved out, Sister Brigid, in her floor length habit, approached Ava when she was on lunch duty. She tapped across the cement assisted by wooden canes that she'd brought from Ireland and needed for leg weakness from childhood polio. She touched Ava lightly at the elbow, and said, "So this is where you begin with us, Sister Ava." Ava didn't know what she meant and didn't have time to ask, as Karen Murray, from the ninth grade, ran up to tell them that Sylvie, from the eighth grade had twisted her ankle. Possibly Sister Jacinta's twenty-four-hour interrogation of her and Sister Anne— what did you know and when did you know it?—was their christening into "true" convent life. That Sister Brigid had never directly addressed Ava before that day would occur to her much later.

A year after that, Sister Anne reverted to being Brenda and went on to get her Master's and Ph.D. in Biology at the Toowoomba Institute of Technology. Of course Ava knew that Brenda was leaving—"Her passion is biology, not a religious life, Sister Jacinta, and this she knew as soon as she felt constricted by our science curriculum." Still, Ava couldn't prepare herself for how disruptive Brenda's departure would be.

One night Ava was able to sleep through the night and the next night she wasn't. She could be started by a noise in the wall or awakened by a nightmare like the one of a man with a giant mouth laughing or the one of herself as an emu carcass afloat in a waterhole. Sometimes she didn't know if it was a nightmare or noise that had awoken her, only that once awake she was flooded with worries—one student's continued absences or another's slipping grades, her suspicion of being sidelined now that her closest convent friends had left, and the fear that she was sideline-able, evidenced by the growing stack of her letters that Bernadette had returned.

One night Ava could easily fall back asleep if awakened and the next night she couldn't. She would have an hour or hours to fill by reading the Old and New Testaments or by revising lesson plans or by composing bonus annotations of the student essays that she'd already graded. Soon Ava was so sleep-deprived that, once awakened, she was unable to focus on any of these activities and instead would roam the convent halls and grounds.

Sister Michael said there was a ghost.

Sister Theresa said a sleepwalker.

Sister Jacinta said, "What nonsense, we have a bit of wind, and we all know it's drafty."

Sister Agnes feared the devil, while Sisters Clare and Mary feared someone might discover their relationship.

Sister Scholastica was deaf and heard nothing. By this time, Sister Theodore had died.

The others sisters didn't care to say.

On these night walks, through halls smelling of borax and ammonia interrupted by the florid scent of the tropics, Ava felt like she was more and more falling away from this world. She tried to anchor herself with physical motion and prayer. The Biblical excerpts that she was drawn to only reinforced her feelings of disconnectedness. Job said to Eliphaz: "*I am hemmed in by darkness, and thick darkness covers my face.*"

Seriously, Job? This is how you cheer yourself up? Bernadette was easy to ignore now:

"*And now my soul is poured out within me; days of affliction have taken hold of me,*" said Job to Bildad, retaliated Ava to Bernadette. As Ava passed barefoot over cool linoleum floors—cleaned by her, Lily, and Brenda too many times to count—as she floated by the darkened convent walls hung with the Stations of the Cross on one side and portraits of Our Lady on the other, she had become a shadow of herself, a spiral of hopelessness that was becoming less easy to harness, no less anchor.

At three one morning, awake from a nightmare where Ava was a spider web with tangled bush flies, buzzing and beating their wings against her, she'd wandered around the convent and grounds until she found herself in the courtyard between the convent and school. She rested on the base of the life-size statue of Nano Nagle, the founding Mother of the Presentation Sisters. She tugged at a loose thread of her nightgown and pulled, letting the seam unravel. Unnoticed, stars and a crescent moon bathed her and the statue, the surrounding buildings, the jacaranda tree beside the convent house, and the oak at the top of the courtyard, in a fine white light.

When Ava first heard the tap of wood on cement, she had found a new thread to pull, and was mulling again over the mistake she'd made of pushing that button back to her mother. As Ava registered the sound as the canes of Sister Brigid, she had re-concluded that it was the sin of pride that she'd believed that she could leave that Jane Pilgrim and presume to be present for her students when she'd abdicated being present for herself and her family. By the time Sister Brigid arrived beside her, Ava's feelings of self-condemnation so filled her that the old nun loomed as a certain nuisance and distraction to them.

Sister Brigid cleared her throat. "Sister Ava?" A moment later when Ava hadn't responded, Sister Brigid struck the base of Nano

Nagle beside Ava's legs with one of her canes. "Sorry, Mother," Brigid contritely said to the figure, before redirecting her attention to Ava.

"Sister?"

"Sister," Ava reluctantly replied.

"We've all traveled a long way to get here."

Ava, still staring into her lap, wound the nightgown's loose thread around a finger.

"Of course, there can be no two paths alike." Sister Brigid stepped closer to Nano Nagle intentionally crowding Ava.

Ava stopped fidgeting long enough to see a series of Janes en route here, armed with altars, button stars, prayers, letters and lesson plans, necessary to reshape and control, touch up with a bit of meaning, all that they couldn't understand and felt no control over.

"Sure, for some this is not the right stop."

'Study, work hard, you'll get in and be a good teacher and a great Sister,' Father Malcolm had assured her. Ava shook her head and shrugged as though the two religious had said something distasteful. Busy Janes like bush flies in the web.

"Not that we have stopped either." Sister Brigid paused, appreciating the moonlit scape surrounding them. "This is not a stop."

"I haven't stopped." Ava said defensively, fighting an urge to cry.

The screams of fruit bats interrupted and, as they watched the bats pass blindly overhead, Ava realized she felt exactly stopped. Like every ounce of energy and each goal she'd set had led to here and here was a stop. The stop. Lily and Brenda moving on, as Bernadette and her parents had, only reinforced this.

"Dear girl, we may look like a convent house, but we're not. We're part of a chorus—a message of compassion and hope— spreading across seas and continents *ad finem fidelis*. Aren't we that, Sister Ava?"

Ava looked up at the old woman in her medieval garb and, through tears, whispered: "I'm a bit stopped."

Sister Brigid, as though she hadn't heard or, more likely, was ignoring Ava, continued: "We're on the move, Sister Ava, not resting on our laurels here. Remember, she who forgets that you'll never plough a field by turning it over in your mind, also forgets that you've got to do your own growing no matter how tall your Father is."

Ava smeared the tears and snot from her face.

"Ecclesiastes says: *He who observes the wind will not sow; and he who regards the clouds will not reap.*" She marked the verse's meter with each tap of her cane. "Which is to say, Sister, that Jesus suffered for us doesn't mean we won't know suffering, but that He's deepened our capacity for understanding it, and made it up to us to make something of that, if we're ever to have the hope of Resurrection. Which is to say, Sister, as a Presentation sister, we don't stop. Come, Ava," Brigid said, offering her hand.

Ava took a breath. And another. She leaned forward into her lap to wipe her tears on her nightgown. Sitting back up, for the first time that night she noticed the moonlight. As she looked over at Sister Brigid, she noticed that the moonlight touched Sister Brigid in such a way that Ava could picture her in the moonlight on the wooden deck of the ship she might've sailed on from Ireland. Before she knew it, Ava saw her fly off the deck and begin waving her canes like batons, directing and encouraging the invisible souls around her. Ava almost laughed. She almost had to remind herself she was very miserable.

But no question how odd, the scene buoyed her. Ridiculous, she'd think in retrospect. What was it? A flutter of hope, some weight lifted, a fellowship reestablished, but Ava knew with certainty that, as dreadful as she felt, she was meant to reach out and fly up with this bold, half-mad nun.

"Whatever you have suffered, Ava, can only make you stronger in understanding." Brigid shifted. Ava heard the scratch of starch in her skirts. And it wasn't the magical nun she saw then, but the pale and thin Irish girl, sweeping out the single room sod house, the embattled young woman, negotiating the crowded dock with her sticks after saying the final goodbye to her family in Cork.

"Or, as Sister Scholastica says, as long as you know who you are, the worst you can do is look like a convent house." Brigid chuckled then, and, after she helped Ava to her feet, she pointed out how the silica in the cement sparkled in the moonlight and how much like an ocean cement really was, and how didn't that just make them a wee bit closer to Jesus, following him on the water as he walked across the Sea of Galilee.

Later Ava would wonder why Sister Brigid was roving about that night and what exactly it was about her peculiar comments that had so eased Ava's doubt. Much later, she would become that Sister, the assuring witness to a young nun's dark night of the soul. That night, Ava, with an image of her parents and Bernadette and all the people she'd known and an appreciation of the many people she'd never know, but who were still abroad with them on this pavement, said, "Yes, all right then."

✦

Five sick men at Depôt Glen and Ted Ackers left a flask of sugary tea for Bernadette. Poole, with gangrenous black legs, could no longer walk. The flesh off the roof of his mouth hung visibly. They all found signs of rot on their bodies—the swelling joints, pussy gums, the splotches of blue on arms and legs—indications of internal bleeding that spoke of a deterioration like Poole's, complications hidden, but felt in kidneys, lungs, and heart—private terrors, which the men publicly mocked and that Bernadette soberly recorded. Besides the physical suffering before her, Bernadette continued to see Jane everywhere in Depôt Glen.

Captain Sturt ordered a dray to carry the sick men—half their party—to Adelaide when the rains finally came in mid-July. Bernadette waited in the light drizzle for their return that same day with Poole's body. She helped unload him then watched in disbelief as her mother wrapped him in a blanket and Jane constructed a cross from two planks that one of the sailors had pulled from their boat for her.

"Come along, Pilgrim." Sturt gathered their party. He recited the Lord's Prayer over Poole's grave with those still able, standing, heads bowed, water beading on their oily forms. Bernadette rested her head on the library desk. She felt exhausted—Jane-tired—and perplexed that there'd ever been a Bernadette with a sister she could protect; with a mother she might draw comfort from; and with a father capable of driving her into the arms of a stowaway. That there'd ever been a Bernadette who'd choose to follow any explorer, no less this one, into the middle of Australia seemed beyond stupid.

Ted, fresh from a lecture, eased into his carrel after he checked on her, relieved that the girl was finally resting.

Undeterred, once they'd reached Fort Grey, Sturt roused the remainder of the party including Bernadette. "The boat is critical! Yes, we may have difficulties getting it across the dunes, but you'll see how worthwhile it is." He ordered Morgan, the sailor in charge of horses, to paint it. It was a sensible move, Bernadette conceded. The wood was dry, split, and warped, not prepared for water in the least. Morgan could also replace those planks.

Their party went out from Fort Grey to find the Inland Sea three times. The first expedition went west to Lake Torrens and Lake Blanche, a formation of dry salt lakes, and lasted ten days. As in Depôt Glen, Jane was everywhere in Fort Grey. Bernadette followed her: "Jane, delay! It's definitely better to delay an hour or more for a trip like this."

The second expedition headed northwest to avoid the salt lakes and ended up further into the as-yet-unnamed-but forever-dreaded Simpson Desert. It lasted forty-five days. "It's better not to come at all, Jane. You're really not prepared for this level of exploration," Bernadette argued, even as Sturt wrote in his journal: *I am sure we shall be stopped in a few days at most by some large body of water,* after he'd witnessed more birds fly overhead and a creek overrun with water-hens.

Bernadette joined Sturt and a much smaller party for the third expedition. They again headed north directly into the Simpson. Despite her warnings, Bernadette saw that Jane had tagged along and had dragged the boat with her. "Bloody bugger, Ship Sailor, go back!" she ordered, knowing that it was actually too late. They passed Cooper's Creek—the future gravesite of explorers, Burke and Wills—when they finally stopped.

Where the Inland Sea would be, they found desert. Sturt wrote that he walked across *"a plain as extensive as the sea, covered with the shivered fragments of former mountains."* The stones, baked by the sun, burned their party's faces. Sturt wrote of plains *"dark with Samphire,"* and plains *"perfectly bare and white with salt."* The salt, blown like smoke over the flats, burned their party's eyes, stung their faces, and caught in their throats. Jane sat on the side of the boat and watched Bernadette. There was no water to relieve any of this.

Although Bernadette saw what Sturt saw, although Bernadette must've known from the outset what they'd find, Jane was still beside her. She saw sand and, for Jane, transformed it into liquid; dunes into waves; and flying sand into water drops flung free from the crests of waves. Steaming stones were rock pools and the burn on their faces was from the sun off the water. If the salt flats were empty—"It's only temporary, Jane. The water, drained in the ebb tide, will reverse with the moon's pull, and, watch, fill the flats again."

To a deflated and listless Sturt, accompanied by his anxious men, who had turned back to Fort Grey, Bernadette, with Jane beside her, shouted, "Hey, look, the sea is here. Look!" As they trudged away from her, she yelled that only Poole would die. If they remained with her—she looked at Jane again—if they remained with them, couldn't they see that there were seagulls overhead and other birds that they could sketch and watercolor. Water-hens. Parraquets. Couldn't they see that they'd brought the boat?

Sturt turned back, shaking his head. He was neither deflated nor listless. "Your true mettle shows, Pilgrim, in how you handle your hopes and expectations when they don't work out." He was grave, sick like Poole, preoccupied with getting his party safely to Adelaide before the true onset of the dry season. First, though, he had to get them back to Fort Grey.

Jane had crawled into the bottom of the boat. After Sturt left, Bernadette joined her.

"Almost forty days, Jane, is how long this expedition lasts."

Like Jesus' test time in the wilderness or Moses on the mountain, right, Bernadette?

"Oh, for God's sake!" And then, "I'm sorry, Jane."

Bernadette remained with Jane in this stony desert and willed the sea to stay. It didn't. It couldn't. The matter of sand, grit and ash, salt and rock, the inescapability of pain, fault and culpability, were more definite than Bernadette wanted them to be. Is this it? Is this all that there is? If there was really no place to escape, bugger it, she thought, and clenching her jaw, she closed Sturt's journal and dropped it beside her chair.

After, without a glance back or a goodbye, Bernadette willfully left Jane and caught up with Sturt and the party in time to hear the mournful chant of native Australians and to witness the Chiefs weep and Sturt give one of them his blanket. She was also there in Adelaide as the men returned to their relieved families and Sturt was reunited with Charlotte Christiana, but the joy of these returns she lumped with the monotony and suffering of the rest, all of which, she impassively considered. She was numb and now concertedly disinterested.

Bernadette pushed the clutter on her desk to the side and turned to a blank page of her notebook. From the basement of the Queens University library, what she reported and discussed were Charles Sturt's discoveries of new territory, inconsistencies of the expedition, the problems of faulty longitudes and latitudes, the repeated journal entries, confusion of dates, the corrupt dynamics of the men together, the thermometer that exploded in the summer heat, and the horses that became prostrate or died. She discussed Sturt's political aspirations, his possible hypochondria, and melancholy. She said, what a silly idea to follow a bird into the center of Australia as if it could lead you to water, an "inland sea." Sturt's courage and resilience wasn't mentioned or that he'd looked out for her as much as he had his own men, and that somehow, long ago already, she'd actually depended on that.

It's unclear if Bernadette turned against herself with these omissions or just, once again, arrived at herself. "Free," is what she was now, she'd say: of Sturt, of her expedition companions, of Jane and her parents, of Andrew. "Free," now of expectations and longing, Bernadette returned to the St. Lucia library, not mumbling in discourse or grappling for insight, but humming and weeping.

Ted heard her and called out to her from his carrel. "Hey, you're really humming."

"Hey? What?" she said.

"Humming," he repeated. "I know that tune!" he said, walking towards her.

She'd lost her bearings too. "Was I?" she answered quietly.

"Yeah." He stood beside her now. She tiredly followed his gaze to the plates stacked at the back corner of her desk and looked up at him with genuine confusion. He was familiar; maybe they'd shared the food.

"So I was." She'd been crying too. She quickly brushed her tears into her palm. I've got to stop doing that, she thought.

Please don't cry, he thought. "'Botany Bay,'" he said.

"Yeah?" Her face was hot and prickly. She blinked twice to mask a stray tear before she looked up at him, stunned a little by the translucent quality of his amber eyes. I must look a mess.

"Yeah. 'Botany Bay.'" Ted, seeing her blush, turned away to give her some privacy with her embarrassment. He didn't mean for his turn to become a retreat, but that look of hers had stripped him of the sense of himself that could regard her as purely as she seemed to be regarding him.

Bernadette, retrieving Sturt's journal from the floor, watched the man walk away.

His backside and hips were round like one of the packhorses from early on in this expedition. She wondered how long she'd hummed and how long he'd listened when she saw that he'd turned back.

He was younger than she'd thought. His hair a dark orange color, his face sprinkled with large, almost square, brown freckles, which she found disarmingly appealing. He squinted in her direction, but didn't look at her directly this time, though she wished he would.

"One I quite like is 'Wild Colonial Boy,'" he said. Without invitation and as though they weren't in a library, he started to sing with gusto:

"There was a wild Colonial boy, Jack Doolan was his name,
Of poor but honest parents he was born in Castlemaine.
He was his father's only hope, his mother's only joy,
And dearly did his parents love the wild Colonial boy…"

Bernadette watched him and listened.

"Come, all my hearties, we'll roam the mountains high,
Together we will plunder, together we will die."

She didn't feel comfortable doing either of these things.

"We'll wander over valleys, and gallop over plains,"

Because—with his face reddening from his effort,

"And we'll scorn to live in slavery, bound down with iron chains."

his hips sashaying side to side, off the beat but clearly in search of one, he seemed strikingly vulnerable to her.

Bernadette, forgetting herself and the past that had led to that self, felt overcome.

The familiar lyrics of the "Wild Colonial Boy" became less familiar as Ted sang until they became insensible—an impossible singing, sounding in her, ancient and immediate, like the singular and various songs above the banks of the Murray and Darling, alongside the Brisbane River and over the creek bed at Mt. Isaac. *We'll wander over valleys, and gallop over plains.* Who could tell where one musical phrase ended and the next began. *And we'll scorn to live in slavery, bound down with iron chains.* The space between her and this curious man had become so vibrant that Bernadette couldn't anymore tell distance as she could where they weren't touching.

PART THREE

CORRESPONDENCE TO THE FAITHFUL

✦

WHEN AUDREY'S TELEGRAM ARRIVED at his brother's property, Billum Downs, Robert couldn't contain his relief. "See Stewart, Audrey's telegram!" he said, waving the paper above his head.

"Good reason to celebrate, hey mate." Stewart slapped him on the back. "A beer and lamb chops night, I'd say." Stewart was starved. The drought was killing his livestock and they'd spent the entire day lugging a heifer carcass to the edge of the western paddock.

As they ate, Stewart watched his brother—an odd duck—but his brother through and through. "Good on ya, mate, about Audrey. Birds like to stick you in the dog house for a time, but don't they always welcome you back with open arms!"

Robert wasn't so sure of the truth of his brother's statement. Audrey hadn't said that he was forgiven, but in a telegram that's not the length of what you can say.

"Audrey is very accepting," he answered, gathering their dishes to rinse. Stewart lit the end of an old smoke.

"Mum was like that. Too few women like Mum and Audrey, Bob," Stewart lamented. He'd just been dumped again for straying, "philandering," Jenny, his now ex-girlfriend, had called it.

"That's right, Stewart," Robert agreed. He turned from the sink to his brother, who was now lighting a new smoke from the butt of the previous one. "Those will kill you, Stewart, if you're not careful."

"That's my bro!" Stewart laughed. "I was wondering when you'd show up!"

Robert looked confused. "It's not a laughing matter. We're family. We have to look out for each other."

✦

There were two bus rides and two Roberts. When Robert Thatle turned seventeen he made a special trip to Rockhampton, where he'd gone every year, except that one time he'd stayed behind with his father, and where, the next year, he'd meet Audrey McBride, his future wife. At Town Hall, he went to an office, where young ladies filled out applications to change their maiden names to their married ones. He filled out a similar form. By the time he left Town Hall that day, in his mind at least, application in, he was proudly renamed "Pilgrim."

More than two decades later, after Robert received Audrey's telegram, he rode the bus from Billum Downs back to Claremont. That optimistic young man of the first bus ride was now older. Where one Robert ended and the other began is difficult to tell: each man some mix of denial and acceptance, fear and redemption, cowardice and courage. Suffice to say, while young Pilgrim felt certain he could escape the world of disgrace and disrepute, the later Pilgrim was only sure and grateful that Audrey felt some confidence that he could going forward.

When that bus pulled up to the Claremont stop, the veranda of Dawn and Sally's Ballet Studio, Robert gathered his rucksack from the overhead bin. Audrey waited for him at the end of the platform in front of a poster of Margot Fonteyn and Rudolf Nureyev in *Swan Lake* and beneath the grooved iron awning still sagging under the weight of red dirt from the storm.

"A lot of potholes between here and Longreach." Robert, nervous, had prepared an opening line. He didn't say this, however, or ask about that dust storm that he'd missed. He stood there wondering about Audrey standing there, about Audrey not moving or speaking, even as behind him Annabel McPhearson and her two-year old Johnny boisterously welcomed Annabel's mother-in-law to town. A tingly rash spread on the back of his neck as his anxiety intensified.

"I received your telegram, Audrey." He glanced up at the roof not registering its warp.

Just as he was about to say "Sorry" and "Sorry," Audrey reached for him, hugging him until he blushed and then she caressed his face, a gesture from so early on in their marriage that Robert was caught off-guard. He couldn't say what he meant to say or even swallow. He couldn't speak for the entire journey home for the tears he held in.

When they arrived home, the house didn't look the same to him; had the foundation shifted? Where it had sagged, it seemed sturdy. Where it'd been sturdy, it sagged. The entire structure rested lower than he remembered and was dwarfed by the gum tree beside it. "Our girls, at school, then…" his voice trailed off as he registered how deserted and lonely the place felt. He followed Audrey into the kitchen, which seemed dim and he said, "Is it dim in here? Seems like it is."

To Audrey, the kitchen looked strange as well or maybe just her with him in it. So much had changed with Robert that he didn't know. She felt older than him, and like a sister. Before this feeling could transform into anything more she said, "Give me my buttons, Robert."

Robert, prepared, reached into his pocket and pulled out a paper bag. He lined up the buttons on the table. He was about to step back for Audrey to admire them, as she'd typically done, when she silently came up beside him and collected them as though they were coins on a dresser. She gently squeezed his arm before she walked out.

Although he'd missed the storm, Robert still recognized its effects: the red dirt in the wheel wells of their station wagon, film on both sides of the windscreen and windows and even grit in the seams of the vinyl car seats. The effects on the house were too many to quantify. After Audrey had left the kitchen, he walked back out to the car with a bucket of cleaning supplies from under the sink. He could manage a contained mess. This was a start.

Robert performed a final cursory wipe of the sparkling windscreen when he saw the girls approach. Bernadette nodded to him as Jane raced up to him. He dropped the rag inside the bucket, wiping his hands on the legs of his trousers and smiled in awkward greeting.

"Jane." He gently touched the top of her head.

"I'm glad you've recovered, Dad," she said. While he knew that Audrey and he had devised the "illness" excuse for work, he couldn't know that for Bernadette and Jane he'd experienced a mental collapse.

Bernadette caught up to them. "Welcome back. Are you better then?"

"Good, Bernadette. Yes, there's the drought. But I'm good." Robert replied, a little disconcerted. "You know, the drought at Uncle Stewart's."

"Yes, the drought throughout Queensland," she replied.

"Come see what Mum's making." Jane solicitously took his elbow and led him back to the kitchen. Bernadette veered off to her bedroom. He set the bucket by the sink and followed Jane to the pantry: the cramped closet barely lit by a tall narrow window in the back. He was reluctant: the memory of the buttons was still fresh and he didn't want to view the shelf where those jars had been. Jane, as oblivious to his thoughts and feelings as to the shelves of dry goods, cans, and jars of buttons, squeezed ahead of him to an oversized sewing basket.

"See," she said, opening the basket like a treasure chest. Before Robert were Audrey's buttons sewn into a swath of fabric. The button sampling picked up the partial light and peeled away some of the darkness.

After a significant pause, "Beauty!" he exclaimed and "I'd like Stewart to see this!" and "Your Mother. Your Mother!" He looked over at Jane. Her right fingers danced along the edge of the sill. She soberly tugged her left plait.

"School okay?" He'd been away too long. His eyes were drawn back to the buttons which, displayed like this, filled him with hope.

"A boy in my grade has burns over his body," Jane blurted out.

A lifetime of buttons well worth recording.

"Everywhere. Boils and scars."

Audrey thought so too. He could see that.

"But he said they didn't hurt but I didn't believe him, but I didn't tell anyone, too." The meaning of Jane's words was slow to sink in.

"So I didn't. Not even to Bernadette."

"The boy's body." Robert still stared at their buttons. "Why were you looking at the boy?"

"He showed me."

The buttons were blurring and the room darkening. "No," he whispered. "He wouldn't have."

Jane straightened. "He did. He took off his shirt after school."

"How was that allowed to happen, Jane?" Robert's voice rose. The crowded shelves had closed in. "You don't get to see naked...nakedness!"

He searched the shelves around him—cereals, cans, bottles, buttons in bottles—when his eyes lit on one of Jane's altars—a ridiculously pink one.

"What is that?" he demanded as though he didn't know. "It's time you take responsibility," he poked the air in the shelf's direction, "take responsibility for your altars. Make an inventory of them, Missie, because I'm sick of stepping on them in the yard or around the house. I could've put my hand in that!" Still poking the air, he berated her, "Faith makes order from chaos, not the other way around, Jane!"

Jane pushed her way out of the pantry, backing away from him. "Bernadette says a proper inventory can only be made by experts in the field." Still searching for a safe place, she followed that with: "Bernadette says I have to be over forty to be an expert." Her voice waivered.

"Enough, Jane! What does Bernadette bloody know? You could've been hurt! Bernadette help you then?"

Audrey, hearing the commotion had rushed from the back of the house, Bernadette from her bedroom at the sound of her name. He looked over at them and back at Jane, her face bright red, her lips quivering.

"Exactly right, exactly right," Robert sputtered twice, before he stumbled away from them and the house and back out to the car.

What did it mean for Robert to become a Pilgrim? Were the delineations of those things that Robert saw and felt and thought clearer, cleaner, better behaved? When young Robert returned from Rockhampton after changing his name, his mother, Marjorie, was confused as was his father, Jack, before he became angry. "We do stupid things, Son," he said. "But, the key, if you have your wits about you, is not to let it become a path of stupid idiot things. Because once that's started, it's near impossible to stop."

✦

Just as Charles Sturt wrote a journal to his wife, Charlotte Christiana, while on expedition to the center of Australia from August 1844 to January 1846, Bernadette wrote to Jane, who was completing secondary school in Mt. Isaac and sent buttons to her mother in small envelopes marked "personal."

Although Sturt and Bernadette traveled together that first year, their narratives portrayed different lands. What these narratives shared was the restriction on mentioning anything that had come before their departure. Sturt says in the journal's first line: *I shall not, my Dearest Charlotte, allude in the course of this narrative to any of the events that occurred prior to the day on which I left the Grange.* Bernadette writes in her first letter from Brisbane: "I'm done with Mt. Isaac, Jane. Now silent on it!"

Besides Charlotte, Sturt left behind four children under the age of nine. Charlotte, who'd experienced firsthand the calamities of exploration, understood that Sturt had left them for lands guaranteed to be brutal. In 1840, she'd accompanied him and his friends on a small venture north of Adelaide when Henry Bryan, Charles' associate from the Colonial Office, became separated from their party. Hours later, three more men disappeared. Sturt's search party found the group, covered in the blood of a horse that they'd slaughtered to quench their thirst. Bryan was never found. "Charles, what's the word about Henry?" Charlotte would ask until it was evident that there would be none.

Charles was going farther this time. Charlotte writes in a letter to a friend: *No one here expects news of a good country. Nothing but desert for my husband to toil through; and no water to ease his labours.*

Jane was relieved to have Bernadette go: the strain and discomfort that last day in the house was unbearable. For Audrey, however, the slackness that the tension replaced opened a void that felt lonely. Robert thought it was good for Bernadette to go. As he told Audrey: "Our daughter has been full of spirit since birth; you can't keep a girl like that still." All three underestimated what it meant for Bernadette to leave for Brisbane, or really, what it would mean for them. Jane wrote: "Lucky you, Bernadette! I bet Brisbane beats Mt. Isaac hands down."

Sturt felt guilty about leaving, which he masked in speeches about destiny, necessity, and the sacrifices needed for the good of the country. To Charlotte he depicted such a fatalistic picture of his condition that soon it was she who felt guilty for doubting him and making his last days at the Grange too difficult. Sturt wrote: *My thoughts then, Dearest, settled upon you, and upon my children. Had I indeed parted from you forever, and were the steps I had taken at such a sacrifice of happiness to ensure future comfort, only to plunge those I most loved into deeper distress? My mind has for some time been afflicted by the most gloomy forebodings.*

Bernadette felt neither gloom nor guilt. When her parents commented on the distance she'd be from them, uncomfortable as she was physically, she blithely loaded her suitcase into the underbelly of the bus, kissed her mother's cheek as Audrey handed her a bag with make-up and food, and said, "Imagine, there's more than eighteen towns between here and Brisbane!" Bernadette ignored her father on her way to saying good-bye to Jane and ended up hugging Jane distractedly. Once the bus was on its way, she realized that Jane hadn't spoken or reciprocated her hug, and that she couldn't recall Jane's expression, so busy had she been tracking her father's more guarded one. For these failures, Bernadette immediately blamed her father.

On Sturt's trek from Adelaide towards the Inland Sea, he catalogued his interactions with flora, fauna, the natives, and the members of the expedition party—largely in that order. He recounted for Charlotte the Darling River's sloping and grassy banks, the weeping and umbrageous trees, and a death-like silence that permeated the spot. *"The Darling River itself is a muddy ditch."* He told Bernadette that he expected this.

Of the bus journey away from Mt. Isaac, Bernadette only catalogued the man-made landmarks of oversize: the Big Banana, the Big Pineapple, the Big Cow, Emu, and Avocado. Jane thought Bernadette was lying until her mother confirmed it: "If you go all the way up to the fronds of the Big Pineapple, you can sit on the balcony, where on a hot day, you'll feel the only breeze in Queensland. And if that wasn't good enough," she added, "you'll also be served pineapple boats: dessert of the gods."

When Jane wrote back to Bernadette, she told her what their mum had said and reprimanded Bernadette for not sending a pineapple boat back for her. Jane left out that their father had claimed that the "Big" category of tourist attraction was a "frivolous and an unwise investment for Queensland." "We are not an inflated people," he'd said. Bernadette concurred. "What are we, Jane, that we build such towers of absurd inconsequence beside dusty paddocks?" She later asked Sturt: "Is this what you expected?"

Sturt's salutations—*Dearest, Dear Charlotte, My Dearest, My Beloved*—reinforced his pleas and promises to Charlotte, consciously and unconsciously shaping his wife's responses. "You are not forgotten as we waste away out here, as Bawley, my friendly, shiny-coated gift horse to you dies of thirst, as we search onward because we must, Dearest, in spite of these conditions—this hunger, thirst, scurvy, and death—yes death, Beloved. I must," he insisted again. *"This sea is my destiny and our future."* It is our responsibility as explorers to reveal our truth such as it is, he told Bernadette. And yes, Pilgrim, you can expect the language of the heart to be more torrid.

Bernadette's letters were more muted. She did not call out to God that no mishap befell the children during her or Sturt's absence. She did not say, *Dearest, I remember, I regret, I yearn.* She did not say, *God, that nothing has befallen any of you even though it is unlikely that I will return to witness it, if that be the case.* For her, style aside, what befell children befell them. There was no getting around it. "Sadly," she admitted to Sturt, "but," as she'd learned firsthand, "still befallen." She was also in no rush to return.

Instead Bernadette's letters to Jane attempted to provide a "rational" testimony of town life, as though her "rational" was more objective then Sturt's more floral style. Brisbane's newspaper, *The Courier Mail,* was fair and comprehensive compared to Mt. Isaac's amateur and provincial *Central County Gazette.* The wider range of nationalities and ethnicities she'd seen in Brisbane—Greek, Indian, Italian, Irish, Thai, Aboriginal, Islanders, etc.—she listed, making suppositions on tensions and alliances and life quality based on neighborhoods, employment, crime, health, accessibility to healthcare, and mortality statistics. "Complex society like this isn't likely in Mt. Isaac, Jane," she wrote.

In one letter, as though she were developing a case study, Bernadette mentioned the drunks, who she'd see on her way to swimming meets on the streets of Fortitude Valley. There was one man, in particular, whose face was bloated and ravaged by weather and drink, who must've been beaten as well. "A face can't get that swollen just on drink," she informed Jane. That she didn't mention the man's employment and health history or even his ethnicity—the key topics that she'd earlier extolled—Jane took as an oversight.

Was it carelessness or a careful shaping of perception like Sturt's, that Bernadette also didn't tell Jane that after the meet, she'd seen that same man, leaning against a hydrant, and although she'd decided to offer him her sandwich and her damp towel, (meager acts, she knew), she didn't, which she blamed on another student, who called the bloke "a lay-about-loser," which had prompted the man to retort, "Bugger off!" initiating a charge of anxiety within Bernadette, which she stifled since it was too late to ward off. "Get a job, mate!" is what she shouted at him over her shoulder.

"Who are befallen children, anyway?" she asked Sturt.

Besides the testimonial aspects of her letters, Bernadette berated Jane to think, to rally, to leave Mt. Isaac behind. "They're smart here in Brisbane," she wrote. "I know you'd be as at home as I am. You can be honest, be yourself."

In another letter she wrote: "I've met a boy, Andrew, and he understands me in a way that surprises me. Here, you can follow your heart and your own opinions."

Although Sturt didn't save Charlotte's letters, it's clear from his responses that she wrote them. About Captain Grey, the new South Australian Governor, who Sturt believed had derailed his advancement in the Colonial Office he wrote: *He may be civil to you, Charlotte, and I will repay his civilities, and moreover I will be grateful for them for your sake, but there is a breach between me and Captn Grey that will never be made up.*

Mirroring Sturt's response, Bernadette wrote about their father: "He may be nice to you now, Jane, but his weakness is insidious and frankly, unforgivable."

Sturt continued: *I made him my bitter foe. Believe me, Charlotte, the Greys hate us both the more because we deserve it not at their hands.*

Bernadette: "Jane, what can I say to convince you? Sure, comfort from prayer—take it. But let's not overdo it."

Charlotte Dearest, if I could have earned my bread in any other way I would have thrown my appointments in Captn Grey's face long ago.

"Don't become a martyr, Jane. They're pitied, not liked."

But, my Dearest Charlotte, I scarcely know what I am writing, and am perhaps wrong in exciting you against those from whom you may have received attention and alas! this will reach you too late to caution.

Bernadette vocalized neither hesitancy nor doubt. She wrote, "Jane Pilgrim, how weak is he? Wake up! Brisbane's sky will never be obscured by outback dust; never abraded by riverbed sand. Yes, marching orders, Ship Sailor!"

What letter can't seduce or proselytize, befriend or comfort? What letter can't, with a word, lift a spirit and, with another or even absence of a word, dash it? Bernadette chose her affiliation with Sturt and, in her mind, Sturt chose her. Is it fair to link Jane and Charlotte even though neither chose or even knew of the other's existence? Under the auspices of exploration and faith, fairness or choice rarely rate. Suffice to say, Charlotte Christiana and Jane Pilgrim equally understood the power of this form.

There is documentation that one night Charlotte's house-companion witnessed Mrs. Sturt read of the *awful perils* through which Charles had passed. The next morning, she found Mrs. Sturt where she'd left her the night before wholly transformed: face drawn, eyes swollen and bloodshot, and her hair whitened like snow. *Too surely,* she wrote to her brother, *our Mrs. Sturt shows the intense suffering caused by the narrative of her husband's dangers.*

Jane, without house companion witnesses, journal entries, or a priest, who was allowed to divulge her feelings, simply wrote back to Bernadette.

Dear Bernadette,

How great that Brisbane is so complex. I bet <u>The Courier Mail</u> would never print Mrs. McSweeny's weekly recipe column.

Miss Perry is my homeroom teacher now. It's a switch from Mrs. Bankman. Perry notices everything. I suppose she makes us feel more seen as much as Mrs. Bankman made us feel ignored. Franca thinks it's because Mrs. Bankman smokes marijuana. Do you think that she does?

Mum and Dad send their best. Dad made a point to tell me to tell you that he wants you to be safe there in the city. You should have heard how he emphasized the "safe" of that. I think that's important.

Dear Bernadette,

You should see the garden I've started. Dad helped me turn the soil and Mum said she knew a place to get manure to fertilize it. I've decided on a banana tree, which Mum says won't thrive this far inland. Dad went to the library and brought back a book on varietals that he said Mrs. Johnson from Delton's recommended. Can't you hear them going on about wattles versus bougainvilleas versus bottlebrush and desert pea. What do I care? I've planted a banana tree, which is small but surviving. Mum is definitely wrong about this.

You're right about the martyr profession being overrated. Now that I've decided against it, I'll have to finish Secondary and sadly delay any move to the big town of Brissy. Bummer.

Dear Bernadette,

The Brisbane sky sounds lovely. Another sight to look forward to for our visit, which is only two more weeks away.
Your Mr. Thompson stood in again for Miss Corbit's history class. I can't tell if he hates me for me or because of you. He mentioned your pin project again as an example of what not to do for our history projects. I'm so mad. He's not even our real teacher. Franca thinks we should all do pin projects.

Do you remember my friend, Gavin Mackay? He's the one who dropped out after Grade 7 and moved to Claremont? Well, there's a rumor that he stabbed a man in a brawl and is now locked up. That's sad to me. Anyhow, Bernadette, ease up on Dad. It seems like he's sad too.

It'll be brilliant to see you next week. All of us can't wait.

Their correspondence changed after Jane and Robert's visit to Brisbane. Jane sent a series of transcripts of the Last Will and Testament of men who had once sailed with Captain James Cook.

*In the Name of God Amen, I **Aneas Aitkin**, Boatswain of his Majesty's Ship <u>Africa</u>, Thomas Newnham Esqr. Commander, being in Bodily health and of sound and disposing mind and memory, and considering the perils and dangers of the Seas and other uncertainties of this Transitory life, do for avoiding Controversies after my decease, make, publish and declare this my last Will and Testament in manner following, that is to say—*

Bernadette was genuinely confused.

First, I recommend my Soul to God that gave it and my Body I commit to the Earth or Sea as it shall please God to order, and as for and concerning all my worldly Estate I give, bequeath and dispose thereof as followeth, that is to say—

It was a strange throwback to their childhood explorer days, or maybe a reference to their mother's Singing Ship, and Cook's account of Keppel Bay.

I give and bequeath unto my beloved Wife, Mary Aitken of Deptford in the County of Kent, and in case of her death unto <u>my daughter Mary Ann Aitken</u> of the same place, all such Tickets, prize money, short allowance money, smart money, pensions together with all Salary, Wages, Sum and Sums of Money, Lands, Tenements, Goods, Chattels and Estate whatsoever, as shall be any ways due, owing or belonging unto me at the time of my decease.

Bernadette expected an explanation of the text at the end of the first letter.

And I do hereby Nominate and Appoint the aforesaid Mary Aitken my Wife, <u>and Mary Ann Aitken my daughter,</u> sole Executors of this my last Will and Testament...On Witness whereof to this my said Will I have set my hand and Seal the Sixteenth day of August in the year of our Lord, One thousand Seven hundred and Eight one, and in the Twenty second year of the Reign of His Majesty King George the third over Great Britain &c. **Aneas Aitken.**

And when there was none, she decided that Jane had mistakenly sent it. Jane's next letter began:

In the name of God Amen, I **Wm. Anderson***, Surgeon of his majesty's Sloop <u>Resolution</u>, having been for some time past in a Bad State of Health and not without any prospect of Recovery, have resolved to make my last Will and Testament—*

Bernadette then considered that this statement on mortality was perhaps part of Jane's project for Miss Corbit's history class.

Noble Arrowsmith *who sailed on the <u>Adventure</u> as an Able Seaman on the Second Voyage and died serving on HMS <u>Resource</u>: I give and bequeath unto my Mother, Elizabeth Arrowsmith, living in Leadenhall Market, London, all such Wages, Sum and Sums of Money...*

By the third letter and will and testament, Bernadette was less patient. Yes, poor Noble Arrowsmith and lucky Elizabeth, Bernadette thought, although she didn't imagine an "Able Seaman's" worth to be much of a windfall, and further, didn't know why she had to read about it.

> **Robert Barber**, *born in Kilkenny, Ireland, who sailed on the* <u>Adventure</u> *as quartermaster during the Second Voyage:*
> *All my Prize Money, Wages, Sum and Sums of Money, Lands, Tenements, Goods, Chattels and Estate whatsoever as shall be any ways due, owing or belonging unto me at the time of my decease, I do give, devise and bequeath the same unto my two Sisters Mary Barber and Ann Barber.*

Good for them, but again, what does this have to do with me? Jane's history project had clearly gone awry for a) she was sending it to the wrong person and b) nobody could possibly care about this to the extent that Bernadette had imagined they'd cared about her pin presentation of the flu epidemic.

> *In the Name of God Amen, I* **William Bee** *of Deptford in the County of Kent, Mariner, do hereby make my Will … that after payment of my Just Debts & Funeral Charges) may go and belong* <u>to my Eldest Daughter Mary Bee.</u>

There was no way to order Jane's bizarre missives.

> *The last Will and Testament of me* **William Bligh** *of Durham Place, Lambeth…I give and bequeath unto* <u>my daughter Harriet</u>*…and each of my* <u>four younger Daughters Elizabeth, Frances, Jane and Ann</u>, *the sum of two hundred pounds—*

In Bernadette's next letter to Jane she requested that Jane coherently assemble her project and submit it to Miss Corbit or to Mr. Thompson or to whomever. Not her! In response, Jane sent another *Last Will and Testament of In the Name of God Amen, of* **James Colnett**, *late of His Majesty's Ship* <u>Glatton</u>. Then **Isaac Carly's**, *of 4th rate Ship of War the* <u>Revenge</u> *and then* **William Bayly**, *late first Master of the Royal Academy in his Majesty's Dock Yard near Portsmouth.*

Bernadette, now infuriated by Jane's obfuscation as well as by the drama in the wills—dying fathers giving their fortunes to their daughters and wife—demanded that Jane cease these letters that weren't letters immediately. Clearly what Jane was telling her with these wills that weren't hers, Bernadette decided, was that Jane was set on killing herself: a self-annihilation or "annulment," which was naturally confirmed to Bernadette when Jane, a few years later—against her advice—joined the Presentation Sisters.

The last letter that Bernadette opened from Jane stated: "Bernadette, in way of explanation of the previous wills and testaments, surely we can be thankful and acknowledge our fathers, who give what they can, when they can, imperfect as that is. If I can do this, why can't you?!"

From then on, so reprimanded, Bernadette returned all letters that she received from Jane, and then later from Sister Ava, unopened. What Bernadette scrawled on the back of that first one she returned said: "Until you wake up to yourself, I'm done on you! In the Name of God Amen!" The postman naturally censored this, covering the Lord's name with thick black ink from the Biro that he carried for such purposes.

✦

Audrey didn't request a ladder, but she was grateful to Robert when he bought her one. It was an aluminum single-sided stepladder two and a half meters high. "It's got slip-resistant traction-tread steps, Audrey, so you can feel very secure going up and down." Robert knew that for her to gain perspective on her button quilt, to properly parse the parts together, she needed a certain amount of height. He'd discovered this one day, when he came upon Audrey standing on the back fence with Bernadette and Jane on each side steadying her. Before her on the grass were two adjacent button-covered blankets that she appeared to be studying. Clearly the set up wasn't ideal for her to implement any changes even if she had any in mind.

"Girls, why don't I steady your mother, while you move the blankets whichever way she likes."

"Thanks, Robert," Audrey said, taking his hand. She directed the girls to rotate one blanket a half turn and place the other blanket below it. They waited quietly as she considered the new arrangement.

"That looks right," she said. Audrey gripped Robert's hand as he carefully assisted her off the fence. From the sewing basket on the ground, she removed a packet of oversized safety pins, and proceeded to attach the adjacent edges of the blankets. The three of them looked on, Bernadette circling the blankets like a surveyor. Audrey, glancing up at them, recognized their discomfort.

"Come on now, I could use a bit of assistance," she said, standing and distributing pins to each of them. They hesitated. "Please, the blankets aren't going to bite." And when they still didn't move, she assured them further. "The buttons aren't going to break if you step on them. I promise." Bernadette and Jane didn't give it another thought and jumped right in. Robert kneeled at the edge—he would never forgive himself if he somehow damaged any one of those precious buttons.

The ladder was better than the fence, but not ideal. Jane later on suggested that they build a tree house, which wasn't really practical since, as Bernadette pointed out, the first limb of the gum tree beside the house was over seven meters high. Bernadette said that what they actually needed was a crow's nest.

Audrey was content. She appreciated their interest and help when they were there, and it was much easier to consider the placement of the blankets sitting on the top rung of the ladder versus tottering on the fence. As the button quilt expanded, the logistics of arrangement became more cumbersome. Audrey would lug the blankets out to the yard in a wheelbarrow, unroll and arrange and rearrange them, necessarily unpinning and re-pinning them as she went. Periodically she'd move the ladder to different sides of the fabric to gain a better sense of the work.

To see Audrey out in the yard like that unnerved Robert. As time passed, she looked more and more precarious sitting alone at the top of the ladder, notebook in hand. Robert tried not to think too much about the irregularities of the ground and the angle of the ladder and that her fall risk increased with the frequency she moved her setup. Amazing to him, that Audrey could guilelessly negotiate these variables. Awesome, actually, her single-minded focus on the arrangement of her quilt in the face of such danger.

"The tennis club is replacing its umpire chair, Robert Pilgrim." Louisa Cawley stood before him at the register at Delton's. "It's 2.44 meters high and has a cushion and a canopy."

"Mrs. Cawley…"

Her hand shot up like a traffic cop's.

"Call me Louisa. I've arranged for the Pro and his assistant to drop it by at your convenience. But Mondays are slower at the club so that'd be best for them." She handed Robert a receipt with date and time—the following Monday at nine—when they planned to deliver it, and turned to walk away.

"Louisa, what do we owe you?"

She looked back at him with a strange mix of bemusement and dismay.

"It's used, Robert. The cushion is faded, the canopy cracked. If Audrey can't use it, chuck it, for goodness' sakes. It's rubbish to us."

✦

The day after Jane's fifteenth birthday was humid and still. Forty-three degrees Celsius, a scorcher. At mid-morning, Bernadette and Jane had set out on a bushwhacking expedition. Audrey had left earlier to help Solicitor Simpson with some case that was about to be settled because apparently his new secretary, Angie, had morning sickness.

Robert prepared a cup of tea and sliced a piece of birthday cake left over from the day before. It was a beauty. Audrey had outdone herself, decorating it with blue marzipan seashells set on white icing with a scattering of raw sugar for sand. Unofficially, they had also been celebrating Bernadette's eminent departure for university. To be fair, he thought, the celebration would also have to be for Audrey, their mother who'd made it possible. Such a feast would set them well for the next leg of their journey. He smiled to himself. The potentiality of "Pilgrim" was undeniable.

The birds were silent. The house was dark and, although cooler than outside, still oppressively warm. Robert had discounted his misgivings about the girls heading off in such heat, listening to Bernadette expertly explain why the bark on striped bark gum trees strips and how their nude trunks in the rain resemble the red trunks of Manzanita trees, native to North America. While she'd elaborated on the fire-resistant strategies of these trees, Robert decided that she, like his brother Stewart, might like to see his statistics on rainfall in Queensland that he'd been collecting along with his data on fires. He made a note to himself to show her these later that afternoon. Theirs was a harsh land.

"You've got to be resilient to survive the cycles of drought, fire, and flood," he interjected. The hope that Solicitor Simpson had finally repaired the office air-conditioner, which Audrey had complained about some time back, crossed his mind.

"True enough," Bernadette agreed, feeling a happy affinity with her father right then.

When Robert finally settled in his armchair with the newspaper and his second cup of tea of the morning, he had a sense that things were right with this world that he and Audrey had made, a private unorthodoxy that he figured most marriages and families eventually became. After a while with the newspaper print blurring and his head nodding, he laid the paper in his lap and closed his eyes.

Robert woke to a commotion in the yard. He'd been dreaming, so at first he wasn't sure if the noise was just a part of his dream. He rose, feeling groggy and heavy and moved languidly through the heat to the veranda and the sound.

At the top of the steps, he looked out into the yard.

"Dad!" Bernadette called out. "Quick! Help us!"

Although Robert saw his daughters coming through the fence and into the yard, he couldn't process the details of them coming through the fence and into the yard. Jane, partially clothed, was half hanging off Bernadette and Bernadette, also partially clothed—shirtless—was holding her there. He located Bernadette's shirt, which was draped around Jane's bleeding shorts. No. No. Fabric doesn't bleed. He looked away from the disturbance of this sticky color to their faces, also bleeding. There it was again.

Bernadette and Jane listed right toward Bernadette's side as they moved ahead. It was all slow motion to Robert: the pauses, the stumbles, the lurches; the calls for help distorted and protracted, deforming in the heat. He felt panicky, aware that Jane and Bernadette this way was nothing he could sensibly cope with.

"Hurry now, Dad!"

They would expect him to rush to them. Of course, Robert would expect himself to rush to them. The tacky feel of the fabric, the sticky skin. What else would he do?

Bernadette called out to him again. What was going on? She could see that he hadn't moved. But it would only take him a second to reach them. He could see that they weren't going to manage much longer. Jane stumbled. "Hold up, Jane, he's coming!" she assured Jane, although now she wasn't actually sure this was true.

"Get Mum! Go on!" Any help, she thought, self-conscious suddenly about her exposed chest until, redoubling her effort to keep Jane moving forward, she forgot this again.

Robert could feel the blood pulsing in his face, his brain. Of course. That's right, their mother. Cement in his legs. But where was Audrey? Was she with the Solicitor working? Or. Was she "not working" with the Solicitor? He could hear his breath amplified in his nostrils and lungs. Or, what if she wasn't with him at all and was with someone else "not working?"

"We're...Jane is hurt. Ring an ambulance. Go on!" Bernadette felt desperate.

When they finally reached the bottom of the steps and he still hadn't moved, Bernadette practically spat at him. "What are you: blind and deaf? Dumb? Must be. Fuck! What the fuck is wrong with you?"

Jane looked in their father's direction, but not at him.

"I'm all right, Bernadette. It's okay. We're home." For her everything had continued to be tremendously thick, slow, and sad. She was so tired. Above them, then beside them, their Dad, sweated profusely, wrung his hands and swallowed and gulped, but didn't speak or move.

"Don't worry, Bernadette," Jane said, shifting her weight more to the banister to relieve her sister. "We'll clean up; we'll be all right."

It was as though a nerve had been struck with these words. Robert literally yelped, and rushed past them down the steps, past the azaleas, until he reached the far corner of the yard where behind the umpire chair, with images of Mary Tucker juxtaposed with his daughters now, young Robert Thatle gasped and gagged.

The day after his daughters' assault, not long after they'd seen Bernadette off at the bus stop, with the will and ardor that Robert couldn't summon the day before, couldn't muster to report the assault to the authorities or to tell Audrey or even to help his daughters inform their mother so that she might adequately nurse them, Robert dug into his memory, surveyed their house and yard until, as precisely as memory allowed, he mapped the locations, described the materials, and documented the prayers, poems or titles inscribed on each altar that he had once accused Jane of "purposefully scattering in every which corner of their home." With each of his excursions through their house and yard, each altar revived and restored, Robert felt as though he'd done more that day, revising its outcome over and over. It wasn't just that he'd met Bernadette and Jane at the fence and carried them across the yard to home and help. Eventually he made his way further to the riverbed, closer to apprehending those men, until one day Robert actually arrived before the men, and was able to whisk his daughters to safety before they even knew they were in danger.

Years later, on the day that Jane became a Presentation Sister, Robert presented her with this inventory of her altars. He didn't notice that Jane seemed confused by the manila folder and inventory. He smiled shyly at her, and thought things do turn out after all, as though it had always been some part of his plan, as though here in this was again some confirmation of the veracity of him and them becoming "Pilgrims." He said, "Yes, Jane Sister—what a fine day for you this is, for us."

Inventory Excerpt:

1. For Saint Josaphat:
<u>Location</u>: dining room
<u>Materials</u>: matchbox covered in yellow cellophane with pipe-cleaner cross
<u>Prayer/Title</u>: I thank the goodness and the grace
<u>Thoughts</u>: My girls: goodness and grace. My family.

2. For Saint Francis of Assisi:
<u>Location</u>: under front steps
<u>Materials</u>: on bed of dry eucalyptus leaves, toy miniature cow, horse, sheep, tiger and elephant (all green plastic)
<u>Prayer/Title</u>: *Lord, a beast but a just beast*
<u>Thoughts</u>: We're beasts, but why can't we be "just" like the other varieties? I wish I would've got you girls a pet.

3. For Saint Martha/Sister of Mary:
<u>Location</u>: above kitchen sink
<u>Materials</u>: prayer card—Lords of the pots and pipkins, etc.— glued to pencil cross
<u>Prayer/Title</u>:
Lords of the pots and pipkins,
Since I have not time to be
A Saint by doing lovely things
And vigiling with thee,
By watching in the twilight dawn
And storming Heaven's gates,

Make me a Saint by getting meals
And washing up the Plates. (Nanna)
Thoughts: I never thought that cleaning might get you to heaven.

4. For Saint Agatha:
Location: beside bath
Materials: mounded cotton balls, dollops of toothpaste and shaving cream on toilet roll reshaped to altar-like dimensions
Prayer/Title: *Yea, a joyful and pleasant*
thing it is to be thankful (Book of Common Prayer)
Thoughts: Very messy altar for me to contend with.
Never thought of this like joy but there you have it.

5. For Saint Mathew:
Location: between kitchen door and hallway
Materials: web designed from green thread strung between two biros, three one-cent, a 20c, 10c, 5c coins at base, mud coating?
Prayer/Title: *How shall we sing the Lord's*
song in a strange land? (Book of Common Prayer)
Thoughts: I don't hear the music Jane. I'm just struck by the weight of the dirty coins.

6. For Saint Paul:
Location: beside carport
Materials: nest of gum-nuts and twigs, one yellow painted paddle-pop stick cut like thunderbolt
Prayer/Title:
Enable with perpetual light
The dullness of our blinded sight. (Book of Common Prayer)
Thoughts: I remember the summer storms, smell of burnt copper, rumbles of thunder with crack of lightning like a bullwhip. I'd lay under the water tower feel the downpour thump the earth.
7. For Saint Peter:
Location: Under kitchen table

<u>Materials</u>: Golf ball covered in Cadbury shiny inside wrapper pocketed in mound of clay
<u>Prayer/Title</u>: (missing word) *did eat angel's food*
<u>Thoughts</u>: Your Mum was a fantastic baker.

8. For Saint Teresa of Avila
<u>Location</u>: behind sofa
<u>Materials</u>: stenciled butterfly, shards of colored glass, magpie feather
<u>Prayer/Title</u>: *I have watched, and am even as it were a sparrow: that sitteth alone upon the house-top.*
<u>Thoughts</u>: Poor sparrow chased away by magpies in this place.

9. For Saint Valentine
<u>Location</u>: cereal shelf in pantry
<u>Materials</u>: pink and red-crayoned cardboard cut in heart shape, bed of broken glass
<u>Prayer/Title</u>: None stated
<u>Thoughts</u>: Pain, a broken heart doesn't stand a chance against love.

10. For Saint Rita
<u>Location</u>: beside Saint Valentine Altar on cereal shelf in pantry <u>Materials</u>: paper doll cut out with pink crayon pox marks, glass splinter in head
<u>Prayer/Title</u>: Scent of Roses
<u>Thoughts:</u> Not a native flower; requires a lot of water.

✦

On the Saturday that Jane Pilgrim came to interview with the Presentation Sisters, there was a tropical rainstorm that originated southeast of New Guinea and came off the Coral Sea onto the Queensland coast. As part of the havoc it brought, it blew down a large branch of the jacaranda tree that hung over the veranda at Saint Ursula's Convent, took out the electricity at the western edge of

Toowoomba, and caused a flash flood at Condamine Creek. Although no persons drowned, the Patrick Donavans lost their dog, Ned. It was strange, people said, that the storm could sustain itself so far inland.

None of these things had happened yet when Jane arrived. She'd come from Mt. Isaac by bus (two actually) and taken a third (the local) to the convent. The winds were wild, whipping the trees and bushes side to side. Once Jane was off the bus, she too had to contend with the whipping wind, which pushed her uphill towards the convent with multiple hands until those same hands reversed direction, pushing her back down, which forced her to lean so far forward that at times she appeared to be crawling. The rain had not yet begun. She would've been more nervous about the interview if it had been normal weather. The break in the humidity and the crazy air both excited and grounded her.

Jane knew this was her last chance. The Sisters had already rejected her two written applications in which she'd laid bare all the details of her life. She'd written four letters after that to convince them to interview her. She'd had Father Malcolm write references as well as her professors at the Teacher Training College, fellow teachers-in-training, and students. Father Malcolm had had Bishop Gray put in a word for her and, ultimately, Jane guessed this was why Sister Jacinta Rathborne finally contacted her:

Dear Miss Pilgrim,

Upon further consideration, we have decided to grant you an interview on Saturday, March 8th at 10:00 a.m. at Saint Ursula's Convent. This should not in any way suggest that we are disregarding our previous evaluations, merely, that we are dutifully acknowledging the strength of your call.

I look forward to meeting you in person.

Yours in Christ,
Sister Jacinta Rathborne

Large raindrops fell on Jane just as she climbed the last of the steps onto the veranda and was met by Sister Scholastica, who looked formidable in her long black robes and veil. Jane curtsied. Then curtsied again when a younger modern Sister Jacinta, the Head of the convent, swiftly approached them from inside. Jane was embarrassed that twice now she'd curtsied to women who weren't the Queen, and that until that very moment Jane had not known she hadn't known how to greet them. Bad start, she thought—oh God, here we go. The rain was thudding against the steps when Sister Jacinta ushered Jane into an outer parlor room, which smelled of stale potpourri.

"Tea, Jane?" Sister Jacinta asked. Jane sat on a straight back chair that faced a framed print of the Sacred Heart of Jesus.

"Please, Sister, that would be very kind," Jane answered, face still flushed from the greeting. "Thank you for seeing me."

"Yes," Sister Jacinta answered in a way that Jane knew was more negative than non-committal. Jesus, in the print, stood with an inflexible posture with one hand in sign of blessing while the other pointed to his red heart centered on a flaming yellow cross on his white smock.

"You've seen my references, then, Sister?" She had to raise her voice to compete with the crescendoing storm.

"Jane, our concerns are not with how you seem, but with how you are," Sister Jacinta said, pouring the tea.

Jane glanced over at Sister Scholastica who, seated in a plush Elizabethan chair, neither looked their way nor showed signs of hearing them.

"What in my application concerns you, Sister?"

"We have to think of the community, Jane. There are too many girls joining for the wrong reasons and before long, or in some cases much later, they realize their unhappiness and either leave or stay despite their unhappiness." Sister Jacinta slurped her tea and added, "The health of the community is threatened with each wrongful entry into the community."

Jane's hand holding the teacup had begun to tremble. Grand-Dad Jack's hand shook this way. Strange that she hadn't thought of him for years and here he was, blustery, smelling of stale beer with yellow-stained smoker's fingers, impossibly attempting wheelchair wheelies. It was such an unlikely memory for a convent interview that Jane knew it was a gift. Her gratitude, immediate and full, made her wish that she could share with these nuns a sense of him—the wheelie and the laughter they'd shared later as he'd raise and lower his paralyzed leg like a boom at a railway crossing so Jane's dolls could pass beneath. Jane grinned in the middle of Sister Jacinta's lecture, inappropriately she realized later.

If Sister Jacinta noticed, she didn't acknowledge it. She studied the intensifying storm outside and continued to list the five reasons not to enter religious life: to love without distraction, to seek peace, to find the answer, to belong, to repay God. This was a speech Sister Jacinta gave often. It was as though she were in a trance, Jane observed, annoyed then agitated by the drone of her disengaged voice. As Sister Jacinta elaborated on each point, it was clear to Jane that Sister Jacinta neither cared that Jane was a dedicated teacher nor understood that she'd overcome her childish religious fervor for a more grounded belief. It was clear that Sister Jacinta was indifferent to all that had been written in her applications and references and, like Bernadette, without saying it directly, focused on a part of Jane's past that was private and inexplicable.

"Sister, you said that I'd have the opportunity to write a final statement, or request, you called it?"

Sister Jacinta seemed stunned by both the interruption and tone of the interruption. Sister Scholastica for the first time stirred in her chair and looked with interest at Jane.

"If you don't mind, the weather, the bus schedule ... I best do that now, don't you agree?" The print of Jesus on the wall was wrong. The red of the heart should bleed into the flames and make a mucky big stain on His smock. Borders like that artist made have nothing to do with Jesus, Jane thought. God's love is a creep and a splatter that a picture like that just doesn't capture.

"Best. Yes, yes," Sister Jacinta said, rising, then sitting, then rising again as though temporarily unable to decide where she was headed. "I agree." She showed Jane to a table in the adjoining room where she gave her a black pen and a leaf of paper at the top of which was the insignia of the Presentation Sisters. After a short time really, no more than five minutes, Jane handed the paper back to Sister Jacinta, thanked both nuns for their time and consideration, and plunged into the rain and wind with a rectitude that surprised both Sisters, who watched her veer away.

What Jane couldn't know, as she paced the bus station later, waiting for the announcement for the next bus (all buses had been cancelled due to the storm) was that just after she left a mighty gust of wind had brought down that branch, which had crushed the convent banister on which she'd leaned earlier. She couldn't know that Sister Scholastica was fervently singing her praises, not for her understanding of the depth of Jane's commitment, but because Jane had reminded her of herself on her first day at the convent in County Cork, over fifty years ago, when she'd thrown herself prostrate before the first person she'd met. How funny that had been and funny this girl, how funny how much Sister Scholastica enjoyed someone curtsying before her. She hadn't known that about herself. Jane couldn't know that in less than a week she would receive the formal invitation to join the Presentation Sisters, a Bishop's order from a Bishop notorious for sending girls who would last with the Sisters less than three years. She wouldn't know Sister Jacinta and all members of the community were obligated to follow his orders, given their vows of obedience—for them a source of tension and frustration. Neither would she know that Sister Jacinta was actually chagrined at Jane's interview because, at heart, Sister Jacinta sensed, even as she was lecturing Jane, that she might prove to be one of their best sisters, her persistence and lack of subtlety unique.

Jane didn't know that the winds had blown out the electrical lines in the part of town where Harry MacKenzie lived, and Harry, who was scheduled to drive the bus from Toowoomba to Emerald, where Jane would get her bus connection to Mt. Isaac, would not report to work for two days. Nor did she know that the Patrick Donavans hadn't as yet missed their dog Ned in their rush to gather their valuables for evacuation.

What Jane knew as she paced and paced was that she was reminding herself of Bernadette on the deck of one of her stupid bloody, stupid bloody ships and how wasn't that ironic. She continued pacing, though, and was filled with thoughts and feelings that could only be described as blasphemous.

The statement that Jane wrote that day for the Presentation Sisters:

On the "Strength" of My Call

Sisters, do you know the truth of my call? It is not Jesus, Mary, or Joseph. It is not the Holy Ghost or the Communion of Saints. It is not a grand love of my fellow human beings. It was my sister's face when I was raped. (Don't get all trauma this, trauma that, for unlike what you want to believe, I am no victim. As I have stated in your application before, I do not want or need to hide in your Order as you insinuate!)

Let me tell you about such faces, Sisters. They strain forward even when held back. They absorb too many details to be told. What those men were to me. What they were to themselves. Have you ever looked into a face that's helpless, furious, and alone all at once? You may talk about lost soul this, lost soul that, but have you ever seen into the face of a soul that's lost? You're wrong if you believe that the sight of souls is for God alone.

You say you are concerned with how I "am" versus how I "seem." I point out to you, Sisters, that you confuse who I seem with who I am. Don't reduce me to a body in a riverbed. I am, I was, even when I was lying in the middle of it, I knew I was a part of something else that included those men and the riverbed yet was more than those men and the riverbed and all that had come before in my life and all that would happen after. My sister didn't know this. She was alone. My call is to reach her.

Sisters, I am called for this. I see my sister's face on so many other faces, and I will go joyfully, passionately, angrily, lazily, and even, if I like, sinfully towards her. This I will do with or without you!

In the Name of God, Amen—Jane Pilgrim

PART FOUR

THE INLAND SEA

✦

IT'S NOT THAT THE PEOPLE of Mt. Isaac had forgotten to hope for rain. They hadn't. The drought, because of the length of it—five years—had taken on a sinister quality that was more difficult to rise above for some, and for others—most, actually—had insinuated itself into their lives to such a degree that after a while even the nuisances of it were difficult to parse from their habit of it, which inevitably dulled their ability to picture anything beyond it as well. Insidious either way—so, for example, after the first year, when Daryl Michaels shot his wife, kids, and himself out on his property, the town people said, "Definitely the drought." Yet when the same thing happened to Jim Roony and his dog, Jim, three years later, they'd said, "Definitely gone bush, you know, the isolation," as though there wasn't a drought, and the livestock rotting in Jim's paddock were different than the livestock in Daryl's, as though the isolation Jim felt, Daryl hadn't, as though the murders of wives, children, and pets were bound to happen regardless.

The inconvenience of dust and dirt was normal now. The dry coughs, the reddish film rinsed into the sink each night that, in the morning, magically reappeared "like fairy dust, Mum," said Dominic Keys to his mother, Mary Ellen, as she dampened a towel to clean his never-changing sweet face. Joe Pearl, the publican at the Imperial Hotel, would say, looking out over his customers—the blokes on his side of the pass-through and the girls in the Ladies' Lounge on the other—that you could tell that they were related by their familial red glow. "Dust, the great equalizer," he'd say with a snicker. "I bet there's not a crack in all Mt. Isaac without a bit of grit."

Throughout the state, sheep and cattle died. Crops failed. Locally, the mine hired some men pushed off their properties and brought down by the drought conditions, but others left the district altogether. Men from the Land Bureau would periodically visit, and sometimes the Drought Research Group came to gather data about pasture cover, supplementary feed reserves, stock sales, and intended sales should the drought continue, which, when it did, they stopped assessing since the stock was dead or technically "depleted." Early on there was talk about erosion—what soils were susceptible to it, and then how it was done: erosion through overstocking and erosion from fallowing and repeated cultivation of ground.

Although there was no finger pointing, some town people were suspicious of the stockmen and farmers who might've been able to prevent the die off of pasture cover, grasslands, and crops. Lack of rain or, technically, "rainfall deficiencies" was quantified in tables to compare to future droughts as though this one was over. The loss of soil nutrients, blown as far as New Zealand in dust storms, was less easy to conceptualize, no less quantify, although in Mt. Isaac and its surrounds it was just a matter of wiping your cheek to know what was on the move that day.

✦

"What do you got there, mate?"

The bus felt stuffy, filled with diesel fumes. Robert Thatle, at seventeen in his new suit, already felt grimy in his rumpled suit. He held a tattered sheet of paper on which he'd drawn three columns, which he'd filled with names that he'd earlier generated. In the first column were Anderson, Richardson, Thompson, Johnson, Robinson, Gibson, Dixon, Pearson, Watson, and Wilkinson. The second column contained color names: White, Brown, Black, Blue, Gray, Green, and Rose; and the third, a greater variety of names from Ainsworth to Knight, Foster to Tidwell, and Vickers to York.

"Surnames," he replied.

"Yeah?"

Robert had decided that an English surname suited him. He was drawn to the fancier names like Partridge or Ainsworth—men who might wear bowler hats and suits with wide stripes—but had discounted them out of respect for his father, who, he knew, would have a hard enough time processing any name change, no less those ones.

"Yes," he curtly replied, hoping to discourage his bus mate from inquiring further. Robert, with time pressure now, had to decide on one of the names before he reached Rockhampton, a deadline he'd set, so that when he introduced himself in that town, he'd be saying something true about himself that the name Thatle couldn't do.

"So, you're planning an identity change, then?" Robert's bus mate had quickly sized him up.

Robert didn't know what to say. Seven years biding his time to distance himself from the disrepute of his family—no one asks for a father with a brothel, a brother enthusiastic about the brothel, and a mother, a mother—anyhow, that, plus his months mulling over possible names, and here this guy acted as though Robert's plan was as simple as a superhero's costume change.

"Give us a look, then. I've got an ear for names," his bus mate said. "True, you're lucky."

Robert reluctantly handed the list to the man. Unbeknownst to Robert, Robert reminded his bus mate of his older brother, Mike, whose body he was on his way to Rockhampton to claim. Robert's way of setting his jaw, his seriousness, was just like him. "What's your Christian name, then? I've gotta have that, you know, to hear the whole thing right."

"Robert," Robert said, wishing now he'd chosen to sit two seats ahead, next to the elderly lady with the straw handbag.

"Robert Robertson. Nah, just joking. I'm Neil. Neil O'Rourke."
Robert wondered if it was too late to move.

"And last name?"

How had he allowed such a private matter to become so public?

"Wouldn't that be bloody ironic if I gave you back your own name?"

Robert felt as held hostage as his list. "Thatle. Robert Thatle." The bus hit a pothole. The unexpected jolt punctuated a surge of anxiety as Robert realized that he'd just introduced himself as Robert Thatle for the last time.

"I'm not gonna pry, mate, but you want a name that captures the reason you're re-naming yourself, or not the reason exactly, but, you know, the image you'd want to get out there."

Robert had been considering his Thatleness since he was a boy. It wasn't right that this bus stranger, Neil, was asking him to reexamine it. There was no way to explain to this Neil that the cruel and fraudulent elements of his Thatle line shouldn't be taken forward even if some less cruel and fraudulent Thatles had to be sacrificed along the way. This was a cleansing he was doing for the sake of generations to come.

"Robert Thompson or Robert Jenkins or even Robert Ellis says nothing about you that could make a strong impression or give a picture." Neil looked over at Robert. 'You're full of it, Neil!' he heard his brother, Mike rebuke, which was true. Suffixes like sons, kins, bergs, and on, he knew, absolutely gave a picture of parents and homes, and even trades.

Robert's mum had to have had some inkling of the activities of August. Blind loyalty wasn't an acceptable trait to carry forward either.

"Do you see, Robert? No disrespect, mate. Well, here, you've got the name Wood. Now with Wood you can conjure something solid, hardy, you see?" Mike was solid: only fool solid Mike would take a stand between a gay bloke and a bunch of drongos on a dark street.

Like bowler hats and wide stripes maybe, Robert considered.

Neil didn't speak, looking ahead at the seat back in front of him. For better or worse, his brother's mettle had bound Mike's life irreversibly to his death. If there was a surname with a "brother of Mike" suffix, Neil would change his name in a heartbeat.

He sighed and lowered his voice. "Do you actually know what you're getting into here, Robert Thatle?"

Robert realized that Neil was genuinely concerned for him, which he hadn't expected. "Of course I do," Robert reassured him.

"Sorry, mate," Neil apologized. "That was out of line,"

"No harm," Robert said, then: "I'm not much of a Wood. Maybe something with more action." Neil had a point. "More purpose."

"Yeah, you look like a man with purpose," Neil said, staring down at Robert's list but unable to focus. Neil handed the paper back to Robert, who, grateful for Neil's insight, was now feeling fortunate to have sat beside him.

"Best to give that name of yours some more thought, yeah," Neil said, before turning his head towards the window. "Wake me before we unload in Rocky, would ya, mate? But with your new name, yeah?"

"Sure," Robert agreed, already generating surnames that might embody his resolve.

When the bus pulled into Rockhampton, Robert rose into the aisle and grabbed his bag from the bin overhead. It was premature. He'd have to wait for the passengers at the front of the bus to collect their things and move out first. He was excited though and he couldn't sit any longer. Neil, on the other hand, made no signs of moving. Robert couldn't know that the last thing that Neil wanted was to arrive, for here there would be no turning back. His brother, Mike, would be claimed and be definitively dead then, and Neil would have to shoulder that loss forever.

In the aisle, Robert stood awkwardly beside their seats, his arms folded around his bag as though it were a small child. Robert, sensing Neil's gaze, said, "Robert Pilgrim."

"Sure? Pilgrim?" Neil said. When Robert nodded and didn't elaborate, Neil said, "Traveler. One who visits foreign lands or what, something else? Journeys far to a sacred site, right?"

Robert's closed-lipped smile seemed tentative.

"Good, good, I like it," Neil reassured him, watching then as Robert's teeth emerged in a full out grin.

The two young men edged down the aisle toward their respective destinies. On the platform there was a moment before they separated. Neil stuck out his hand. "Mr. Pilgrim."

"Mr. O'Rourke." As they shook hands Neil said, "I reckon there's a bit of Pilgrim in all of us, which would make us related." Neil, shaking Robert's hand, was then shaking Mike's, like he knew his brother would always be there in fellows like this, and to Robert's surprise, Neil pulled him close and roughly hugged him, before Neil abruptly turned and crossed the street. Robert stood bewildered, not knowing how to take this strange reenactment of his father's send off from earlier that day. Such hearty bookends had to be auspicious. "G'day, I'm Robert Pilgrim," he practiced.

✦

Almost incidentally, Audrey followed the ute out of Mt. Isaac that day. Belinda had been visited. The broken lamp had been left for repair. Back in the car, Audrey didn't have a clear idea where she was headed, only that she didn't want to return from where she'd come. She'd just pulled out of the lot when the ute cut in front of her. A fast brake, a jerk, and she said, "You can't just do that, Mister." When the vehicle turned left then right, she did too. When it merged with the highway, she tailed it out of town, the sand storm ramping up around them.

Audrey's initial impulse, defensive and assertive both, shifted as she adapted to the driver's pattern of slowing and quickening. When the vehicle braked, decelerating some, Audrey answered with her own braking and deceleration. When it sped up, so did she. Soon Audrey felt as though she was a part of a conversation; that the fluctuations of speed were like words of greetings, then troubles confided and comforted. Mt. Isaac, meanwhile, was falling further behind them. As Audrey adjusted her speed again, she pictured Robert in the kitchen, separating buttons from glass. This was enough in her mind that when the ute pulled over to the side of the road she almost passed it.

"Do you know Gilgin Downs?" He was a young man, maybe late twenties, blond. His cheeks were tanned and scarred from acne. He didn't look at her—her makeup and outfit had lost their crispness since the morning—but scanned the horizon as though he expected his mate in a semi filled with bauxite pellets to materialize at any moment.

"I think so," she said. She could hear sand particles sweep over the car.

"Cig?"

"Sure." Audrey didn't smoke, or hadn't since secondary school when, with her friends, smoking was more of a social gesture than habit. He leaned across his passenger seat and through the window, clearly not bothered by the dust, and lifted the packet to her. Even as she leaned through her window to take the cigarette from him and then leaned further forward for him to light it, she saw that he still didn't look at her, but examined the lighter, his dashboard, his hood, then the horizon again. She dusted off her cheek.

"Follow me then, yeah?"

She'd agreed, feeling a buzz from the cigarette that although wasn't completely pleasant, wasn't completely unpleasant either.

Gilgin Downs, an abandoned cattle property, was due west between Mount Isaac and Moreen, the state-owned bauxite mine, and was below a large escarpment. When Audrey followed the ute driver down the rough dirt road, her concern wasn't about the isolation, but that if one of her tires blew out, she didn't have a spare. She was relieved to see the Queenslander house on the rise ahead and relieved to finally park behind him. The dust from the driver's ute, infiltrating her car, made it difficult to breathe. While the dust settled, she studied the Queenslander house: the spiky burgundy branches of the wild bougainvillea had penetrated the open veranda and blocked the front windows and door; the termite infested steps leading up to the veranda had collapsed or disintegrated completely; and the right corner of the corrugated iron roof nearest her, reddened with rust, had lifted off the house like a wing.

Once out of the car, she was only half aware of the stillness, the wind temporarily slack like they'd entered the eye of a storm. She watched the driver get out of his truck, and pause. Curiosity and an odd impatience for how the day would play out, these were her feelings as she watched him—a taut man with sharp angles—look to the right of the house to the corrals where once cattle had been herded, horses—brumbies probably—broken in, and where now the posts had slipped and rotted off their foundations at odd angles. Audrey felt a surge of adrenaline even as she remarked to herself, this is a lonely place, Audrey.

Less than a meter from her, the ute driver dropped his cigarette and ground it into the dirt with the heel of his work boot, a familiar action hard for her to place. Audrey smoothed her dress, expectantly waiting for him to resume the conversation that they'd begun with their cars. He paused by her hood, tracing a scratch with his thumb, before turning his attention to the front tire, which he kicked, saying to nobody in particular: "That balding tire is about to blow."

"Oh," Audrey said. "I know that," wary suddenly of her impulse to apologize.

"Right," he said.

It wasn't exactly criticism or exactly disinterest Audrey sensed, but an undertone of dismissal. Louisa Cawley and the khaki man—that's what this reminded her of—his speaking to her as if he were speaking to "nobody in particular." Audrey's adrenaline shifted.

The driver pulled out his pack of cigarettes again and extracted one with his teeth. This time he didn't offer her one. Audrey stared in disbelief as he lit it. On having a closer look, had the driver determined, as part of being a "nobody" that she wasn't the type of woman who "should" smoke? He leaned up against the hood oblivious to her look. Solicitous and protective like Robert; how could that go wrong? *You just leave it there, Mrs. Pilgrim. Louisa said to go ahead and plant it where you stood.* How had all these people deemed her so incapable that she might need their help and so mute or dim-witted that they should speak for her?

A whirl of sand sprung up and almost immediately dissipated in the empty corral. I did this. Her mother had praised Audrey's talent for getting along with people. Encouraged or not, she couldn't remember, Audrey had honed her skills in being agreeable, conciliatory, and accommodating without a thought for herself—which, was that the point? Somehow that "her" of herself had been sacrificed and "her" life kept at an arm's length and life also then kept at an arm's distance. She'd done that for them.

The driver took a long pull off his smoke. Until Belinda.

Now Audrey didn't want his stupid cigarette, this man who'd cut her off and who wouldn't look at her. Audrey lunged forward, yanked the smoke from his mouth, threw it in the dirt, and shoving him away from her hood, shouted: "You just piss off home!" Though uncomfortable, he smiled, which infuriated her. She punched him in the arm and would've again if he hadn't caught her arm and pinned it to her side. "I'm serious, piss the fuck off now!" Belinda's words felt powerful. She hit him with her other hand and twisting, freed her pinned arm and then launched herself at him again, pounding her fists against him until he pulled her tight into his body and held her there as she flailed.

The ute driver didn't speak or move, didn't seem phased at all by this Audrey Pilgrim in his arms.

Still holding her, he guided her into the car. He held her down, hesitant for a second, deliberating although he wasn't a deliberating man, then pushed her back onto the seat, and maintaining a hand on her chest, he unfastened his fly with the other hand. Half standing, leaning in and on her, powered by a sinewy strength, he unceremoniously fucked her as she yanked his arm from her and bit her lip and pushed up toward him. He fucked her as each possibility of breath was pounded from her, his elbow knocking the steering wheel, which fueled a fury now matched by Audrey's, that raged at Audrey and raged back at him, who not Audrey or ute driver, but bodies to each other, were raged at and raged at until this rage precipitously fell away from him, then them, and he slumped forward and he and Audrey caught their breath.

Her and the driver's faces were sweaty from their efforts, their breath deep and quick as though they'd run a race. As he pulled himself away from the car seat and Audrey, forever later it seemed to her, she heard her own breathless voice ask, "Bill's your name?" She felt herself travelling simultaneously in slow motion and fast wind through time past her brother and parents, past Robert and her daughters, past the hospital to here where the driver had just stepped back from her, and was now "righting" himself.

"What did you say?"

Audrey didn't move. "Bill. It's on your shirt." He looked down at his name embroidered in white on the navy uniform shirt issued to him by the garage. He wiped the sweat pouring from his face on the inside of his collar.

"I'm a mechanic." He said this reflexively; conscious now of the lady laid back on the car seat with her thighs still spread. For all that had occurred on this day and in this last hour, Audrey felt suspended in time, her adrenalin gone, yet singularly present. Her thought, sluggish as it came, was of cooling, but with that no real wish that this would happen. Truthfully, her thoughts didn't move much beyond that name on the driver's chest, a smudge of grease she'd noticed under his jaw, the soreness between her legs and warmth throughout her.

"I go by Billy, though," he said, his breath steadying as he stood at her door, nervous and stand-offish like a lone teenager at the edge of a crowded dance floor.

"Yes. Billy," she repeated, studying the ceiling of her car, aware gradually of her back and bum stuck by sweat and semen to the vinyl seat that she'd soon have to clean.

"Hey, umm." Billy moved into the doorway. "Umm." His hands were rough, fingers cracked—Audrey registered this—as he gently closed her thighs, pulling the front of her dress down. Tenderness—Audrey registered this too—and, understanding that he was fully seeing her, centered Audrey beyond her physical sense.

"You'll be right then, yeah?" He backed out again to face the house.

"Will you do something for me?" Audrey said as she slowly pulled herself up.

"How do you mean?"

She really had no idea what she wanted from him, just that she did want something.

Billy glanced sideways at her as he lit them both cigarettes. "Thanks."

"I'm better at motorbikes than cars. I like to fix them more I mean. I'm good at both."

"I'm sure." Audrey now pulled herself out of the car and, after a moment leaning against it, smoking, she dropped the cigarette and walked slowly towards the shade of the house. Billy followed her, but not directly into the shade. At the steps, she turned to face him but couldn't see his features since her eyes hadn't adjusted from the shift of light. "What's your full name, Billy?" she asked, dabbing a cut on her lip with a ball of tissue she'd found in her pocket.

"Billy Turner." He was a guileless bloke, actually. Audrey saw that he didn't give it another thought to meet and screw a middle-aged woman in the middle of nowhere, and she now, likewise him. Audrey Pilgrim—touched by the heat—abandons her family and enjoys a smoke and screw with the mechanic, Billy Turner. Oh, Audrey.

"Umm," Billy stepped into the shade beside her, "What did you want exactly?"

Billy surprised her, remembering her request, which already seemed asked hours ago. Audrey was unable to look at him, which she realized wasn't about the quality of the light. What she wanted, which before hadn't been clear, was, simply—was it simple? No, maybe it could never be simple—contact.

"Do you have any water?" she asked.

He moved directly to his truck with an efficiency that she pictured he'd move from engine to engine at his garage.

"Here." He handed Audrey a green plastic cordial bottle and stepped back from her.

"I'm not going to bite, Billy." He did have reason to suspect she might. The water was warm and dull, but refreshing. He stepped closer, wary, but closer, and looked away towards the barren paddock as Audrey, with her same tissue, now dampened with water, turned to him and began to remove that streak of grease embedded in the pock marks at the base of his jaw. Hers a surreptitious view, she inhaled the smell of his damp smoky face combined with the pungent oily odors of his uniform, and stood awake to the vibrancy of her body as she patiently labored under his jaw with her tissue.

✦

At the riverbed, Bernadette waited for all sounds of the men to be gone, and then waited for a pocket of time to pass where there was no sound, which would make them safe, this pocket. It had to be long enough that there'd be no chance of the men's return, so the calculation of this no-sound pocket was critical. She hoped Jane understood that that was the reason she didn't call over to reassure her. If she made a mistake on the sound pocket, the timing, well— well, it'd just be worse, that's all. She just hoped Jane could tell this too.

Jane and Bernadette lay in the riverbed for almost two hours after the men left.

"They're going to pay for this, Jane, you wait and see." There was no clear way to deal practically with their torn, soiled clothing. Each girl looked at her sister and saw that her sister was worse off than herself. Bernadette brusquely cleaned herself.

"I'm going to be sick again, Berna…"

"They're going to wish they were dead. You watch." She held one arm around Jane, one hand at her forehead, steadying her as she vomited, as her mum had done for each of them with their bouts with flu. Bernadette wished their mum was with them now.

"I shouldn't have joked about Saint Paul…or Charity. I, I don't know."

The bank was steeper than either girl remembered, the soft sand hard to climb. Jane kept losing her footing and sliding back down the bank. She couldn't keep hold of Bernadette. She couldn't straighten up.

"Don't be stupid, Jane. Here: now take my hand! Try again. Up!"

The sisters, traveling side by side, filled the narrow path. Bernadette felt the squeeze of the bush as it closed in around them. At first Jane, dizzy, and still bleeding wanted to sit, lie on the path and rest, sleep, which Bernadette wouldn't allow for fear that she wouldn't be able to get her up again.

Bernadette encouraged Jane to steadily keep on, while fighting her own urge to bolt. All vegetation and insect, animal, and bird life she'd savored on the way in, she now resented and felt burdened by, felt as an antagonistic entity to resist at all cost. Her sight, like a scythe, cut away all that had betrayed them: the eucalyptus, wattle, oak, bottlebrush, and high grass hiding those men from her until it was too late. The clicks, hums, and sighs, caws and chirps: a mass of nature noise colluding to drown out the men's voices.

Jane's thoughts ran mixed. From "Dear, dear Bernadette" to "thank God, it's over" to "I'd like to rest a little, Bernadette," to "isn't everything greener than before, Bernadette—isn't it?" to "I wonder if after Saul was struck blind if when he saw again, things were as green as this" to "we'll be fine, Bernadette; it's okay, I'm sure it's alright for me to sit for just a moment."

Bernadette said, "Jane, this was not a God thing and shut up now about the saints." She said, when they got home, watch, Dad will help and make it right. She said, they were like explorers on their last legs, but they wouldn't be stopped, they had legs. She said, all passion isn't that; she said, this fucking bush, Jane, whose idea was this, this fucking bush!

Jane sat finally and couldn't be argued out of it. Blood down her legs and she thought I'm bleeding to death. Oh, how sad and beautiful to die here in this bush and it was as though birds she'd never heard called and coddled and peeped and squawked and laughed to welcome her. And she wished then that she knew all their names and had made some record or, at least, seen Bernadette's sketches so she could be prepared and be able to appreciate the beauty she hadn't noticed enough before, that she was now about to join.

"Let's go!" Bernadette saw the fresh blood, saw Jane's face drain. "Get up!" She pulled her with all the strength she had, and Jane said, "Oh Bernadette, always in a rush."

Bernadette said, "Bloody fuck! Get going," and then, recanting, "Jane, I know this is hard, but we can't stop here, we—this isn't—come on, Jane, do it for God or whatever, but help me get you back. Help me please, Jane. I don't—shit, I can't, I can't just do this now without your help!" Bernadette had taken off her blouse and had wrapped it around Jane's bloody shorts.

Jane's arm was around Bernadette's neck as they moved forward on the path. Jane worried for Bernadette now, worried for her worry until her mind drifted again to her friend, Gavin, and his burned body and then in the next instant to the web, the crystalline form of patterns spun there, and a longing for the pleasure to be held in that tension, to rest in a web like that, and then she thought it's coming soon, we're almost there. Good, good, some beauty to cheer Bernadette, too. And she pictured herself at rest on the path while Bernadette wrote something in her book, and she could rest, and there might be something pretty, something not completely caught in the web's threads, that they could pick out, and she could sit and rest just a little while, while Bernadette drew the bug or butterfly that they'd saved.

When they came upon the web, Bernadette, with a single arm stroke, pulled it apart. There was no time to object. With Bernadette pushing them forward toward their house, Jane's thoughts moved to herself with the web's threads hanging and sticking, caught against their skin and clothing, clumped and matted, the inflamed edges of Gavin's wounds and crying, she said, "Bern, they've wounded us, haven't they?"

Bernadette, pulling Jane closer again, her arms trembling with fatigue, said, "Tell me that prayer again, Jane." How far now, not far, it had to be a matter of one hundred meters, no, one hundred and fifty, Bernadette said, "Speak to me in 'eths.' I bet you can't, Jane." With a slight uphill to their fence and a section of scree-like stones on the incline to get through, she said, "You'll see soon how safe we'll be." And calling then, calling loud, a shout really, after Bernadette saw the welcome figure of their father on the veranda, she thought: it won't be true that this fury life will raze all hope from us.

✦

For the people in Mt. Isaac and its surrounds, it became normal to normalize the drought. The devastating effects of drought were not easy to see. Yet when the stark facts of it were exposed, those who would, gamely took stock, while those who wouldn't, dusted themselves off and moved on: best they could; facts be damned.

PART FIVE

THE SINGING SHIP

✦

AFTER THE GIRLS MOVED away, Robert and Audrey settled into a rhythm of life that, though comfortable, was not without the occasional upset wrought by the secrets that they kept from one another. Just as Robert had his compartments, where facts over time were gentrified, Audrey's shift into an ever-present present meant that the past and her feelings and regrets stayed past, except—and it was a large exception—where it played out daily in the creation of her button quilt. Maybe it was their respective styles of denial that nurtured their relationship in those later years, for they did grow closer.

Robert would help Audrey with her quilt in the interstitial time between his duties at home and work. His focus was still primarily the button inventory, even though it had become less precise over time as a result of the prohibitive number of buttons that arrived and that the donations were often from clubs. After Jane left, he also assumed the job of arranging the blankets in the yard as Audrey directed him from her umpire chair. As time went on, he could definitely see that there was more that he could do.

One evening Robert announced, "We're at a crossroads, Audrey. As I see it, I can either dedicate myself exclusively to the button inventory or help you more with your pre-production needs." At the time, Audrey was separating the colors of newly arrived buttons, which Robert had already logged, into soup bowls and over-sized mugs.

"Sure, Robert, I'd be glad for the help. The inventory though, I know that's important to you." She paused to stretch her fingers and hands. Her knuckles cracked. Funny how much more stiff they felt with the cold weather. When he didn't respond, she looked up at him, uncertain how to interpret his silence. Hopefully, she hadn't discouraged him. "Of course, you predicted it, Robert: my hands have become more stiff and sore over time," she conceded.

"It's a cost-benefit calculation in the end," Robert replied. "By and by you've got to give Father Time his due." Audrey smiled. "Which is to say, Audrey, our hands together will get this quilt done."

He was a kind man, her Robert, more caring than she could've hoped for. Whatever you could say about him, you could never fault him for endeavoring to make things right by their family. She forced a laugh, wiping a tear away. "Goodness, yes, Father Time."

He marched through the kitchen to the pantry. "Is that tin of lard still in here?" he called out. And, a moment later: "I believe we can poach the chamomile from Jane's tea." And a moment after that: "For the eucalyptus leaves, we've got the entire bush. I've told you, haven't I, about my mum's remedy?"

Once Robert was on board, even before he retired, the quilt rapidly expanded. The system he developed allowed Audrey to spend more time on button selection and arrangement, which in turn meant she could sew more. What was strange to Robert was that until he made this shift, he didn't realize that the inventory, which he'd believed would close the distance between them, had actually expanded it. Robert's helpful insights about the production of the button quilt surprised Audrey, as did that she could be surprised by him at this stage of their marriage.

"Perfect, Robert: I'd never thought of that," she said to him when he arrived one day with two six-packs of beach pails and shovels of assorted colors. "For the buttons?"

"That's what I thought too, Audrey," he said, beaming at her. "I borrowed the label gun from work to make tags for them."

✦

At Robert's retirement luncheon, he and Audrey sat with Hamish Templeton, Delton's prior executive manager, who, until recently, before his prostrate condition had worsened, had been mobile. His son, Cameron, who'd inherited his father's position, gave the first toast after the meal. Cameron gave a history of Delton's, acknowledged it was a shame that none of the Delton family could attend that day, and then spoke of his own father's commitment and dedication to the store, reminisced about times he'd visited his father at work, giving a shout out to "Ron," whom he must've seen on one of those occasions. "This town owes this man," Cameron said of his father. "Without him and Delton's, there'd be no local place to buy your household goods." He turned to Robert then and thanked him for his many years of service to Delton's Department Store and he lifted his glass and said: "Well done, Ron Pilgrim. You'll be missed."

Mrs. Johnson, who still worked in the Linens and Fabrics Department, spoke next. "Do you know that Robert, Robert Pilgrim, visited my department every week?" She perused the luncheon group with a pleased smile. "We all know—maybe not you, Cam—about his wife, Audrey's, famous quilt," she said, acknowledging Audrey. "Well, I'm honored to have assisted Robert in selecting his buttons for the quilt, and I'd like to think that my tastes might've even prevailed." She gave a chortle and, walking over to Robert and Audrey's table, said, "Here's a box for the road. Good on you both."

Retirement luncheons can be awkward, and so far this one had delivered. "Thanks for all this," Robert said, rising. "It means a lot to me that you wanted to honor me today, for I've enjoyed my work at Delton's and working alongside all of you. To serve here..." He trailed off. What did all those years of service mean? "I liked waking up and knowing that I was headed to Delton's. I liked that it's allowed me to provide for my family, and to provide a bit of help to other families with their purchasing needs. And yes, Mrs. Johnson, I liked to buy my buttons from you for Audrey." He could feel himself getting choked up by the finality of the event. "Delton's though, the requirements of my work, actually taught me to be a better help for my wife. Her project ..." He trembled with the strain of keeping his emotions tapped. "Well Audrey's project, that's my ..." he looked over at Audrey, "that's what's key." That last part came out as a sob-hiccup.

Robert sat then. Audrey took his hand, and as Cameron pulled Hamish in his wheelchair away from the table, Audrey whispered to Robert: "What a job we have ahead of us."

✦

It was the month before Audrey's accident. Robert had just returned from Claremont, where he'd purchased a three-pack of blankets, more spools of colored thread and four large spools of twine. He knew that many of these supplies he could easily buy locally at Delton's, but he also knew that Claremont was the place that Audrey had always gone to make her purchases. She hadn't asked him to make the longer trip or even asked him to replenish her supplies. Robert had taken stock of the number of buttons accumulating and calculated that it was only a matter of time before there'd be a bottleneck.

Robert unloaded the quilt supplies and stored them in what was once Bernadette's bedroom, which had long been converted to a sewing room. He didn't hear Audrey but assumed she was around. He'd taken the car after all. He passed through the dining room where the latest quilt section was spread and, as was his habit, folded back the completed portion. He called out for her and when she didn't answer, he looked out back, where she'd typically go to examine one or more blanket patches.

As he suspected, Audrey was sitting in the umpire chair studying a single quilt patch below her. Robert didn't want to disturb her, but he was curious about what she was looking at. He could see a glittery shine radiating off the ground. The day was heating up, the humidity rising, details evident to Robert by the pungency of the nearby eucalyptus tree floating to him in the breeze. He heard a caw behind him and, although it wasn't mating season, he half expected the swoosh of a magpie's wing as he walked out to join her.

There from the edge, looking down at the blanket Robert was struck by the brightness and brilliance of a mass of white and metallic buttons of assorted shapes that shimmered in the light. It was abstract to him, but splendid. "Splendid, Audrey," he said.

"Come on Robert," Audrey gently prodded. "Join me up here."

Robert had spools of thread that needed to be matched to the requisite colored buttons. He had a packet of sewing needles that needed to be threaded. He had the box of buttons from the Castlemaine Brewery that needed to be sorted and distributed into pails. The blankets would need to be unpackaged. It was crucial to spread them out so that the creases would break down before Audrey began to sew.

"Robert?"

He hesitated, but then slowly climbed up the five wooden rungs of the umpire chair. Audrey shifted to the edge of the seat to make room for him and steadied him as he squeezed in beside her.

What he couldn't see before, which was now evident from this new height, was that the beauty below was in the shape of a ship.

I could love you, if you just asked. That time was this time. This time they were above the picnic below and all the messy and painful digressions that had been a part of that couple. Only this time, all that there was between them was love and the warm breeze touching them as it swept towards the ancient bush behind them. "Singing," he whispered, taking Audrey's hand.

✦

Sometimes time stalls or you stall, and your every day is the same—day in, day out—until one day something changes. Bernadette hadn't spoken to Jane for over ten years. After their fight, and once Jane had become Sister Ava, Bernadette had effectively erased her, transforming her into a stranger, a Sister Ava character, who sent holiday cards, suggesting a friendliness that a typical stranger wouldn't. Eventually Bernadette treated her mail as though it was sent from a malevolent stranger, insisting to the postman that he return-to-sender each missive addressed from her. "I don't need to see them, Francis. You send them right back when they arrive."

The postman, Francis Jean, whose grandparents had emigrated from Southern Italy and who happened to be Catholic, was skeptical about Bernadette's mail. He didn't believe a convent nun could mistakenly send all those letters only to have each one dependably returned. There was something fishy about the set up and that Bernadette, a university professor, couldn't write her own return-to-sender note or, even better, send the poor nun a note to tell her she's got the wrong professor. For these reasons, Francis unfailingly delivered Sister Ava's mail, feigning forgetfulness—"Oh, no, did I miss that? Yeah, sorry!"—on those days when Bernadette brusquely handed one back to him with her own mark of rejection.

After Ted moved in with Bernadette, he only gradually became aware of the depth of the Sister Ava mail situation. When he asked Bernadette about it, she mentioned a senile nun, confined to a convent in Toowoomba, who'd for years been fixated on her. Bernadette's dismissive tone suggested that she had it handled and had for a while, which was par for the course for Bernadette, so Ted left it at that. He did wonder why the postman still delivered the nun's mail, but, with the never-ending negotiation of his love and live-in relationship with Bernadette and the speed at which the two of them negotiated and worked at their careers, these thoughts never lasted long.

It came up again, of course.

One afternoon, Ted arrived home early from his lab to find the message machine blinking with two messages. He'd cancelled his anatomy seminar lecture because four of his six medical students were out with the flu, and gauging from the coughs and sniffles of the other two, they'd be next. When he set his briefcase in the hallway by the machine, he was mentally staking out the herb bed that he intended to plant that afternoon: thyme beside oregano, basil beside parsley, then sage and rosemary. Parsley was so invasive though, he thought as he pressed the play button. That'd be as brilliant as bringing bunnies to Australia.

"Hello? Bernadette? I think this is your number. This is Ava. Jane, your sister. I'd rather not leave this as a message. Mum's fallen. It was a bad fall, Bernadette. Maybe you should call me. She's dead. Mum's dead."

An immeasurable quiet filled the line until it was broken by this woman's quick inhalation before the machine cut her off. The next message was the continuation of the first.

"Sorry. The funeral service is this Sunday in Mt. Isaac at 11:00. Dad is all right. Considering. She fell from the escarpment above Gilgin Downs. She'd not been herself lately. Is what they said. Anyway, it's slippery up there. They said that too. And that it was immediate. She didn't suffer. Oh. (Another inhalation) You can ring me at 212-089. Dad at 986-633. The circumstances, well, I'm sorry this is how we'll finally meet again."

Ted replayed the messages twice more. After he wrote the message on the pad beside the phone, he replayed them again. What am I doing? I've got to call Bernadette. Her mother has just died. As he decided this, after almost a decade together, he realized Bernadette wasn't someone he considered as having a mother, which was absurd of course, and, as this occurred to him, he realized Bernadette wasn't someone he considered being a mother, which meant he didn't consider himself as a father either. That the call had come from a Sister Ava didn't trouble him yet.

The immensity of what Ted had to convey to Bernadette slowed him. He put the kettle on, but decided to shave instead, a habitual delaying tactic that irritated Bernadette. Ted had never known his mother so the possibility of having a mother to die and the impossibility of having to hear and to accept her death at this late stage horrified him. Ted debated whether to drive back to Uni to tell Bernadette there, or to wait for her to come home, or could he somehow catch her in-between. Putting off the call and playing out scenarios, Ted realized was only delaying telling Bernadette this sad news, only delaying the pain and grief that would arrive with it.

Ted reported the news carefully as though he were translating it from a foreign language. Bernadette listened, but didn't respond. After an agonizing silence, Ted repeated it, adding how sorry he was and should he pick her up or start the trip arrangements to which Bernadette replied after another silent stretch, "Ted, I don't know a Sister Ava so I certainly don't know this Sister Ava's mother!" And before the pause could become a silence: "I spoke to Mum this morning. There's no way that she's dead."

The distance from Brisbane to Mt. Isaac was still roughly 965 kilometers as the crow flies, and still further depending on which land route you traveled by, what combination of bus, train, and car. Mt. Isaac for Bernadette was a remote speck that may as well have been in another galaxy where another Bernadette Pilgrim once existed.

Bernadette had received a letter from her mother the day before last. It was the same day that she'd returned a manuscript she'd reviewed for a colleague in Sydney. The arrival and departure of this mail could be verified by Cindy Beans, her secretary at Queens University, if anyone were to ask. The letter had been a surprise in that her mother rarely wrote to her. And strange, in the personal nature of it, but Bernadette would be glad to show it to anyone as proof that Audrey was alive. Australia Post could be slow, but not slow enough that something like this could happen in the meantime. This was just the kind of rumor that "that Sister Ava" would spread.

Bernadette strode angrily out of her office and stood over Cindy's desk. Cindy slowed. The Professor had the explosive quality of a shaken up soft drink about to be opened.
"Any post?"

Cindy routinely placed Bernadette's mail in her inbox after the 10:00 a.m. delivery. "Like what?" Cindy nervously licked her bottom lip. Although it was the afternoon, maybe if Cindy just knew what the professor needed, she could somehow accommodate her.

"Any post? You know letters, postcards? A postcard! Mail!"

"No, that's it for today, Professor." Bernadette's deflation was immediate. "But maybe tomorrow," Cindy said, registering this.

"Good! My mother is traveling and I expect she'll send postcards."

"Oh, I'm sure she will," Cindy assured her. "Where'd she go?"

"London. First to London; then on to Europe. She'd always planned to visit the Continent." Cindy Beans wished Bernadette's Mum would send her a postcard soon. Bernadette thought, what am I saying? This just can't be. Not this.

"Is that right? Fantastic!" Cindy called after Bernadette, who had turned back to her office with a bleak expression that worried Cindy.

✦

It was cold still, more winter than spring; a layer of frost coated the dry grass outside Mt. Isaac's parish church, a modest structure of wood and glass. As mourners filed into Saint Stephens, they visibly relaxed as their chills dissipated into the communal heat. We're no different than animals in a barn, Father Malcolm observed from the side. Although Bishop Gray had offered to preside over Audrey Pilgrim's funeral mass—the baptism could be postponed, but the highway dedication was higher profile and trickier to reschedule— Father Malcolm gladly did it. The Pilgrims had been part of his congregation since his arrival in Mt. Isaac. Their daughter, Jane, had essentially left their family for his family so the whole thing felt entirely personal.

Most of the congregants he'd known for years. He watched Louisa Cawley, their former mayor, now more active in the church since her divorce, place the hymn numbers on the board up front. She was more of a softie than people realized. Earlier she'd been quite upset telling him about her visit with Audrey the previous week.

Apparently, Louisa had found Audrey pacing back and forth in her backyard, searching the ground as though she'd lost something. "Are you okay, Audrey, I asked? She looked a little startled, but assured me she was. She then invited me to sit in the umpire chair. I went up—I didn't want to be rude—telling her the fantastic news that the representative of the State Art Council agreed to exhibit her quilt in Brisbane and if that worked out, fingers-crossed, on to the National Gallery." Louisa had suspected that Audrey hadn't recognized her— what with the yard search, lack of greeting besides the chair invitation, and that when Audrey had finally sat on the ground, she'd exclaimed:

"Lovely," referencing the grass not Louisa's news. "After a while—it was quite peaceful up there, Father—Audrey just out of the blue said 'Thanks for the chair, Louisa. What a difference you've made.'"

Rare for Louisa to show her emotions, Father Malcolm had held her hands as she'd collected herself. "You can be sure, Father, I'll get Audrey's quilt to Canberra even if I have to carry it there myself!"

The Pilgrims had had a rocky ride no doubt. Rumors of Audrey's depression, Alzheimer's, suicide—the whole gamut—seemed to be at play now in town or at least in Father Malcolm's parish. Reports of her past promiscuity had also resurfaced. Hardly helpful considerations at this juncture, but people always savored misfortune or controversy.

Luke 6:37: Do not judge, and you will not be judged. Do not condemn, and you will not be condemned. Forgive, and you will be forgiven. Give, and it will be given to you.

His homily on tolerance wouldn't be shelved anytime soon that's for sure.

Regardless, today: Father Malcolm brought himself back into the toasty room with his parishioners, where he signaled a hello to Joe Pearl and his lovely wife Sandy, who was chatting with Mary O'Neil still in that black veil. Behind them Brad and Mary Ellen Keys and their disabled adult son Dominic sat with Bill Turner from the garage, who—good man—had hired Dom as a "helper." Across the aisle from them were the Simpsons and the Delton's crew and, behind them, a handful of firefighters from Mt. Isaac's Fire Station. There were also plenty of family and friends that Father Malcolm hadn't been introduced to. It was a good showing. Sadly, the notable absence in this crowd was Bernadette Pilgrim, who, Ava—God bless her—still insisted was on her way. Regardless, today: Father Malcolm brought himself back again—today it was his honor to officiate this funeral to ensure that Audrey Pilgrim, singular person that she was, received the decent church service and burial that she deserved.

✦

The distances were not the same as before, and Ted was not Andrew. When Ted hung up with Bernadette, he bawled as though his mother had just died. The incongruence between the truth that he felt and the truth that had been expressed to him winded him as though Bernadette had taken her fist and belted him in the heart. He finally walked out into the yard to compose himself.

Bernadette breezed into their house as though she'd just arrived from a European tour. Ted met her near the door and, as they hugged she said, with a studied lightness, "You mustn't take any notice of that mad nun." She registered his flushed tear stained face, adding, "Mum's in Europe, Ted. She just left."

She didn't understand why Ted was so upset, why he'd be provoked to tears. "Ted?" This grief doesn't belong to you, she silently rebuked him, when, to her surprise, Ted pulled her into his arms.

"Oh, Bernadette," he quietly said, "This isn't right, this isn't right," and he started to rock her as though she wept and needed comfort.

So we shouldered our Matildas and turned our backs on town. Why this line came to Bernadette she didn't know, only that she felt she could use it as some line of action or maybe defense: a necessary filter to what was playing out between them. *We shouldered our Matildas,* she repeated, as a tool to steel herself from Ted's unasked-for embrace; *turned our backs on town* with the creeping sense of panic as she tried to push away from him and he pulled her in closer. When Ted said, "It'll be alright, Bern," she thought, what is he saying? Why is he saying that? And shoving herself away from him and he from her, she shouted: "What is wrong with you, Ted? My mother is alive!"

✦

The first postcard Bernadette received from her mother simply said, *Greetings from London!* Also: *Love, Mum.* It was dated three weeks after Sister Ava's message and, though postmarked domestically, it suggested it had been sent from London, England because beside the date was printed *London, England.* Four weeks later, a postcard arrived from Frankfurt, Germany, of the turn of the century Julius Pintsch Factory, with two smoke stacks in the center of a large rectangular brick complex. "*Dear Bernadette, Did you know that this factory manufactured the Edelmann Typewriters, the second mass produced typewriter in Europe!*" it said. "*And do you realize that if someone hadn't had the <u>courage</u> to move on from the Edelmann, we'd never have known the Smith Corona or the IBM Electric typewriter or the computer! Love, Mum.*"

✦

Ted brought up Sister Ava's messages each night over dinner, that sacrosanct time for them when they enjoyed the respite of the shared meal and conversation after a full day at work and before they'd break for more work or a good book or even a bit of "telly." That week they ate Shrimp Caesar, lamb chops and potatoes, pasta primavera, left-over chicken teriyaki, vegetable curry that Ted made from a spice packet, and fish and chips from Gordon's down the street: meals that would never sit right with either of them again. Ted, unsure of what he was doing, was sure that he needed to do something. With gentle persistence, he told himself, you could tease out the truth.

"This Sister Ava knew your name."

"Of course she did, Ted. She's been posting me cards and letters for years."

"Yeah, but there was a familiarity."

"She's been posting me cards and letters for years."

"But what's this about her name being Jane?"

"Ted, her name probably is Jane. Nuns change names."

"Not in the modern Catholic church they don't."

"Well, clearly this Jane did change her name." And after an uncomfortable pause —Bernadette had not spoken Jane's name in years—she said: "Anyway, who made you the authority on the modern Catholic Church?"

Bernadette hated Ted that week. She hated Sister Ava too, and the dreadful machine where she'd left that message. When Bernadette could no longer bear Ted's inquisitions, for that's how the dinners felt to her, she'd retire to her study to work, but would more often end up re-reading her Mother's last letter. Some clue would be revealed in it if only she looked hard enough. With the uncertainty about her mother's fate and that Bernadette couldn't bring herself to speak to Jane for fear of what she'd have to face—more complications than a person should have to face—Bernadette, as best she could, buried her fears and grief.

My Dear Girl,

This morning your father took four more sections of the quilt to the cleaners. It's an unwieldy piece. Too much to look at now that it's almost done.

✦

Robert and Ava received condolences from the stream of mourners entering the church. Robert's brother, Stewart, with his wife, Tammy, who had arrived the night before from Billum Downs, helped direct mourners to their pews. Ava recognized her mother's old boss and family, the Simpsons, and a host of other Mt. Isaac townspeople, including her old friend, Franca, who fiercely hugged her on her way to be seated. Her convent friends had come as well: Lily with her husband, John, and Brenda with her partner, Sue. There were plenty of people Ava didn't recognize and may have been curious about, but she, even after her father was seated inside and the congregation assembled, lingered in the vestibule hoping that the next face in the door would be Bernadette's, that somehow her sister's bus or train had been delayed, maybe her car had had a flat, maybe there was a chance that her answering machine was out-of-order, or maybe— Bernadette was an academic person, a professor—maybe she was just returning from a conference abroad and had had no time to tell them that she was delayed but on her way. Ava slipped outside into the cold air where the street and surrounds were unequivocally silent and still. "Come, Ava." Sister Jacinta had followed her. "It's time." Ava stalled a moment longer before she let Jacinta guide her to the front pew beside her father as George Volasheski played "How Great Thou Art" on his accordion at Robert's request.

✦

"Why don't you ever speak about your family?" Ted handed Bernadette the jar of mint sauce for her lamb. "I mean you know all about my brothers, George and Ed."

"Who speaks about brothers and sisters they don't have, Ted?"

Bernadette, there's no easy way to advise a person. No good way to caution. But, those things that you're most certain about can become hazy with time. And what you think you'll never forget, you do forget. And after a while you become this vacillating and forgetting person.

Aging isn't straightforward, Bernadette.

After the first, Audrey's postcards arrived punctually every four weeks. There was one from Barcelona and one from West Bromwich mentioning, really celebrating, the historic typewriter factories in each town as well as providing tidbits on successful management of secretaries intermixed with advice about "letting go." After months of postcards, a commentary about typewriter manufacturing had emerged, each postcard with a peculiar—it wasn't exactly nostalgia—fascination with these intricate machines as precursors to the computers used by secretaries worldwide. It was as though Audrey were using her tour to teach Bernadette about typewriters, the secretarial landscape, and, how was this possible, acceptance.

The best secretarial/manager relationships are partnerships not dictatorships. In my day Bernadette, the best way to achieve this was through open, mutually respectful lines of communication. Shared tea breaks are nice too.

P.S. the Olivetti Typewriter is Valentines red, which made me think of the vice versa principal: Just as every Mum has to let their beloved child go, every child has to let their beloved Mum go.

Bye now, M

Bernadette couldn't openly admit that, even more than Jane's wills, Audrey's postcards disturbed her. How was she to interpret the oddness of having your "mother" visit towns of obsolete typewriter factories and lecture you about secretaries when Audrey hadn't been an active secretary in more than two decades and, as far as Bernadette knew, had no interest in typewriters. And what about the adages that were neither in her mother's handwriting, nor of a subject that her mother would ever choose to write about as far as Bernadette knew. How was Bernadette to interpret, when, a month later, Audrey, now in Belleville, France, *"the site of the famous Continsousa Etablissments where the Contin typewriters were made"* persisted?

Don't be overly concerned with number of words per minute; often quality trumps quantity.

Likewise, having a good parent for a short time beats having a bad parent for too long.

Bernadette refused to be ruffled by the postcards' domestic stamps and local postmarks. And refused to directly consider the postcards' authorship.

Promise, Love, never leave yourself nowhere to go. Be active about your options. Make plans before the forgetting begins. That's right, plan to forget.

✦

Although Robert did later question Audrey's insistence to view her quilt from the escarpment above Gilgin Downs and his decision to help her, questioned her growing detachment from the quilt that she'd dedicated herself to, later wondered about those tender episodes mixed with ones where she was so lost in thought that she hardly recognized him, at the funeral that day Robert numbly shook hands with the hands offered to him and nodded back at the sympathetic nods that he received. At the Peace Be With You part of the mass, as he shook Ava's hand, he said: "I don't recognize all these people. Do you think they're our button people, Sister?"

✦

"My mum died giving birth to me. My dad raised us. Why don't I know a thing about your parents?"

"My dad died…" Bernadette faltered. She pushed back from the table and, rising, slammed the bowl of rice against the tabletop. "I can't. Get your own bloody curry!"

Cindy Beans' solicitous announcements about the arrival of Audrey's postcards exhausted Bernadette. She felt more and more hemmed in to a stance that, although chosen, felt increasingly claustrophobic. She didn't like the publicity of postcards or that Cindy was tracking them. On those days a postcard might be due, Bernadette, best she could, tried to avoid Cindy, checking her in-box when she'd stepped away from her desk.

Very excited for today I'm in Berlin at the Senta Typewriter Factory. Frister & Rossman manufactured these portable typewriters as well as, get this: SEWING MACHINES. This secretary quilter couldn't be happier!

While Bernadette knew that the postcards weren't actually Audrey's, to Ted she insisted they were. "Mum is in Leicester." "Belleville now"—each destination pointedly saying, you're wrong not to believe me, Ted. "See," she said, holding the first card up for him. "See," her hand trembling, "you were unkind to question me on the worst week of my life." Ted refused to comment about the first card or any of the cards that followed it, optimistically noting that at least Bernadette had admitted that the week itself had been grievous enough to be termed "worst." "You tell me, Ted. What dead mother sends postcards from Europe's typewriter towns?"

Like me, I know you get swept up. Mind that, Love. I can't be certain, but I think how we make our path does influence where it ends.

All love is uneasy. Don't shy away from that, Bernadette. I can't remember just why I say that now, but it's, I think, important to say to you.

✦

The grief that Ava experienced over the death of her mother was offset by her anger towards Bernadette for not responding to her phone call, and worse, not coming for their mother's service, and by her relief at the immense support given her newly widowed father.

After Stewart and Tammy returned to Billum Downs, the ladies from the town's organizations and associations coordinated meals for the grieving man for well over four months. It wasn't just Robert's fellow workers at Delton's like Mrs. Johnson of Linens and Fabric, who regularly bought by fruit salad, but the customers—Marcy Phelps, Julie McInerny, and Jan Tyndon, and even their adult children—who he'd served, never imagining that they might reciprocate with cakes and casseroles and invitations for Sunday dinner. Even the men were generous with invites to the pub, local footie and cricket matches as well as lawn bowls after Sunday services.

Many were people that Robert had never met, but who knew him because of Audrey's quilt and included him as she'd included their buttons into her life's work. When Robert looked at the situation this way, and he tried to during the day when he deliberated on what to do with the leftover pails of buttons and at night, when alone under a square of Audrey's quilt that he couldn't yet bring himself to reattach, it helped lessen his sense of loss and even slightly comforted him that Audrey might've somehow planned it this way.

Ava, on her return to St. Ursula's, called Bernadette at the University, where she assumed Bernadette could less likely dodge her call.

"Good Morning. Professor Pilgrim's office. Can I help you?"

Ava was momentarily lost for words, wary of how her feelings might affect her ability to communicate.

"Sorry. This is Cindy Beans. I'm Professor Pilgrim's secretary." Cindy sensed that the person at the end of the line was reluctant to speak. The professor's students could often be bashful when they called.

"Hello Cindy. This is Sister Ava Pilgrim, Professor Pilgrim's sister."

"Seriously? Seriously! I didn't know the Professor had a sister."

It was a delicate phone call really so Ava said, "This is a delicate phone call, Cindy."

"I can be discrete; it's part of my secretarial training," Cindy immediately responded.

"Our Mother was a secretary once, before she became a quilter."

"Seriously! Like me? I didn't know that either."

Ava could hear the kindness in Cindy Beans' tone. Bernadette was fortunate to work with someone so good-natured. That was something positive she could say to Bernadette. Cindy, excited to learn more about the Professor from her secret sister, then asked:

"Have you heard from your Mum? Professor Pilgrim seems quite concerned that she hasn't received any post from her since she's been on holidays overseas."

There it was: Bernadette. Unadulterated Bernadette. And at first for Ava, no breath or words.

She collected herself and finally, calmly, told Cindy that their Mother had recently died and that no, there would be no post from her and yes—after Bernadette's phone number was verified by Cindy—Bernadette knew that. Bernadette had also known about their Mum's death early enough to come to her service. This last part Ava didn't share with Cindy as Cindy clearly cared about Bernadette and Ava didn't wish to undermine that beyond what she had.

"Shall I tell her that you called? She's in a lecture currently."

"No, that's not actually necessary." Ava felt hollow and heavy, bleary and clear-sighted. Is this how surrender feels? Or is this just defeat? Whatever it was, Ava knew that there was no more to be done here: no more letters or calls to be made. Ava could understand Bernadette's rejection of their father and even partially understand Bernadette's rejection of her—she'd relentlessly pursued Bernadette to deal with their father and, most likely, Ava was too much of reminder of what they'd suffered together. Who knows? But this, this was gratuitous. Their mum had been Bernadette's advocate, had praised her independence, had called for Ava's forbearance in dealing with her strong personality, had assured Ava that however much they fought … enough, Ava. "I appreciate all your help today, Cindy. Really, you're very kind. Take good care. God Bless."

Whereas Ava experienced a cheerless closure that morning, Cindy Bean's world was upended. She felt terrible for Professor Pilgrim, who was clearly so grief struck that she couldn't admit that her mum, a secretary like Cindy, and an artist on top of that, was gone for good. Maybe she could help though—maybe her sister, Sister Ava's call was a call to help. Cindy slipped out to the newsagents, where she bought a postcard of Trafalgar Square and a stamp. On the card, she wrote:

Dear Bernadette,

Greetings from London!

✦

"Some properties and towns aren't big enough to be mapped, are they?" said Ted, laying the dinner plates on the table as Bernadette dumped their fish and chips from the newspaper onto them. "What's Mount Isaac like?"

She pushed a serviette across to him from where she sat.

"Your faculty bio says you were raised there. Like I was raised in Southport. But you knew that."

Bernadette ate a chip then salted the rest. She tasted the fish. "Local chip shop sells flake: shark meat," she said, examining her piece. "Plenty of sharks in Southport, but you knew that, yes?"

Ted silently watched her performance. "Bernadette, I ordered last week's editions of *The Central County Gazette.*"

Bernadette rose, scuttled the fish and chips in the sink, and wordlessly retreated to the bedroom. Oh, Mum, how I miss you.

I'm getting closer, Ted thought, or maybe just meaner.

Bernadette would say that she was Ted's humming girl from the library. Ted would say that she was his weeping one. Yet it wasn't just her vulnerability that he'd fallen for, although he knew that some men were susceptible to that and a whole lot of nonsense about saving and caregiving. He had fallen for her vulnerability, so ill hidden, and her reckless determination that no one should see it, and bizarre insistence that no one could. As he sang to her that day in the library, he'd felt riveted because he'd never felt anything like it. He'd hung around even in the face of a stream of boyfriends, so that when her other beaus abandoned her for easier matches, he remained. Sometimes he wondered if she was testing him, and at other times he wondered if he was testing himself. Ted knew that he'd finally made it to her, entered that private lexicon of her soul or the place it might be (he was a skeptic about these things), when, after they'd slept together, Bernadette confided how once, when a boyfriend came out of the shower, his pink legs reminded her of a bowerbird she'd once seen, and she'd felt disappointed when she'd looked up the rest of his pale body.

The awareness of his own pale body wasn't something that Ted felt until recently. As their relationship deepened, he'd felt like an insider with Bernadette and assumed that he was. Now he realized there was much that Bernadette kept from him, a load of pain kept hidden. The success of marriage, his father had always told him, what allowed his and his mother's relationship to flourish, was the twining of people's inside details. "The sacred unburdening," he'd call it. Ted couldn't bridge the gap by himself. Only Bernadette could supply her details. For the first time, Ted understood with certainty that desire alone wouldn't be good enough, wouldn't last. Yet, with gentle persistence, he told himself again, you could succeed at anything, even love.

Remember Bernadette, it's not enough to open your arms to life. You have to open your arms, thighs, and expose your entire body, mind, and soul to it. Love, you have to walk straight at it.

You are of my heart dear girl—

> *Your mother,*
> *Audrey Pilgrim*

✦

After the ocean covered the Arafura Plain and the Great Australian Bight, the land link between Australia and Papua New Guinea had been severed; after epic inland floods and droughts and new arid zones that had to be abandoned altogether; after the Dutchman, Willem Jansz, landed on the tip of Cape York and Captain Cook arrived on the east coast a century later; after the freed convicts, the pastoralists, the massacres of Aborigines, and the gold rush with its surge of immigrant miners and entrepreneurs and the rebound legislation restricting them all; after "world" wars and advances in modern warfare—chemical, incendiary, atomic, and germ—and the Royal Horticultural Society commended Melbourne's Botanical Garden for its rose, lily, and lavender collections; and, not so far offshore: the fall of Saigon, the Indonesian invasion of East Timor, and the "granting" of independence to Papua New Guinea; at the advent of the Web, mass communication, and social media, only a year after the death of the Queensland quilter, A. Pilgrim, Bernadette and Ted separated and Bernadette relocated to a flat in Kelvin Grove.

"This is not the type of leaving we typically do." Captain Sturt sounded irritable. Although it had been more than five publications since Bernadette had considered Captain Sturt and his expeditions, his arrival on a late night at Kelvin Grove didn't surprise her. Bernadette was trying to organize him, situate him back at the meeting place with the Chiefs for the friendship ceremony on their return from the Central Australian expedition. She'd glossed over it before, which now, years later, still bugged her.

Bernadette sat before the flat's picture window, looking beyond her reflection to the street and parked cars and oak trees bathed in an orangey, almost dirty light from the street lamps. "I've missed something, haven't I, Captain?"

"This is not the type of leaving we typically do."

How and why this had any bearing on the return leg of their expedition, Bernadette didn't know. "That's past," she corrected. "This is the return," she added, as though Sturt was confused. There was a possibility that Bernadette had misunderstood. "What type of leaving do we typically do?" she then politely asked.

It was quiet in the apartment. Because it was still sparsely furnished, it seemed larger than it was. Ted's and her place had evolved into a cluttered but cozy space. Here rugs would reduce the echo and please the neighbors downstairs as well.

"I have a question for you, Pilgrim." Sturt interrupted. "You wrote: Quote: *Charlotte Christiana was once described as 'the woman who allowed a husband to go on and on trying to prove something to himself about himself, while she grew sadder, and sadder, and sadder.'* With respect to her sadness, do you blame her for that, for taking that stance about me or am I to be blamed for being that man, who had to prove himself, which put her in the position of being that sad?"

"Actually, someone else 'once described' her that way," Bernadette replied.

"So, you have no stance on Charlotte Christiana's sadness?"

"Stance?"

"So, you have no opinion about the levels of her sadness?"

"No, I'm sad she was sad," she quickly countered.

"Really?"

"Really, yes, there can be no one as sad as me about the degrees of sadness she was contending with." Bernadette honestly didn't know where he was headed.

"So, Pilgrim, it doesn't bother you that the toll of my self-proof—if indeed that is what it is—is Charlotte Christiana's sadness?"

"You're an explorer! Explorers explore!" Bernadette felt defensive, but this was true. Sturt, hopefully, would feel enough validated to move on. When he didn't respond, she added, "Which is not to say that I'm not sensitive to Charlotte Christiana's sorrow."

"So, Pilgrim, as far as I can tell, you have a host of loved ones who are tending toward the Charlotte Christiana model."

Bernadette scraped her chair back. She hadn't anticipated this.

"Would you think differently of me if, say, I had Charlotte Christiana growing sad at the same rate as my friends, Duncan and Fitz?"

"I'm sorry about the rate of Charlotte Christiana's sadness. I am. But I can't speak to the increasing sadness of Duncan or Fitz. I don't even know who they are." Bernadette couldn't believe this.

"Or would you think differently of me if, say, I really wasn't off proving something to me about me, but simply was avoiding something about me?"

Bernadette tracked the fruit bats flying like swallows between the lamps and trees. Those bats needed to settle.

"There's a distinction, and here in this, Pilgrim, is what you've missed; is why this isn't the type of leaving we do."

Bernadette shut her eyes to shut him out. Focus now, Bernadette.

In the cypress grove, it was late in the day and although sunny, there were no shadows. An older native man, the Chief, was seated on a log, drawing figures in the dirt with a stick. Two even older men were crouched beside him. There was no sound in the grove although Bernadette saw signs: tears on the face of one man and the other men's mouths open in what must've been chants. Beside her, Sturt stood before the Chief, assisted by Medical Officer Browne. Behind her, the expedition party, loosely assembled, looked on. The suspicion on their emaciated faces and jealousy about this friendship ceremony didn't need words.

Bernadette was surprised to see Jarri, of her and Jane's childhood expedition days, standing beside the Chief. No longer a boy, he wore a Coca Cola T-shirt printed with the lyrics, *I'd Like to Teach the World to Sing*, and lighting up a smoke, he said, "G'day, Bernadette. Long time no see. Where's Ship Sailor?"

"Let me, as leader to the Central Australian Expedition, present you with a token of our friendship." Sturt interrupted him, and handed Bernadette his blanket to offer to the Chief. The blanket must've smelled rancid: smoky, faintly of ammonia and rot: Sturt in the desert and along the Darling River for months unbathed. The blanket must've been heavy, too: caked with dirt and sweat, infested with bugs. Yet Bernadette could neither smell it nor feel its weight. She couldn't feel the warmth of the day, although she could see sweat shine on the faces of all the men in the grove. It dawns on her, that without reliable senses, she's misreading all the signs.

Jarri laughed. "No duh! If you can't feel anything, how do you expect to exchange anything? That's right, you don't exchange shit, Bernie!"

What the hell! Bernadette squelched her impulse to leave the grove.

"Lose land. Lose family. Lose sky relations." The Chief was now audible. Sturt smiled and bowed as though the Chief had graciously accepted his blanket, which he hadn't because Bernadette still held it. Jarri good-naturedly took it from her.

Chief asked, "Where are you from Englishman? India? Australia? Cheltenham?" The Chief knew Sturt's history.

"Brisbane? Mt. Isaac? Meralamgee riverbed?" Jarri added, winking at Bernadette. "She's missed something," Sturt informed Jarri.

Somewhere southwest of Menindee in a flat in Kelvin Grove,

Bernadette feels exposed; naked, she needs the blanket back. Jarri cradles it. Bernadette tries to get Sturt's attention, but he is ignoring her. Bernadette reworks the scene again and again each time Sturt ignores her, which is every time. Always he remains one step out of reach and deaf to her pleas to intercede with Jarri about the blanket. Bernadette appeals to the Chief, but the Chief stares at the dirt before him, unaware of her presence. And why she would think that the naked Native people would care about her nakedness is a question she ignores, as she does why she keeps, in each revision, voluntarily giving the blanket to Jarri. That she is desperate for this dirty blanket, this cloak and token of friendship, is all she knows right then.

"I own this meeting," Bernadette declared, in an attempt to reassert control over the situation, before beginning to rework the scene. This time I'll start with a hand on Sturt's elbow. He'll feel me beside him. And when this time I need his help, he'll help. This time I'll sit in the dirt in front of the Chief. He'll see me. Bernadette was repeatedly confronted with a landscape where no one touches or hears or recognizes each other, where explorer, Native, and woman, although occupying the same space, exist at such different times that overlap and understanding and cooperation seem impossible. In this place of her making she was alone.

"Can't manipulate everything, poor bugger," Jarri congenially said as Bernadette looked up to see her reflection in the windowpane: an aging woman, longing, like a child, for her family and home, and for Ted. She felt even more exposed. As though her want were weakness, Bernadette reproached her.

Although this Bernadette wasn't someone Bernadette wanted to see, she stared at her. Maybe if she stared long enough she could stall time and suspend her attention to everything around her: not have to recognize the jealousy of Sturt's men was made of longings like hers, not witness the heartbreak of those men in the grove, whose ancestral home was about to be stolen and colonized, not appreciate the empty room behind her. Just by looking at herself, she wouldn't actually have to attend to the longing in that woman's face along with those of the men in the grove, the sorrow of the Charlotte Christianas and Teds and Janes all about her.

Bernadette Pilgrim, with her sights filled with her own reflection, felt the weight of everyone around her "growing sadder and sadder and sadder," but couldn't sensibly parse anything together to responsibly act. Bernadette, her sights filled with her own reflection, didn't recognize that everyone in the grove but her had ceded their present and that her present was rapidly dwindling.

Sturt knew. He cleared his throat to get her attention. Bernadette saw that not much had changed. Everyone in the grove was arranged the same. Something was different though. She looked over at Jarri, who was now spreading Sturt's blanket on the ground while singing "Botany Bay." She didn't know which part of this upset her more. Jarri stood and, like he was rubbing it in, saluted her like Ship Sailor, saying, "You'll manage, hey. That's what you do on expeditions."

"Keep it, Jarri! Keep your bloody blanket! I'll get my own!" Bernadette shouted at him. And louder, "I never wanted a blanket in the first place!" Bernadette Pilgrim, in impervious denial once again, carefully avoiding her reflection, gracelessly swallowed enough cold medicine to knock her out for the rest of the night. Sturt called after her: "This is not the type of leaving we do, Pilgrim," as Stowaway Andrew, not without a speck of irony, welcomed her to the world of happy-go-lucky ne'er-do-wells. "Champagne, Bernadette?"

Sturt and his party remained with the Chiefs and Jarri in the grove. Audrey Pilgrim joined them, as did Charlotte Christiana, Poole and Banks. The insects hummed and clicked, the birds screaled, chattered, and screeched above their heads. Sweat pocketed, pooled then poured down their torsos, soaking them. They rested together on the fragrant blanket, since they were also susceptible to the sedative effects of Bernadette's medication. Here they waited for their poor fellow Bernadette to wake up to herself.

The next morning was overcast. Bernadette gulped down coffee hoping the caffeine would buck the dread that the night before had stirred up. Why did thinking and writing about Sturt always become some crazy psychodrama? She wished she'd chosen someone more normal to follow although she couldn't imagine anyone who was more normal.

It was the beginning of the weekend. She wondered if Ted would be fixing breakfast for someone else yet. There was no shadow or depth to the gray day. Jane hasn't written to me in over a year. Since Mum's death. These quiet admissions held Bernadette at the front window a moment longer, the mug heavy in her hand, a shrill car alarm down the street, penetrating the room. She watched a truck back up into the neighbor's drive, the sides decorated with yellow, blue and red crate paper woven into the railings, reminding her of the nerves and veins and arteries of an anatomical model Ted had once shown her. Bernadette didn't wait to see what was loaded onto the truck for she'd gone to shower, readying herself for the drive to Toowoomba.

✦

Saint Ursula's convent life, for the most part, suited Ava. One of the few complaints she had was that the convent's wear was showing.

"Surely the archdiocese could afford to give us fresh paint?"

Sister Jacinta agreed, explaining that St. Ursula's was a lower priority than its sister schools in Brisbane after which she said: "Focus on what you can control, Sister." Jacinta often spoke to Ava as though she were speaking to herself, which wasn't always evident to Ava, who found her at times both tone-deaf and intrusive.

"Maybe Sister, since our sister schools don't have to contemplate their peeling wallpaper, they can solve the permeable boundary problem that is rampant in our intentional communities." Needless to say, this was another of Ava's pet peeves.

Day to day, however, Ava barely noticed the convent's decline or cared about porous boundaries. She lived in a routine where she would daily call on the support of her childhood saints, acts of faith and nostalgia both, to address her immediate needs. For example, when she was upset that the feral cat that she'd been feeding had been poisoned, she prayed to the Saint Francis of Assisi she remembered from under the stairs, with his dry altar bed of eucalyptus leaves and gum-nuts. After she'd falsely accused Micky Riley, their janitor, of poisoning the cat, she turned to the Saint Josaphat of the altar in the dining room with cellophane and pipe cleaners to intercede and help Micky forgive her, after he'd rejected her apology. For Ava's students, blessed with more intense awkward and rebellious phases than usual, access to her saint support was indispensable when her didactic skills failed her.

It was funny how Ava had to continually relearn the connectedness of them all. After dinner the night of the cat's death, Sister Mary, Sister Elizabeth, and Sister Amina dropped by to assist her with kitchen duty, each sharing their own pet fatality story. Ava recalled her Saint Martha altar and recited its attached prayer, which her Nan had given to her:

> *"Lords of the pots and pipkins,*
> *Since I have not time to be*
> *A Saint by doing lovely things*

And vigiling with thee,
By watching in the twilight dawn
And storming Heaven's gates,
Make me a Saint by getting meals
And washing up the Plates."

The absurdity wasn't lost on them. The sisters had laughed at themselves, grieving together for their beloved pets as they powered towards sainthood, dishtowels and sponges in hand.

What Ava began to realize though, was that while, yes, access to the saints via her father's inventory mattered, the creation and use of her own inventories were equally important in deepening her faith and forging community. In some of her inventories, Ava listed struggles (petty and profound) and short- and long-term resolutions, and action items based on these resolutions towards uncovering the better self of herself, where she now trusted God resided and had faith—granted, not unwavering—that even if it took all her life's work to get to Him—a given—she could. So far, she had compiled eleven volumes.

The fourth volume contained the joys and disappointments, surprises and sorrows that the older nuns divulged to her while she changed their linens or helped bath and dress them. Ava would read the joyful and surprising parts back to them on their darker days. Occasionally, as long as Sister Jacinta wasn't around, Ava would share with them excerpts from Volume Nine: bawdy nun jokes she'd heard from her students as well as the gardeners and workmen who tended the convent.

"If they have walkers in heaven, I'm coming back here," Hedvig informed Ava one day in the infirmary, as she assisted the older nun from the bed to the chair beside it. Hedvig's legs wobbled as though they might buckle and her entire arms blanched from the firmness of her grip.

"My guess is that walkers stall forever in Purgatory. Theirs is a thankless job, Hedvig." Hedvig considered her walker's metallic frame, which had kept her upright and mobile these last years, realizing that she could do no better or worse than she'd done. She dragged it closer, keeping a hand on it as though at any moment someone might snatch it. Ava heard Jacinta's quick clip along the corridor grow louder. "Maybe if it had a bit more color. Could we paint it, Ava? A drab walker in heaven won't do."

"Sisters!" Jacinta stood at the infirmary door.

"Sister," they returned.

"Ava, your sister is in the courtyard." Ava stared at Sister Jacinta as though she hadn't heard. "I took it upon myself to prepare afternoon tea for you and your sister. It's on the tray in the reception area." Family disrupted. Jacinta knew that Ava's sister in particular was a master at this.

Ava walked quickly towards the courtyard, not so much cognizant that it'd been twelve years since she'd seen Bernadette, but that Bernadette had been waiting for her as long as it had taken Sister Jacinta to prepare the tea. As she advanced down the corridor of the residential wing of the convent, Ava passed station after station of the cross—Jesus condemned, His Cross, His Falls, His Mum. It had been just over a year since their mum had passed. Ava turned to the wall on the other side to see Our Lady of Fatima, Our Lady of Lourdes, then back to the stations—Simon and Veronica's help, the Nails, the Death, and after, after. What would Bernadette look like? What would they say to each other; would she be sorry? *I hope she's all right. I shouldn't have left Hedvig so abruptly. Was kind of Sister Jacinta, the tea, doing that. Finally, she's come. She's come. We adore you, O Christ, and we bless you. Because of Your holy cross You have redeemed the world.* Here we go.

When Ava stepped into the courtyard, face flushed and slightly out of breath, Bernadette had her back to her and was examining the statue of Nano Nagle, the founder of the Presentation Sisters. Bernadette had decided ten minutes earlier that a real resemblance to Nano Nagle was unlikely and now, staving off an impatience that made her want to leave, Bernadette analyzed the statue's figure: height lengthened to embody power and a face depicted as demure, devoted, and dictatorial all at once. She'd never met such a body and face so brimming with values.

"Bernadette?" Ava rushed across the cement to her. "Bernadette, how well you look." Ava went to hug her, her arms extended, her face—Bernadette did recognize this although only later—filled with excitement and anticipation and no trace of judgment.

"Don't get all nunny with me, Jane." Bernadette intercepted Ava's hands, squeezed and released them, pushing her away like a boat from shore.

Ava, startled, confused, then hurt, silently led Bernadette through the courtyard up the stairs of the convent house to the parlor room where Sister Jacinta's tea sat cooling on a tray. As she watched Bernadette settle in the Elizabethan chair, she thought, *We adore You, O Christ, and we bless You,* and, biting her lip, Oh surely not this. Bernadette thought. What am I doing here?

"I suppose you don't mind living with all these women?" Bernadette swirled her wrist in a gesture Ava interpreted as more dismissive than inclusive.

"Well, it's like being part of the crew of one of our old voyages, Bernadette." Time had not softened her impatience and temper. "We all try in our, well, yes, flawed ways to get along, to be effective teachers, and, always, at the same time, to be better human beings." Bernadette scowled. "Have a scone. They're fresh."

"You're doing that nunny thing again, Jane."

Ava, self-conscious, noted that Bernadette was dressed as if out of a fashion catalogue, and that she herself looked "nunny" in her habit and was, in fact, a middle-aged nun. That thought aired, Ava relaxed, as though the unconscious holding in of it was what was distressing her. She prepared a cup of tea with a generous portion of milk and three heaping teaspoons of sugar, admiring Bernadette's dress that accentuated curves much like their mother's. Her mother had once compared the whiteness of refined sugar to the color of The Singing Ship, she remembered. A gracious thought.

Bernadette glared at the picture of the Sacred Heart of Jesus over Jane's shoulder and said: "I had to leave Ted because he was so insipid. I'm serious, Jane, the man would do anything I said. How can you trust that?"

Ted, who's Ted? Ava supposed that Ted was someone a typical sibling should know.

"Tea, Bernadette?"

"Yes, good. No sugar."

"Is he someone you've been seeing?" It disconcerted Ava not to know anything about her sister, really. She thought she'd be accustomed to it with Bernadette by now. But, never mind, here they were talking. Here, Bernadette had come to her like one of her students with love problems. Here was her sister, who'd missed their mother's funeral and burial, talking to her about love.

"I suppose you don't understand men stuff, though, right?"

Ava handed the cup to Bernadette, who nodded thanks. "They're people, aren't they, Bernadette?" Ava saw a fly land on the jam and suddenly felt sorry for Sister Geneviere with her germ phobia, at the same time aware that Bernadette's glare included her, accusing her of what, she wasn't sure.

"Are there lesbians here, then?"

"Please, Bernadette…" Why did she always make it hard?

"You must be full of doubts?"

"It's normal to have doubts," Ava answered. Her thought, as fleeting as she might admit, was how her life might've been, had Bernadette shown up at those times when Bernadette was expected. "You know the quilt was huge by the time Mum died."

Bernadette set her teacup back on the coffee table. Jane had no right to bring up that blanket now.

Ava watched Bernadette's eyes travel over the room's discolored walls and peeling wallpaper, collecting evidence, she was sure, of a cheap religious life and vindication of Jane's stubbornness at not leaving the convent when she was advised to. Bernadette was thinking, No need to put yourself through this, Bernadette.

"It's bigger than this room. And tremendously beautiful. Dad still sleeps under a square." Neither of them had touched the scones. "Any interest in seeing it?"

Bernadette didn't respond. Fool for coming. Ava read from the mild grimace on Bernadette's face that she'd already dismissed Ava, along with their parents, and that she'd come to see that Jane was shipwrecked here and should be given up for lost. She thought of saying "I'm not lost," but instead said, "Do you listen to the wireless ever? I like the music on 4BC, but also I like ABC for their news and talk programs." Instead of what Ava could tell Bernadette about the funeral and their father's adjustment to a widower's life, it seemed suddenly more important for Ava to convey her own pleasure from listening to the wireless, for Bernadette to know that Ava's students actually thought she was a difficult but insightful teacher, attuned to their hopes and troubles. "I pray for you daily, Bernadette," Ava said, adding, "You know, I pray for us all, actually."

"Oh, Jane, you don't change, do you?" Bernadette stood. The immensity of the distance that she'd put between them was as plain to her as the impossibility of retracing her steps. What good was an unfamiliar family, Mr. Ted; what would you know, Jarri? Sturt? Who was he but a subject to close the book on? Jane was at least cared for here, Bernadette dismissively thought, and stepping out of the parlor she muttered, "How can you stand the smell of mildew in here?"

Ava had had a host of things she'd wanted to tell Bernadette.

Somehow it was hard to fit her life and faith into a language that Bernadette would understand and accept.

She considered if that had always been the case between them. Hardly possible, although she wasn't sure anymore. Even before Bernadette had stepped off the convent's bottom step, Ava was telling her about the first days at the convent—about Lily and Brenda who'd left—and how after, she'd had that crisis of faith, but she stayed because this was her community. She knew that now. As she watched Bernadette turn down the path by the roses and rhododendrons that Sister Michael had tended until her death, she mentioned how funny and wonderful this group of women could be, (how they'd rallied around her after their mum's death), but couldn't always be, because of those same fears and hurts that other people had, and sure they were peculiar and struggled, but wasn't that everyone? As Bernadette turned and looked over her shoulder at St. Ursula's and Jane, Ava was mentioning her students to her: how hard she worked to keep them safe and secure and make them secure in themselves and how sometimes she saw that same look on their faces that she'd seen on Bernadette's at the riverbed and she'd do anything to remove that. For that strain and singleness—that look—just wasn't the case, wasn't true. By the time Bernadette reached her car and was driving down Piedmont, Ava was practically shouting that the point, that the point was not the expeditions or voyages, the floating—no, it wasn't—it wasn't the floating or even drowning, but the water, them together in the water. And that that was okay and she and they were all okay because that was the point.

Later that afternoon of Bernadette's visit, Ava asked Sister Jacinta to see her own file. From it, she took the record of her interview with the Presentation Sisters. The next day, she photocopied the document titled On the "Strength" of My Call in the teacher's staff room while Mrs. McKinney, the Ancient History teacher, complained about the colored chalk in her 9B classroom that kept going missing. Ava wrote a note at the bottom of the copy before she slipped it into an envelope, addressing it to Professor Bernadette Pilgrim at Queens University in Brisbane. She took a stamp from the stamp basket, which was kept on the side table in the convent office. And she walked to the postbox at the corner of Bellevue and Bonny Avenue to mail it. A breeze whipped her veil high onto her head and swept across the nape of her neck, which felt like a caress, which pleased her. She wondered if the breezes were like this in Ireland and if Nano

Nagle had felt such a breeze as this or Martha and Mary on the desert steppes in the Holy Land or her mum seated high up on her umpire chair. So many breezes, she thought, turning back toward the convent. *And we bless You. In the name of God. Amen.*

✦

Bernadette was waiting for Ted in her office at Queens University when Cindy Beans brought her the day's post. She hadn't felt this good in ages. She'd just heard that she was being awarded the Australian Academy of History Morris Hullup Prize for her distinguished work in preserving Australian history. She'd received other awards, but this one she truly hadn't expected. Ted, ironically, was one of the first people she'd wanted to tell and there he was: his appointment sandwiched between her eight o'clock lecture and eleven o'clock appointment. How Ted became scheduled Cindy couldn't explain, except that: "He, Professor Ackers, said that you and he had footnotes to revise before the paper's final deadline. Final, final, he said."

Cindy had a way of flabbergasting Bernadette. She considered reminding Cindy that Ted was an Anatomist, that Anatomists and Historians didn't typically share critical work, that although Ted— didn't she know this already—and Bernadette had lived together for years, they didn't any longer so he couldn't just pop by to visit whenever he liked. Theirs had been a swift and amiable parting. Yes, she'd given Ted her new number, which he hadn't called. She couldn't feel hurt by this, since she'd left him. She'd had to. He'd gradually insinuated himself into her past, insisting that she attend to it as though somehow he considered her past his or, at least, enough affecting his that he should get a say. He'd spun her up and been personal in a way that no one had any business being.

Cindy, Bernadette knew, sensed that something wasn't right with the schedule. When she was nervous, she'd repeatedly lick her bottom lip and every so often clear her throat. She did this now.

"Shall I bring you and Professor Ackers tea, then," she said, "when he arrives?"

"That'd be terrific," Bernadette replied, adding: "I just heard that I received the Morris Hullup Prize, Cindy."

"That's fantastic! Congratulations. That's hard to get."

Partnerships not dictatorships, Bernadette repeated to herself, acknowledging the stack of postcards set beneath her Charles Sturt paperweight. "Shall we celebrate with lunch sometime next week?"

"Yes, I'd really enjoy that, Professor."

"When Ted comes, get some tea for yourself, Cindy," Bernadette said, wondering what exactly Ted had meant by "final, final." With that she uncapped a red marker and began her review of Lucinda Phung's graduate thesis about the drover boss, Edna Jessop.

Bernadette was through the Intro section when Cindy interrupted to hand her the day's post. She didn't realize at first that the letter was from Jane as there was no return address on the envelope. Neither was there a *Dear Bernadette* or *Love, Jane* or even, *Yours in Christ, Sister Ava*, although Bernadette knew Jane wouldn't actually write that to her. In fact, it wasn't a letter at all, but rather a Xeroxed page of an essay handwritten on the Sisters of the Presentation of the Blessed Virgin Mary stationary, dated more than a decade earlier and titled *On the "Strength" of My Call*. The only fresh writing was at the bottom of the paper. The question: "Who won't you forgive: Dad, me, or you?"

Bernadette skimmed it:

Sisters, do you know the truth of my call? It is not Jesus, Mary, or Joseph. It is not the Holy Ghost or the Communion of Saints. It is not a grand love of my fellow human beings. It was my sister's face.

....Let me tell you about such faces, Sisters....You may talk about lost soul this, lost soul that, but have our ever seen into the face of a soul that's lost?.... My call is to reach her.

Sisters, I am called for this. I see my sister's face on so many other faces, and I will go joyfully, passionately, angrily, lazily, and even, if I like, sinfully towards her. This I will do with or without you!

In the Name of God, Amen—Jane Pilgrim

After she read it a second time, Bernadette rose and shut her office door. She still held the uncapped red marker in her hand.

Identifying feelings can be tricky. Sometimes a person doesn't know how alone or lonely they are until someone points that out. Sometimes once a concept like that is loosened, it flows too loose and free and can be overwhelming. Of course, people are often wrong about what they point out.

Behind that door, Bernadette's reaction to Jane's statement, *On the "Strength" of My Call*, was all of these things and none. It was "yes, I am like that, aren't I," and it was "no, that's not me, she's wrong, I'm not that way at all." In no time, *sister's face* was underlined as was *such faces* as was *a face*. She circled *helpless*, *furious*, and *alone*, and crossed out each time *lost* was used, which was three, leaving *soul this, soul that, a soul that's*. In the margin, she wrote *soul?* and scratched it out. Beside the line about *those riverbed men* she wrote, *private"* At the end, she ticked *joyfully*, *passionately*, *angrily*, *lazily*, and double ticked *sinfully*, and even though she didn't write it, there was an implicit *Good!* in the margin.

Around the words *father*, *forgive*, and *you*, Bernadette drew boxes as if to give them their own space.

After her furious annotation, she walked from one side of her office to the other, staving off her growing, sickening understanding that she'd, for years, punished Jane for following this 'Call' that had ultimately been provoked by a look on Bernadette's face that day at the riverbed and an understanding of Bernadette that she couldn't refute.

When Cindy announced Professor Acker's arrival over the intercom, and Ted let himself into her office seconds later, Bernadette looked startled, pale, and Ted noticed that her fingertips were covered in red ink.

"Bernadette, are you all right?"

Ted immediately saw that she wasn't. Her smile was more like a wince. She turned away from him and the door and towards the bookshelf, which she scanned as though searching for an antidote to her unstated condition.

"I admit the appointment was over-the-top, Bernadette."

She didn't move or indicate that she'd heard him.

"Truly, I thought Cindy might catch me out." Then, a beat later: "Okay, I knew she wouldn't."

"Ted, do you suppose I have a soul? Or that I did once and it got lost?"

Ted, dumbfounded, paused. He fought an urge to immediately reassure her, a rabbit hole he didn't want to go down just then. "I'm an Anatomist, Bernadette."

"Yes, so you are," she quietly agreed, turning back to him and looking at him so directly that Ted blushed and looked away unsure if she'd meant to make him feel as diminished as he did. After all he'd planned to say to her, what was he afraid of now?

"What I can tell you, as myself, an Anatomist," Ted said, doing his best to recover, "is that certain things fit together perfectly. I mean think of our bones—206 of them—177 that we can voluntarily move. They all fit—ball and socket, hinged, sutured—just so." He did an exaggerated shrug, letting his arms fall into his lap as he noted her eyes follow them tiredly, just tiredly. He didn't like this fatigue. There was more at stake here than their relationship, he realized, although he must've known this all along.

"Sure, the bones are something, but the joints, that's where the marvel happens: cartilage, synovial fluid, and ligaments that twist this way and that. Decorative and functional both. Exquisite." Her eyes had wandered back to his face or, at least, to the left side of it, maybe his ear, he thought, maybe she was seeing his ear.

"Muscles are not to be underestimated. Have you ever considered their forms?

They're beyond delightful. Sensual, yes, that's what they are. Twisting ropes of filaments—spindle, fan-shaped, fern-shaped, diamond and square..." Ted wanted her eyes back on his, another chance of her directness that had dropped away from his face and now rested on his collarbone. As he described the synchronicity and beauty of muscle motion, his hope to draw her back to him was becoming less certain. Yes, he could go on to describe the fascia and skin, nerves and neurons, but what about the fluid systems of blood, lymph and air. The further he went into this body, the further he was from an answer for her, a line to her, a line between them.

"I'm a flesh and blood man, Bernadette," he said finally. "I can't talk or tell about souls."

He let the silence well between them that before he'd tried to fill, and he studied the bookshelf that Bernadette had stared into earlier. His eyes bored into the corner of the third shelf when he told her that he loved her, never mind the status of her soul. He looked at her directly when he said this love was simple for him and, he added, most complicated, stroking his jaw as though it'd been struck. "I resent you, Bernadette, for lying to me. And leaving. And yeah, I resent you for making yourself stupidly lovable and un-leavable." Ted didn't want to go further. "And as much as there's all this love,"—he stopped again—"I've got to leave, Bern. You know that, right?"

Bernadette Pilgrim, between words and sense, between body and soul, couldn't recall now the age when all pieces of herself weren't perfectly muddled. Charles Sturt, she thought, why you, and looked to Ted—all flesh and blood—she'd tried to hear him, but had she been deaf too for all these years? She looked away from Ted to the paperweight and postcards, and thought of Jane's Wills and Testaments, the good anchorage of the *Endeavor*. She saw her father steady her mum on the railing of the back fence; Jarri and Jane march bravely ahead. Are expeditions voluntary—hers with Sturt, Jane with hers? Any of them?

This girl's like a bucking bronco. Not bloody worth our trouble. That was said to her once. *Slap her hard right down!* And that. *You don't want us to have another go with your sis?* And that too. But also pointed out: was a sea with waterhens, a boat in a desert, three deserts, a soul. *Feel that? And this! And this!* But also, there was a make-up compact, a box of pencils, letters to return, sausage rolls. Is this that blanket, Captain? Mum, your quilt? Straight at it. I'm walking straight at it, Mum.

In those tears, whether it was a gasp or sigh, in that involuntary inhalation after, what Bernadette remembered too was that the light raining over them through the tree branches that day at the riverbed was like gold water. She'd adjusted her head in the sand so the beams might touch her face. The man had paused, and a question had swept his face which, when he saw she saw this question, opened a doubt in his eyes. Although it seemed too late for him to stop—he didn't stop—that he was a man who might be sorry, might've been different elsewhere, that she'd still have to get Jane and her home, and that damn for sure how the beauty of that light insisted itself, all bled together in the container of her body, which, quiet then, the man pushed further into the riverbed with the weight of his body.

Bernadette silently cried.

"Professor Pilgrim, your next appointment is here."

"Cancel it, please," Ted, said. He felt adrift in his sympathy for Bernadette, aware but not understanding the source of her suffering. He feared that if he went to her as he'd done before, she might retreat. Still, Ted rose, stepped forward, extending his hand and handkerchief to her for what seemed like forever.

Travelling northeast from Moorundi with Sturt and his expedition party almost two thousand kilometers, and travelling southeast from Mt. Isaac with Audrey, Robert, Jane, and Jarri nine hundred and seventy kilometers, through dry seasons and wet, through bush lands and deserts, through sandy riverbeds and swollen and flooding ones, Bernadette, like Sturt before her en route to Charlotte Christiana, made her way home to Brisbane and her office at Queens University and Ted Ackers standing before her with his hanky.

"You really should get that freckle on your cheek looked at," she said, sniffling and accepting it.

"Excuse me?"

She had a chill; goose bumps raced up her spine and neck and down the back of her arms. Yet the office was warm. Beads of perspiration stood out on Ted's upper lip. His hazel eyes almost shimmered.

"I'm cold." Her tone suggested that this should be evident, but also that she'd just discovered that this should be evident. It didn't account for her tears, which were still streaming down her cheeks or that she had a hanky to wipe them and hadn't. "Is Cindy going to answer that phone?" Ted hadn't heard the ring outside the door until Bernadette mentioned it.

"This freckle here, Bernadette?" Ted had noticed that one of his freckles had turned scaly, a sign of change, which was never a good sign for skin in Australia. Even as he pointed the freckle out to her, he wondered at this shift and that here he was pointing out a freckle to her as though this was the most natural thing that you'd do after your ex-lover asked you if she had a soul and then you'd told her how much you loved her, even though you still had to break up with her, and she'd responded by standing mutely before you for a good five minutes with tears gushing down her face.

Bernadette pulled on a cardigan, which didn't have any effect on her temperature, and wondered how concerned she should be over this freckle. Her dad had always insisted that Jane and she wear sunscreen and hats outside.

Bernadette blotted her tears then blew her nose. Strange how fast the past could return to you and then pass away from you, like certain images and voices were independent of people and time, and that, depending on where you stood, they could fly at and through you. These ones had thrown her and she felt that bone-tiredness that a colleague had once described as an early sign of her cancer. She sighed. No duh, Jarri, it was the same bone-tiredness she'd felt, but resisted, coming from the riverbed that day. And that she knew very well that Jane knew.

Ted cleared his throat as though to restate his presence. Bernadette noted the way half his body seemed inclined toward her with the other half held back and she recognized in this stance some quality of braveness. "I'm sure it's nothing, Ted, you know," she said. "It's not like you don't reapply your sunscreen." His hair was already thinning, and really, he had freckles he'd have to have seen to. Warmer now, she felt her fatigue lifting.

She watched Ted sit and settle back in his chair. Who she saw though wasn't just this Ted, the good and consistent man, whom she'd perversely tried and taken for granted, but he became possibilities again: Ted, Ted Ackers, Theodore Ackers, Dr. T.F. Ackers, and Theodore Filbert Ackers, with some, at least, of the mysterious complexities and contradictions that each name held. Hard to say if he looked different to Bernadette too, but people do when viewed from new angles. Such an affection and query in Ted's eyes, she saw, and a light too, she decided, coming from within him that if she could just make her way inside to—and yes, open herself to receive it and yes, Jarri, open herself to give it—was sure to illuminate her as much as his bone, muscle, and blood.

Ted had set aside the paperweight on Bernadette's desk and was now flipping through her stack of postcards, shaking his head. He glanced over at her with dismay.

Bernadette braced at first then relaxed: "Cindy channels my dead mum. I thought you knew that about her, Ted." And then seemingly apropos of nothing, she said, "I used to call my sister, Jane, 'Ship Sailor' when we were kids. Silly, really."

✦

When Ava called to tell Robert that she, Bernadette, and Ted would be visiting the following weekend, he wrote the news on a Post-It and stuck it to the refrigerator door. Once that was done, he forgot all about it. He had more pressing matters.

Louisa Cawley had demanded that he turn over the last square of Audrey's quilt.

"It's time, Robert," she'd said. "The Queensland Arts Council was flexible about hanging Audrey's quilt in an incomplete state, but the curators at the National Gallery, though not insensitive to grief, still expect it to be complete. It's been over five years, Robert. You can't expect them to wait forever."

He'd agreed, which was easy to do over the phone, although he couldn't actually picture himself handing it over.

When Louisa called again to arrange a pick-up time, Robert told her that he first needed to have the quilt cleaned and when she called again, he told her it was away being cleaned, and when she called two weeks later, he wasn't sure what to say because he'd never removed it from his bed.

There was also the problem with the buttons: they kept coming. On the one hand, Robert was happy that all sorts of people still thought that Audrey was alive and still quilting. On the other hand, with each button packet that arrived, it was a reminder that in fact Audrey wasn't alive and wasn't quilting. The buttons seemed to quantify Robert's grief. After the beach pails filled, he resorted to storing the buttons in muck buckets. He figured it was only a matter of time before he'd have to upgrade to oil drums. Although of course, like grief, Robert had no end game about the buttons, he had at least come up with the solution for the quilt.

Ava didn't tell her father that Louisa had called. More than the quilt business, Louisa had been concerned that Robert hadn't been accepting invitations and was actively isolating himself. Bernadette said that their father was probably sick of Louisa and her nosy friends and, knowing him, had become involved again in a compelling inventory. Ava ignored her. "We'll see."

Friday afternoon, Ava drove from Toowoomba to meet Bernadette and Ted in Brisbane. Early the following morning, they caught an hour and thirty-five-minute flight to Emerald, where they rented a car and drove the remaining distance to Mt. Isaac. When they knocked at the door no one answered so they let themselves in. The door was unlocked, which was still standard for places like Mt. Isaac.

"What are you doing, Dad?" Bernadette said as they stood in the entranceway of the lounge room looking down at him on the carpet. She shared a look with Ava and Ted since it was fairly clear what he was doing.

"Hi Dad, have you been working on that for long?" Ava asked.

"G'day Robert. Good to see you again. You've got yourself a project, I see," Ted added.

"Your mother never let on how difficult this was." Robert had folded Audrey's quilt blanket so that only a rectangular section was exposed. Beside it was a section of blank blanket on which he was setting out buttons that roughly matched the buttons sewn to the other blanket and roughly matched their arrangement.

"How far have you got?" Bernadette kneeled beside him.

"Louisa is really putting the pressure on," he said. "Maybe a fifth.

I glue the buttons down first then sew them. Your Mother didn't have that step, which is good because it really slows you down."

"Right," said Bernadette.

"Can we give you a hand, then, Dad?" Ava was already scoping out the pails and muck buckets of buttons. "Do you think we might even call in some others to help?" She could see that this was beyond what the four of them could accomplish in a day and a half.

"Sure, Sister, if you like."

Bernadette and Ted cleared the dining room table of dirty dishes, newspapers, empty needle packets, and scraps of thread while Ava called Father Malcolm and Louisa Cawley. While Ava refilled the pails with buttons from the muck buckets, Louisa called Doreen and Mrs. Johnson. Doreen recruited a member of her quilting bee at the same time as Mrs. Johnson, across town, drew up a meal and snack plan for the day and a half ahead. Father Malcolm brought in Casey Phelps's daughter and the Pearls' son, an aspiring chef, to help implement Mrs. Johnson's plan. He also called Bill Turner, who volunteered himself and his mate, Dom, to shuttle between shops, the various kitchens, and the Pilgrims' place. Naturally, Joe Pearl offered to buy free rounds for everyone once the project was complete. By the time that Robert and Ava had moved the quilts to the dining room, spreading Audrey's quilt over the floor and draping his over the table, and Bernadette had begun to thread needles with the thread that Ted had selected to match the particular buttons, which matched particular buttons on Audrey's quilt, unbeknownst to them, the operation was well on its way.

Over the next day and half, with the help of an ever-expanding support group, the quilting team worked together in a marathon of selecting, matching, gluing, and sewing buttons to Robert's blanket. The Pilgrim house, almost incidentally, was cleaned and stocks resupplied to accommodate the activity. Late Sunday afternoon, once Robert sewed that last button down, firefighters Neil, Rod, and Mandy carried both quilts out to the yard and spread them before the umpire chair with a sizable crowd in tow.

"Up you go, Dad," Ava encouraged. Bernadette and Ted stood by as Robert ascended the rungs. A quiet had come over the group. Their weary yet excited camaraderie was palpable. Robert, sitting in the umpire chair, felt as moved by this group—his daughters, Ted, Father, and friends, even regular strangers—who'd rallied to help him, as he did by the symmetry of the blankets. Yet, with them, he was at a loss for words. Audrey, if you could see this, he said. Audrey, look at all our buttons. Look how many people, he said. If you could see this, Audrey: the Pilgrims, everybody. Just look!

After some time had passed, just before it reached that awkward stage when people would be looking to each other unsure how to deal with Robert's apparent stage fright, and Bernadette would be heading up the umpire chair to get him, Father Malcolm said: "So what do you reckon, Robert? Respectfully, I think we've put together a fine forgery."

PART SIX

A LAND THEY HAD NEVER SEEN

✦

AUDREY STOOD AT THE RIM of the escarpment above Gilgin Downs. The breeze she felt she was sorry that Robert couldn't feel down below at the base. The trouble with the quilt was that as it grew larger, Audrey kept losing her perspective on it. She'd gone from standing at the edge of the quilt to standing on the fence rail, to sitting at the top of a ladder then umpire chair, to standing on the umpire chair all to achieve a decent view of the quilt's activity. Robert, on her last birthday, had somehow convinced some men at the Mt. Isaac Fire station to bring their ladder truck with its large telescopic ladder so she could be raised above the quilt. That had been wonderful although temporary.

Audrey had to convince Robert that this might be a solution. Together they'd driven to Gilgin Downs, exploring below the escarpment until they found a relatively flat area of ground to lay the quilt, which corresponded to an accessible overhang above, from which to safely look down. As soon as they'd found this spot, Audrey had immediately wanted to drive home and get the quilt.

"The quilt has no backing, Audrey. You don't want it to get dirty or torn, especially since we've just had the last sections cleaned. And safety-wise, dusk isn't the best time to hike up and down an escarpment or even reload the quilt on the car. Did you check the forecast? We can't be certain that a storm isn't brewing. And what with cloth buttons and fabric backing, it could be a disaster drying the quilt afterwards." Robert balked.

Audrey watched as Robert, far below her, finished unrolling an enormous bolt of sheets that they'd spent the last week sewing to serve as a loose under-cloth to the quilt. Packing the quilt and sheet rolls into the station wagon hadn't worked. Even with the back seat folded down the quilt had been too large, although they'd squeezed in the sheets. They'd ended up hoisting the quilt onto the roof of the station wagon and securing it with rope. That was yesterday. After the effort of loading the car, Audrey and Robert had agreed to postpone the viewing until the following day when they'd be fresh.

Audrey was nervous and excited. She hadn't seen the quilt in its entirety for years. Even when she was at the top of the fire ladder, she couldn't view it in a single frame. After a while she felt as though she was stuck in the center of the quilt action, operating on instinct like a silkworm spinning a cocoon around itself. Attach this border to that one, let the color flow this way over the span of three blankets, let this figure be in counterpoint to that one, that one from five blankets ago.

From this height, off in the distance Audrey could see that the roof of the Queenslander house had now collapsed. Soon the structure would be unrecognizable: just a ruin with only a single side of the wood frame remaining, pieces of metal scattered in the dirt. She sighed. Soon there would be nothing there to suggest that families had ever lived on that barren piece of land. Robert stood and stretched before he continued to systematically roll out the quilt over the sheets.

Recently Audrey's belief in the resilience of her creative instinct, her trust that the work would coherently come together, had flagged. Each time she tried to envision the full quilt she couldn't. Last week, she'd mentally staked out sections in the yard. Back and forth she'd paced, lining up color motifs and figures and themes. After one, maybe two, or even three lengths, a section would drop out, figure arrangements would become confused, colors would shift and change so that she'd be forced to start again. Audrey vaguely remembered that, in the course of this, Louisa Cawley had dropped by, a welcome pause in the back and forth of trying to retain what she remembered of what she'd made.

Robert was almost done. Audrey moved closer to the edge. From her roughly five-story vantage point, she could finally see the quilt in a single frame. All her images and motifs disappeared into a flat of mixed color. "Oh," she said. The land and sky fractured into a mosaic of which her quilt was a fragment and, instantly the lines between these disappeared, leaving a seamless expanse of earth and air. "Oh."

Audrey's quiet declarations resonated in the breeze along with the bush sounds and chorus of voices—the original occupants still here on this piece of earth along with the residents of the Queenslander house and donors to the button quilt—all around her. Slowly dawning on Audrey was that if the quilt was inseparable from the landscape as the landscape was inseparable from the quilt, she, just as they, had been woven in here, suspended in space and time from the very start. Audrey laughed as Robert down below looked up at her and waved.

✦

Ava, Bernadette, and Ted arrived in Canberra, the capital city of Australia, nestled in the Australian Capital Territory (ACT), in mid-September to visit Audrey Pilgrim's quilt, displayed at the National Gallery. Their visit coincided with Floriade, an annual flower festival, which was marketed as "Australia's Celebration of Spring," in which designers would choose a theme to transform Commonwealth Park with flowers. Ava and Ted were happy for the bonus attraction, but Bernadette, although appreciative that even dusty paddocks could transform into a sea of flowers or, in this year's case, become a spread of flowers in the pattern of heavens, informed them both that she'd be hard pressed to take more delight in this spring than in any of the last ones. "A concerted resistance to the passage of time is essential for a long life," she told them, as though their strategies for reaching their 70s shouldn't have been successful.

Although Floriade was promoted as "the" celebration of spring, naturally throughout Australia there were others. After a cold, dry, wet, or snowy winter or at least the likelihood of one of these, people were glad to be outside to appreciate the beauty that the industrious gardeners amongst them had achieved. "Bernadette, you can't dismiss the miracle of millions of planted bulbs and annuals in bloom," Ava had responded. She'd become quite the flower festival groupie over the years. Besides going to Toowoomba's Carnival of Flowers yearly, Ava had also visited New South Wales for the Bathurst Spring Spectacular Festival and had once travelled with Jacinta as far as Western Australia for the Kings Park and Botanical Garden Wildflower Festival. "Floriade, I promise you, will not disappoint."

Audrey's quilt stretched over the entire wall of the high-ceilinged gallery, dwarfing them and another visitor standing nearby.

"Strange, fanciful even, this artwork, isn't it?" said the woman.

"I'm from Queensland on tour here in Canberra. Good to come to Australia's Capital. See some flowers; and, what with the rain showers, some art as well."

"Definitely good to go places and see new things," Ava replied, glancing at Bernadette, who she knew would be vexed by the mere mention of the flowers. Bernadette had aged into a more edgy version of their mother: her white hair was braided into a twist behind her head, and many of the lines etched into her face had deepened. Not surprising, when Bernadette concentrated it appeared as though she were scowling, which had been challenging at times for her students, but even more so later when she'd worked with support groups for victims of violence. "Why they don't recognize my empathy is beyond me, Jane," she'd said, before asking Ava to coach her on how to appear more receptive and supportive. To watch Bernadette struggle to reveal the softer version of herself had been perversely gratifying to Ava, something that she and Ted frequently joked about.

"It's like the artist has projected Floriade's "celestial bloom" from the ground onto the wall: stars, planets, Black holes, and galaxies up there in buttons instead of tulips, daffodils, violas, and the other colorful flowers. Tell me that's not the Southern Cross up there?" she said, pointing high on the wall to the top right corner.

Before Ava, in a flash of metallic gold, her own Southern Cross constellation emerged from the quilt. With it came the image of her mother clearing a spot for her at the table as her dad watched. All white blaze in the square beneath the Cross: The Singing Ship and her dad steadying her mum on the top railing of the back fence and Bernadette ordering her and Jarri to unfurl the sails. A swath of green with shards of vertical gray and Bernadette again, shaving their father at the Tremble Family Nursing Home. Ava's eyes rested on "their" square at the bottom left corner. As with everything now, it was fast: all that Ava saw in the quilt's various sections was gone as quickly as it had appeared, leaving her feeling unaccountably bereft.

"She's sewn them onto woolen blankets, hasn't she?"

"Actually, they're synthetic blankets," Bernadette corrected, debating whether it was worth explaining to the woman that the quilt was special beyond its components. Like Ava, Bernadette saw flashes of her and her family's life, buttons hailing from particular days— discrete messages posted to her from her mother—that if she considered any one button for too long drew her into the quilt as though the quilt were an ocean with currents, shifting depths and life that she could no longer comfortably track or even at times recognize. Yet the quilt provided some solace even as it stirred in her an essential discomfort, danger even, that was no less real even though she couldn't identify its origins. She looked over at Jane as though she might contest or confirm Bernadette's experience of the quilt. Jane had shrunk with time, becoming more stooped. Under the gallery light, her tears almost twinkled. Stop that, Bernadette thought, stepping closer to her and grabbing and tightly squeezing her hand.

"If the blankets had been made of wool they may've come from our sheep." It wasn't bad talking to these seniors, the tourist woman thought. She smiled, imagining for a moment her and her brothers' mob of sheep loose around them. The gallery was definitely big enough.

Bernadette felt unmoored in the light airy gallery, apart from the button quilt and the three people who stood beside her. She thought, buttons killed my mum and good that she didn't use hooded pins. She thought, how many buttons would you trade for a boat in a desert with Chiefs and Charleses and Charlotte Christianas? She thought: Camels! Impossible to stay astride them and saddle up, Onwards all! Maybe she was ill that these were her hodgepodge thoughts that day. Bernadette released Ava's hand. "Mind you don't cry more, Jane. At this age, we can't afford to get dehydrated."

Bernadette, a bundle of arthritic pain and poor circulation, left them to rest on the bench in the center of the room. She considered elevating her leg to reduce the edema, but decided against it for some semblance of dignity that an un-elevated limb might grant her. The bench was hard and Bernadette made a note to herself to request a cushioned bench for this position in the gallery.

Ted, very oddly, seemed to be conducting the buttons with his hands. Bernadette noted the Band-Aid on his outer ear, where he'd had a skin cancer removed. "I don't know what to make of this pasty thin-skinned man I've become," he'd said to her last week. She'd felt a little responsible. She'd given him a copy of Muybridge's book with photographic plates on locomotion, which he'd studied for hours, comparing himself to the naked old man rising from a chair, the naked old man bending to drink water, the naked old man carrying a bucket, and ascending a staircase. She was about to scold him for perseverating on the naked old man when she'd had an unsettling sense of their frailty, so ended up reassuring him instead: "Your pasty complexion accentuates your eye color, Ted," which was true.

Bernadette definitely was coming down with something. Ted was making her dizzy.

"Your mum's made rock art on steroids!" he called over to her.

Ted and Bernadette had visited many rock art sites in their post-retirement travels in the Kimberleys, at Devon Downs Rockshelter, and Camarvon Gorge. Even though it was impossible, they'd spent hours trying to decipher the meaning of the figures. But there was really no way to know if a kangaroo, say, was meant as a meal or a mythical being or a representation of natural forces. Maybe it could be a clan or even a designation of territory. It was dizzying how little she knew. Don't even get me started on the chemical stability of pigments.

She closed her eyes, took a deep breath, and imagined herself wandering with Ted in the caves again. They'd also spent hours picturing artists applying paint and wax to those rock faces, blowing pigment around stencil-like objects to produce those intricate figures. Bernadette felt a weird slip, a something uncomfortable inside, and somehow those artists are one artist and that one artist is Jarri and somehow she is before Jarri on the wall as he cheerfully blows pigment around her. Quickly somehow, she is out of his frame, but still enough in the cave that when Jarri etches more figures into the rock surface, Bernadette feels that scraping and pounding in her head and, nauseated now, she really just wants her mum.

"Do you think that's a swarm of Bluebottle Jellyfish?" The tourist woman pointed left center. "Or, like at Floriade, it might be planet earth from space too. Honestly, this art is a lot to take in. It'd be nice if the buttons could actually tell us what they were."

"You have no idea what a clamor that would cause!" Ava exclaimed, clapping.

Bernadette, startled by the clapping, opened her eyes again to the wall of buttons. How they did it, she couldn't fathom, but the red ones lifted off, like a flock of red-headed parquets, the heads of so many hooded pins, crimson flashes in a sea of dark opal, pealing through the air above her. What the hell! She quickly closed her eyes.

Unaware of the commotion behind her, Ava explained the quilt's history to the tourist and directed her to Robert's online inventory, which was essential, she emphasized, to fully appreciate the piece. The rain seemed louder than before for some reason. The tourist woman was right; there was a lot to take in. Ava couldn't imagine, though, a better testimonial to people's need to express and commune, to place and be placed, to be and become, than their parents' quilt and inventory. More to herself than to Ted and the tourist woman, she said, "Sometimes you can get so caught up with looking to God and the holy ones, that you miss what's been playing out before you all along." Ava stared long into the bottom left corner, then called over to Bernadette: "Wouldn't Mum love that that last square is ours." And to herself: *In the Name of God, Amen.*

The rain outside was torrential. The tourist from Queensland was reluctant to leave these kind seniors to face the deluge. She had to go though, for her trip was at its end and, back at the station, her brothers would need her to help prep the ewes for lambing.

"For sure you have to ride the Floriade Viewing Ferris Wheel," she told them. "You won't believe that by looking down you actually feel as though you're looking up, and there, clear as day, is the night sky." Ava and Ted affectionately assured her that they'd visit Floriade the following morning.

PART SEVEN

WEIGHING ANCHOR

✦

HOW POSSIBLE IS IT to accurately express the tangled and conflicting thoughts, emotions, and physicality of Bernadette or Ava or Ted, or anyone really? How possible is it to express even the fine modulation of the physiologic state—with what effect of age?—of heart and lungs, blood and lymph, muscles and bones, digestion, and those nerves throughout the body, serving up the orders for the minute adjustments necessary for Bernadette to sit on that bench and Ava and Ted to stand before the quilt in that gallery in Canberra.

Bernadette, a speedy entanglement of mind and sensation, tried to focus on one thought until she forgot that that was what she was trying to do, and she was transported to the center of another thought.

My leg has gone numb, she noted.

Can anyone truly describe a living being functioning simultaneously within themselves and without, describe the dynamic processes of life as though it were still? Bernadette Pilgrim, for example, was a woman in tension, a feeling in opposition, a woman apparently immobile on a bench yet in a spur of unseen activity; she was a woman resisting an impulse to look forward, staring back over her shoulder at exactly the same time as she resisted an impulse to look back and stared ahead.

I should really prop this leg up, she thought.

This strain she projected outside herself. The movements of her family before her she slowed as her chest tightened, the pounding in her head crescendoed, deafening to the point that she was certain that they could hear it too—couldn't they? —see the numbness now spreading up her side. Just as her state had become untenable and it was occurring to her to call for help, Jane and Ted hooted with laughter as though they'd overheard her worries, and Bernadette, startled to a moment of propriety she imagined a woman in her seventies should have, looked sternly at the quilt before she simply— can it ever be simple?—let go or, more accurately, went.

How sensible is it to even try to understand what happens in that instant between now and next? For that instant, Bernadette realized that to explore was to salvage, to record a story was to remember one, that an injury and a gift could exist in the same strike, that her choices were hers but also not hers and her thoughts were strangely inseparable from others—dead and living—and her companionship and love of Ted was the same as her mother's with her father, the same as Jane with her God and saints, the same love of Sturt and Charlotte Christiana, and a flesh and blood Jarri with his kin and land; and that the anger and cruelties that she'd inflicted were also the same in part as those she'd experienced, documented in her work, and later fought against. And striking—in the mundane nature of it—she realized that a drought and a flood would forever exist on the same plains in a ceaseless rhythm that covered and uncovered the earth with water, regardless of who or what lived and died there, and when.

What Bernadette knew was that Bernadette Pilgrim would always just be Bernadette Pilgrim. Which is to say, for all that she shared with the cosmos, she was still singularly herself and—fortunate or unfortunate—her passions and drive, her preferences and prejudices, her mistakes and misguidedness were not in this instant likely to disappear. And this was her surprise, which annoyed her and propelled her on. As Bernadette sank deeper into the recesses of her body, and, literally, off the bench and onto the gallery floor, these understandings of the intractable nature of Bernadette Pilgrim were what carried her on.

As Ava and Ted rushed over and tended to Bernadette on the gallery floor that day, Bernadette was already west of Ayres Rock, following a fellow on a half-dead horse, who told her that he needed a sign more than anything in the world, more than water, tucker, shade, and rest. He'd been on his horse now for over six days, and Bernadette, a good three meters from him, smelled the rank truth of this. Naturally, she thought of those old explorers trekking across our deserts: the Gibson, Simpson, the Great Sandy and Victoria, and her mind expanded to the Sahara, Mohave, Kalahari, Namib, Gobi, and

Thar Deserts. Bernadette wondered if the man was delusional, so strung out from the elements that he'd lost his wits enough to think that he didn't need water to survive. How far can a man go to forget his horse's condition? What kind of sign was worth what he and his horse had become? It was these questions that Bernadette meant to document before she ran to accompany him into the shimmering salt flats before them, likely unaware of Audrey pressing a cordial bottle into one hand and Robert pressing his list of water hole GPS coordinates into the other, unaware of Ava and Ted at her side, Captain Sturt and his expedition party waiting in the wings, and Jarri ahead of them leading the horse.

✦

The rain followed them from Canberra back to Queensland. After Bernadette's funeral and burial, it continued for more than forty days and forty nights. There were floods everywhere. From the air, the land looked like a spread of muddy water with tree and roof tops dotting the surface. Throughout the state there were fatalities, possessions lost, and property and infrastructure destroyed. Ava was surprised that Noah and his flood wasn't the framework that first came to mind to understand it, but the one that her mother had once read to her of Tiddalik, the giant frog, who had drunk the world's water, and who had to be cajoled into laughter by the animals to replenish it. Now, unlike the Dreamtime story, Tiddalik seemed unable to stop laughing, now all the animals, who'd cajoled him to laugh, had drowned. How now to make the laughing frog stop? It was an unnerving and impossible dilemma. Ava was positive there was a solution but, for the life of her, although she kept trying, she couldn't tease it out.

Like most residents in Toowoomba, the Presentation Sisters had been evacuated from the convent and relocated to a shelter that the Salvation Army had set up. They'd been told that it was only a matter of time before the shelter would need to be evacuated as well. The forecast was more rain. Ava rested on a cot, in a line of cots, where the older nuns, like herself, also rested. She led them in the Rosary and after, led them in a rendition of "Botany Bay," in tribute to her sister and to Ted, who had gamely sung it at Bernadette's service.

"Farewell to old England forever
Farewell to my rum culls as well
Farewell to the well-known Old Bailey
Where I used for to cut such a swell

Chorus:
Singing Tooral liooral liaddity
Singing Tooral liooral liay
Singing Tooral liooral liaddity
And we're bound for Botany Bay

There's the captain as is our commander
There's the bosun and all the ship's crew
There's the first and the second class passengers
Knows what we poor convicts go through

Taint leaving old England we cares about
Taint cos we mis-spells what we knows
But because all we light fingered gentry
Hops around with a log on our toes

These seven long years I've been serving now
And seven long more have to stay
All for bashing a bloke down our alley
And taking his ticker away

Oh, had I the wings of a turtle dove
I'd soar on my pinions so high
Slap bang to the arms of my Polly love
And in her sweet presence I'd die

Now all my young Dookies and Dutchesses
Take warning from what I've to say
Mind all is your own as you toucheses
Or you'll find us in Botany Bay"

EPILOGUE

AT THE TIME of the Pilgrim family with their buttons, altars, and inventories; the time of royal families, prime-ministers and presidents, entertainment and sports stars, and reality TV personalities; at the time of policies about these people versus those people and distinctions between foreign and native, us and them; at the time of the Web, mass communication, and global access and interdependence; extreme disparities between rich and poor; at the time of fundamental challenges to the principles of reason, human rights, and environmental custody; and 11,000 to 13,000 years after— to be precise—the ocean had advanced a meter a day and the intertidal zone had stretched, and those who were there on the Arafura Plain and the Great Australian Bight had been forced to retreat, the ocean had begun to rise again.

This time they knew of the massive ice floes, fragmented from the Antarctic and Greenland ice sheet melting as they drifted north, and the Arctic sea ice melting as it drifted south and the lakes in the lobes of the earth's ice shields emptying and the seas' rise. How did they forget that their place, where spring could be autumn, heavens could be on earth, and cement could be as fluid as the desert that could be a sea, never a "plain" or "bight," was formed of the bodies of their ancestors?

How could they not understand that all that the Pilgrims or Thatles or—so many of us—couldn't see or wouldn't do didn't mean that these things couldn't be seen or done? On the voyage inland, there are no shortages of ways, no inevitable outcomes. And while there's also no guarantee of that corroboree or that picnic feast, laid out for them on the grassy slope overlooking Keppel Bay, they can be guaranteed that there'll be an unbearably beautiful chorus as the wind off the ocean flutes through our bodies—the hollow riggings of this Singing Ship.

END

AUTHOR'S NOTE AND
ACKNOWLEDGMENTS

This is a work of fiction. There is no town in Queensland named Mount Isaac and no Queens University in Brisbane. Some of the characters in this novel—Charles Sturt, Charlotte Christiana Sturt, and his expedition members, James Cook, Sir Joseph Banks, and other explorers are historical persons. I'm indebted to the journals of some of these historical persons. In particular Charles Sturt's *Journal of the Central Australian Expedition 1844-5* and *Narrative Of An Expedition Into Central Australia* with the Introduction and Notes by Jill Waterhouse, James Cook's *The Journals of Captain Cook* and excerpts from *The Wills of men who sailed with Captain James Cook.* Also helpful were more recent books about Sturt and other Australian explorers: Edgar Beale's *Sturt: The Chipped Idol*, and Alan Moorehead's *Cooper's Creek: The Story of Burke and Wills.* As a work of fiction, while I used some details of Sturt's expedition into central Australia, this is in no way meant as a full and accurate account. While the majority of conversations by historical characters are fabricated, others are drawn from the journals and, where possible, I've delineated these. I do believe this will be obvious. I am indebted to the Millay Colony, the Vermont Studio Center, Virginia Center for Creative Arts, and Yaddo, where I was able to develop this work. I'm grateful to the generous readers of TSS, who have provided invaluable feedback and support along the way: Andrea Barrett, Kevin McIlvoy, Cynthia Phoel, Peter Turchi, and, especially, Genanne Walsh, and Tracy Winn. Much thanks to Christine Stewart, the editor at Del Sol Press, for her insightful feedback and patience in these last days. Thank you also to my family, friends, and colleagues at ZSFGH, and to Lewis Buzbee, Maggie Estep, Carey Kozuszek, and Kate Myers, for their early support. And lastly, John Thomson, whose good company and steadfast support has meant everything.

BIBLIOGRAPHY

Beale, Edgar. *Sturt: The Chipped Idol*, 127, (sec.) Sydney: Sydney University Press, 1979.

Berra, Tim. *A Natural History of Australia*. San Diego: Academic Press, 1998.

"Botany Bay." n.d. Last modified 1994. http://folkstream.com/010.html.

"Come lasses and lads." n.d. Last modified September 29, 2009. http://song-archive.livejournal.com/49610.html.

Cook, James. *The Journals of Captain Cook*. New York: Penguin Books, 1999.

Day, David. *Claiming a Continent: A New History of Australia*. Adelaide: Angus & Robertson, 1997.

"Exile's Lament (Australian)." n.d. Last modified October 1999. http://traditionalmusic.co.uk/folk-songsLyrics/Exiles_Lament

Hallack, Cecily. "The Divine Office of the Kitchen." n.d. Last modified December 4, 2010. http://forums.abebooks.com/discussions/AbeBookscom_community_forum/General/

Kelly, Sean, and Rosemary Rodgers. *Saints Preserve Us!* New York: Random House, 1993.

MacGinley, M.R. *Roads to Sion: Presentation Sisters in Australia 1866-1980.* Brisbane: Boolarong Publications, 1983.

Moorehead, Alan. *Cooper's Creek: The Story of Burke and Wills.* Melbourne: Nelson Publishers, 1963.

Mountford, Charles P. *The Deamtime.* 38. Adelaide: Rigby Limited, 1965.

Mulvaney, D.J. *Encounters in Place: Outsiders and Aboriginal Australians 1606-1985.* Brisbane: University of Queensland Press, 1989.

Mulvaney, John, and Johan Kamminga. *Prehistory of Australia.* Washington: Smithsonian Institution Press, 1999.

Murray, Alan. *Nothing But Scrub.* Moorooka: Moranbah Silver Jublilee Committee, Belyando Shire Council, 1996.

Muybridge, Eadweard. *Human and Animal Locomotion Volume 1.* New York: Dover Publications, Inc., 1979.

Pyne, Stephen. *Burning Bush: A Fire History of Australia.* New York: Henry Holt & Company, 1991.

Robson, John. "The Wills of men who sailed with Captain James Cook 1: A to D." n.d. Last modified January 09, 2005. http://pages.quicksilver.net.nz/jcr/~cookwills4.html

Rumsey, A. and J. F. Weiner. *Emplaced Myth: Space, Narrative, and Knowledge in Aboriginal Australia and New Guinea.* Honolulu: University of Hawaii Press, 2001.

Stewart, Douglas, and Nancy Keesing. *Bush Songs, Ballads, and Other Verse,* 12,58. Sydney: Angus & Robertson, 1967.

Sturt, Charles. *Journal of the Central Australian Expedition 1844-5*, Edited by Jill Waterhouse. 2, 15, 20, 22, 37-38, 44-46, 48-52, 55, 65, 67, 70, 83, 85-87, 90-91. London: Caliban Books, 1984.

The 1928 Book of Common Prayer. (n.) Oxford: Oxford University Press, 1993.

ABOUT THE AUTHOR

Rebecca Winterer was awarded the Del Sol Press 2016 First Novel Prize and selected as a finalist for the Black Lawrence Press 2016 Big Moose Prize. She's received fellowships at the Millay Colony, the Vermont Studio Center, Virginia Center for Creative Arts, and Yaddo, and has had a story published by *Puerto del Sol*. She holds an MFA from Warren Wilson College and an MS in Physical Therapy from Columbia University. Raised in Queensland, Australia, she now lives in San Francisco, California with her husband. *The Singing Ship* is her first novel.

CPSIA information can be obtained
at www.ICGtesting.com
Printed in the USA
LVOW11s0242181017
552826LV00002B/221/P